S0-AXX-719

PENGUIN BOOKS

Tu

Patricia Grace is the author of five novels, four short story collections and several children's books.

Awards for her work include the New Zealand Fiction Award for *Potiki* in 1987, the Children's Picture Book of the Year for *The Kuia and the Spider* in 1982 and the Hubert Church Prose Award for best first book for *Waiariki* in 1976. She was also awarded the Liberaturpreis from Frankfurt in 1994 for *Potiki* which has been translated into several languages. *Dogside Story* won the Kiriyama Pacific Rim Fiction Prize in 2001 and was longlisted for the Booker Prize.

Patricia Grace was born in Wellington in 1937. She lives in Plimmerton on the ancestral land of Ngati Toa, Ngati Raukawa and Te Ati Awa in close proximity to her home marae at Hongoeka Bay.

Also by Patricia Grace

NOVELS
Mutuwhenua: The Moon Sleeps
Potiki
Cousins
Baby No-eyes
Dogside Story

SHORT STORIES
Waiariki
The Dream Sleepers and Other Stories
Electric City and Other Stories
Selected Stories
Collected Stories
The Sky People

FOR CHILDREN
The Kuia and the Spider
Watercress Tuna and the Children of Champion Street
The Trolley
Areta and the Kahawai

OTHER
Wahine Toa

Tu

Patricia Grace

PENGUIN BOOKS

PENGUIN BOOKS

Published by the Penguin Group
Penguin Group (NZ), cnr Airborne and Rosedale Roads, Albany,
Auckland 1310, New Zealand
Penguin Books Ltd, 80 Strand, London, WC2R 0RL, England
Penguin Group (USA) Inc., 375 Hudson Street, New York, NY 10014, United States
Penguin Group (Australia), 250 Camberwell Road, Camberwell,
Victoria 3124, Australia
Penguin Books Canada Ltd, 10 Alcorn Avenue, Toronto,
Ontario, Canada M4V 3B2
Penguin Books (South Africa) (Pty) Ltd, 24 Sturdee Avenue, Rosebank,
Johannesburg 2196, South Africa
Penguin Books India (P) Ltd, 11, Community Centre, Panchsheel Park,
New Delhi 110 017, India
Penguin Ireland Ltd, 25 St Stephen's Green, Dublin 2, Ireland
Penguin Books Ltd, Registered Offices: 80 Strand, London, WC2R 0RL, England

First published by Penguin Group (NZ), 2004
5 7 9 10 8 6

Copyright © Patricia Grace, 2004

The right of Patricia Grace to be identified as the author of this work in terms of
section 96 of the Copyright Act 1994 is hereby asserted.

Designed by Mary Egan
Typeset by Egan-Reid Ltd
Printed in Australia by McPherson's Printing Group

All rights reserved. Without limiting the rights under copyright reserved above,
no part of this publication may be reproduced, stored in or introduced into a retrieval
system, or transmitted, in any form or by any means (electronic, mechanical,
photocopying, recording or otherwise), without the prior written permission of
both the copyright owner and the above publisher of this book.

ISBN 0 14 301920 1
A catalogue record for this book is available
from the National Library of New Zealand.

www.penguin.co.nz

Dear Rimini and Benedict

Left Papakura by train . . .

Today I'll write . . .

Dear Benedict and Rimini

MAORI BATTALION MARCHING SONG

Maori Battalion march to victory
Maori Battalion staunch and true
Maori Battalion march to glory
Take the honour of the people with you
We'll march, march, march to the enemy
We'll fight right to the end
For God, for King, for Country
Aue! Ake ake kia kaha e.

WORDS BY CORPORAL ANANIA AMOHAU
28 (MAORI) BATTALION

Tumatauenga – god of war.

Te Hokowhitu-a-Tu –

1. The many fighting men of Tumatauenga.

2. The name given to the Pioneer Battalion of Maori volunteers during World War One, 1914–1918.

To the memory of Sergeant Edward Gunson
28 (Maori) Battalion, D Coy, Reg 815133
(1915–1983)

Dear Rimini and Benedict,

Dear Rimini and Benedict,

You didn't deserve ill-humour and rebuff, and I had no right to send you off with empty hearts when all you were asking was to get to know your 'father'.

'Father' is what you said.

You probably think I'm still a bit loony. It's probably true.

After you'd gone I kept thinking about my war notebooks. Everything I could tell you, more than I could ever tell you about your 'father', is contained in them. It wasn't war that interested you, you said, unless there were matters to do with soldiering that were relevant to you getting to know him. I've tossed and turned about whether I should pass the diaries on to you because I never meant them to be read by anyone else, not only because there are details in them that none of us ever speak about, but also because I didn't want anyone to know the truth about what really happened to me.

The latter reason is unimportant now, and never was important to anyone except me. A further reason for not wanting the books read is because I decided that I should keep Ma's secret, even though I could never understand her reasons for secrecy.

But you have a right. I give them to you because I know you have a right.

When I first began the notes I intended them to be simple recordings of times and places, jottings to do with my journeys and experiences of a war, which for me took place in Southern Italy. Brief scribblings and a few musings is what I started out with, as you'll see. But the notebooks came to mean much more to me than just somewhere where I could doodle a few dates and place names. As you read on, thanks to Brother Pita, thanks to both my brothers, you'll come to passages more illuminating of information you seek. You have a right, and even though there are some things I wish you didn't have to read or incidents you didn't have to know about, I'm pleased now that I didn't burn the books as I had resolved to do, or that I didn't throw them into the Tory Channel on the way home from war, which is what I tell those stickybeak journalists I did, when they come sniffing.

So, though I've thrown out almost everything else extraneous to my occupation of space on this planet, the notebooks are still with me.

The afternoon that you came, when I heard Fritzy barking and looked out to see who was coming, I was surprised all over again, just as I had been surprised on seeing you at age fourteen when you came to visit me in the loony bin about six years ago. You are your fathers' memorials, the likeness being so strong that I thought I was being visited by ghosts – which wouldn't be the first time. Old Fritzy certainly doesn't discriminate about who is one and who is not. I was caught off guard, having been away from the family for so long and expecting to be left alone. I know I wasn't as welcoming as I should have been.

But it is best that I live alone. I'm all right back here under our mountain. It's best for everyone, though I'm pleased now that you came, and grateful to have something to hand on to you.

Sometimes events coincide in such a way that you feel there is something more in the air than coincidence. Benedict, when they gave you your name I know it wasn't because of the bombing of the Benedictine abbey. You hadn't been born at the time of the bombing. Nor was it because of the later event which occurred in a town beneath a mountain, because you were already named by the time we entered the town. No, you were given your name because your father wrote home describing the astonishing sight we came upon as we rounded the base of Monte Trocchio on our approach to Cassino. No one knew then that you would be his remembrance.

No doubt when Jess came to Ma's door with you, Rimini, you would have come with given names. However, your arrival, your handing over to Ma, would have coincided with the receiving of a telegram. You would have been given your new name because of what the telegram contained and not because the truth was known by then. You'll both come to understand what I mean about there seeming to be more circulating than pure coincidence at times.

People have dreams. Some dreams are simple meanderings that help whittle away stagnant hours. Others dreams are reachable, touchable, pliable, so that you can take them and shape them into something that seems to be real. These shaped dreams are bound to be affected by other people, or by events large and small, and in reaching out towards them sometimes dreams are caused to topple, or fragment, or become somehow elusive.

Never mind. You find them or mend them, and when you re-examine them, you may see that their shapes have altered, or that they have changed you in some way. Perhaps they have become smaller, maybe more refined. Perhaps you have. They can be ungainly or misshapen or small, but it doesn't matter. At least they exist and they belong to you. You have a dream. However, sometimes you can use up your dream and there is some condition, maybe just your own pigheadedness, that prevents you from pursuing another. Where are you then?

Stop.

Verbiage isn't what you want from me after all these years of silence.

Here's a final note before you read on. Perhaps you're thinking I made an error with that apostrophe several paragraphs back. You'll understand as you go through the notebooks that it was no mistake.

I hope I'm doing the right thing. I hope you won't be hurt by certain revelations, but I'm certain it's truth you're after.

With love,

Tu

Left Papakura by train . . .

1

away

30 June 1943
Left Papakura by train at eight o'clock last night and arrived in Wellington at eleven this morning to find my family waiting on the wharf to see me off. To my surprise Ma was there. She made sure to tell me she hadn't come because she forgave me, but only because I was her son who she may never see again. Felt a bit guilty at first.

Others had come besides Ma and my sisters. Ani Rose and friends from the Club were there – as well as some of the back-home relatives including Uncle Ju – bringing all kinds of packages which they piled on Choc, Tipu and me. Though it was good to see them I couldn't wait to get on board.

Eventually we were brought on to the wharf where we began embarkation, but finding it impossible to carry all the parcels friends and family had heaped on me I had to give some away. Once on board I found a handy position at the rail on the upper deck and could see family and friends down there among the crowd looking up. We were so packed together that they couldn't see me at first. I took my lemon squeezer off, sweeping it from side to side to catch their attention, and at last they managed to pick me out and began waving. It wasn't long before there was water between us and land. What a relief.

Passed through the heads at dusk and stayed on deck until the lights of Wellington were out of vision. Had a good look round before deciding to turn in to bunk and jot down these few notes.

No regrets.

July 1st
The New Zealand coastline remained in sight for most of the day. Presumably it was the south of the South Island we could see. This p.m. the ship began to roll a little and Choc said his gut was sloshing around. We're now heading west, having lost sight of New Zealand at about 7 ac emma. Some of the boys weren't too happy about seeing the last of our country for a while, but I was excited that we were on our way at last.

Not so long ago I was a schoolboy taking part in athletic champs, running a barefoot first in the fifty-yard sprint. After bracing the finishing tape I kept on running. Off I ran, out of the iron gates and away to war.

2nd
Slept well and now settling down to life at sea. The weather holds fine although the swell increased during the day and some of the boys were seasick. Attended Mass. Very uncomfortable trying to keep balanced in such a confined space with the ship rolling so much – especially when kneeling – but at least I did my duty. Still heading north-west.

3rd
Fine weather continues and we're keeping the same direction. Ship beginning to stink of sick as many of the boys have been affected badly by the motion. They don't want to mess up their cabins so they're all lying out on the decks swishing about in vomit. Tipu and I stood Choc up by the rails and threw two buckets of

water over him. He felt better after that. We went off and found Ruby and did the same.

When I first arrived at camp I found that Choc and Tipu were already there. I hadn't seen these backhome cousins since they moved away from our mountain a few years before. Ruby is their mate from Taihape.

Settling down to a daily routine. No drill or exercises so far but we have lectures instead. Quite dull really. However this afternoon we were supplied with two hundred cigarettes from canteen funds. Decided to take up smoking.

4th

Feeling queasy today, not from seasickness but from too much smoking. Anyway I decided to persevere as I am quite keen on this smoking, so I lay down on a clean piece of deck to counteract the dizziness and kept on puffing. I think I'm getting the hang of it.

Sighted land and another ship this afternoon, which created some interest. Passed through Bass Strait (I think) and left land behind again.

Couldn't eat eggs.

5th

Presume crossing Gt Aust. Bight and sighted land in the distance. A huge school of porpoises put on a great show to starboard this morning, leaping and diving in unison. Every so often they moved off and we'd see the water churning with them further out. After a while they would return, shooting along below the surface to begin their antics again.

The water is calmer now and the weather quite warm. Very hot in quarters so some of us have been sleeping out on deck.

6th

Making about four hundred miles a day since leaving NZ. Nothing to see but water. Anyway we amused ourselves by preparing for a concert (us Maori boys) which we put on earlier tonight. We did some of our club items including haka 'Utaina', and there were two or three solos. A group of boys, all brothers and cousins from Tauranga, sang a bracket of Ink Spot numbers: 'It's a Sin to Tell a Lie', 'My Prayer', 'Prisoner of Love' and 'When the Swallows Come Back to Capistrano'. They sang without accompaniment and sounded every bit as good as the real Ink Spots. It was just a short concert but we had some fun and received a good hearing.

7th

Not much to report except that a cruiser escort picked us up. At least that was something to look at, though we'd been hoping to sight land. We watched the cruiser for an hour or so then brought out the ukeleles. One of our relations from Opunake – we call him Bootleg – stood on his head and played his uke while singing a song without words. His big upside-down mouth and his rubbery lips were opening and shutting as he mimed the words to 'In the Shade of the Old Apple Tree'. Hard case. Plinkity plink. Plenty music, plenty singsong. Plenty laugh. Should reach Fremantle at some time tomorrow.

8th

Headed into the Port of Fremantle this morning half expecting leave, but were disappointed in that respect. Later this afternoon we all went ashore and marched through town. The town is very old and the shops have been boarded up, giving the place a neglected look, but the people gave us a great welcome. We were ashore for a very short time before coming back on board. Hoping to have leave tomorrow.

9th

Went by train to Perth. Trains are old-fashioned and slow, and pulled along by engines half the size of the ones at home. In Perth we spent some time at the zoo viewing these strange Australian animals with their pouches and hoppity legs and swivelling ears. I couldn't get over the birds with all their bright and beautiful feathers. They are of colours I've never seen in my life and didn't know existed in nature, or anywhere. Our birds at home are deeper toned. So are our trees by comparison to the trees in this country. We cooled off with cold beer after that as the weather is very hot. They say it hasn't rained for seven months. Later went to the pictures and saw *Manhattan Moon*. Returned by train with fresh fruit and grapes.

10th
Still in Fremantle. We were taken for a picnic to one of the beaches today. Marched there accompanied by a brass band. The weather was beautiful and sunny though the water was surprisingly cool. Had lunch and returned about 3 p.m. feeling refreshed.

11th
Spent another day in Perth where, first of all, we had a darned good feed of steak, eggs, chips, tomatoes, tea and piles of bread. We were having a good time in the pubs round town and talking about going to one of the dances later. But part way through the day we heard that some of our Battalion boys had been involved in a brawl with Yanks back in Fremantle. We were told that a couple of them had been knifed by the Americans and that one had died. It was very upsetting. News soon spreads, and some of the boys took their revenge on the Yanks there in Perth and so created another brawl. No one was seriously hurt in Perth.

12th
We learned today that another of the boys died as a result of the stabbing. Naturally we've been feeling very sorry and sad about this. Two of our mates gone and we haven't even reached the war zone yet. That would be the worst thing that could happen – to go to war but to die on the way, for nothing. I couldn't help thinking of the families at home.

We attended the funeral this afternoon where our Battalion sang the hymns 'Aue Ihu', 'Piko Nei te Matenga', as well as our Maori version of 'Abide with Me'.

16th

We thought we'd be on our way today, and after all that has happened most of us would be pleased to leave here. However we remained in port and further leave was granted. The whole shipload took off for the pubs in Perth and by afternoon the entire town was rowdy and rolling. Not being used to drinking, when I came out of the pub the fresh air hit me and my legs buckled. Choc and Bootleg took me to the town gardens and shoved me in among the roses where I slept for a couple of hours. When I came to, the boys, who'd been round the souvenir shops, were out on the grass throwing boomerangs. The pubs were shut by then. My mates were still drunk though and I still wasn't feeling too good myself.

We all went off through town, which was still rocking. Officers on picket duty were going round in trucks with Aussie provosts, keeping an eye on everything. While waiting for the train we filled in time skylarking round the railway station with the boomerangs, most of which ended up in pieces by the time our train pulled in. Off we went singing.

17th

This morning we were given a send-off by the military brass band, which played 'Auld Lang Syne' as the boat pulled out. The Aussies have shown us great hospitality.

So we're on our way again and have begun practising for another concert which will be held on Wednesday. It's been raining but not enough to get wet or even to cool us down. The heat is terrific. Heading north-west. Sweating all day.

18th

Still heading NW as far as I can tell and the heat is unbearable.

2

iron

It's not so much the heat that is unbearable. It is the last diary entry that is unbearable. After writing it the pen came to a standstill and the ink congealed. It's a disappointing sentence. 'Still heading NW' is a dull use of ink, and having the day's date above seems to weigh the whole thing down even more. Just because the days are quite monotonous shouldn't mean that writing has to drag as well.

What if someone wants to read this one day – Ma and the family, or maybe a kid in fifty years' time? What will they make of 'terrific' or 'unbearable' to describe the heat? Will it give them any idea of how this old one-eye sun boils round day after day in a close-up, white-hot sky? What will the words mean to someone in latitude forty?

I enjoy writing in the notebook – like the smell of ink and paper, and always want to do my best to keep a neat hand despite the motion of the boat. But I've come to see that writing a daily journal can be stultifying. I have to get out from under dates now. It doesn't matter which days are hot. I don't need to repeat hot, hot, hot, every day. I don't need to guess which direction we are heading in just to have something to write down.

So now, coming back to my journal after being stymied by a sentence a week ago, I've decided I'll write only when there are enough words in my head to create a flow on to paper through a warmed-up pen. In this way sentences will be freed, I hope. They'll shake themselves out and find room to grow, maybe. And it won't matter if what I write turns out to be a mixture of thoughts, ideas, observations and memories, because it will still be a kind of record of what is going on.

There was a sentence that I wrote on our second day at sea, which came not so much from a warmed-up pen but from excitement and a warmed-up heart. As it arrived out on to the paper I was pleased with it, and I've thought of it and been happy with it ever since.

'Off I ran, out of the iron gates and away to war,' I wrote. Even though not perfectly true it's close enough to the truth and it sounds like a good beginning to something. There's a promise there I think. A kid might read it in fifty years' time and hope that there will be more, that the sentence will crack open and leak its information, or expand in some way, on heartfelt desire.

Rangi, in one of his letters home, didn't go on and on about the conditions as their ship neared the equator, but he did tell us about two men from the engine room committing suicide. The way he told it, without many words at all, showed how he felt, showed his acceptance, but also explained something about intensity and heat in the way that 'terrific' or 'unbearable' never could. Fortunately there haven't been any stokers throwing themselves over the side on this trip, so the best I can do is to say that even without clothes or covers the heat won't let us sleep at night, not even out on deck; that drinking water is available all the time now and we are allowed two salt water showers a day. Each afternoon we have siesta for a couple of hours, and we had one good day of hard rain when we put on our togs and walked out, hissing and sizzling and steaming like hot irons.

I had it already planned, my escape from boredom and boyhood. I'd gone over the escape many times in my head and the carrying out of the plan was only waiting for the right moment. As I crossed the finishing line, on my way for yet another athletics trophy, I knew the time had come.

Enough is enough.

If there'd been someone just a step ahead of me, someone to challenge me over the last few yards, or even if there'd been someone breathing on my shoulder, perhaps then, right then, would not have been the time.

I'd worked hard to get all my exams behind me so that I could leave school, but Brother Pita, supported by The Uncle, thought another year would stand me in good stead until I could take my place as a law cadet in an office that my uncle would arrange for me.

I knew the reason they'd sent me back to school was so that I'd give up the idea of enlisting and also because they didn't want me manpowered into essential war industry in the city. School was to be my prison until the war ended, even though I'd already matriculated, even though there were no more challenges left for me on the sporting fields.

So here I was at seventeen years of age, a school kid running in schoolboy races, when all I wanted to do was become a soldier.

On deck early this morning we saw flying fish for the first time, hundreds of them, and I remembered another of Rangi's letters where he mentioned the flying fish but didn't describe them. How old was I then? Fourteen I think. I imagined, when I read his letter, that these fish would be many coloured, with wings that could take them anywhere. I thought that they would be able to fly skyward, swoop like hawks, dive like terns, or flick and jink about like fantails. What I saw were shoals of little fish, the largest no more than a hand-span in length. They were black on top and white underneath and came flying out of the wash, skimming the top of the water at a terrific rate. They used their wings as gliders, cruising along, catching the wind currents before entering the water again with a whack and a splash. They travel quite a distance above water before disappearing. I'd say about twenty-five to thirty chains.

Although this description is as accurate as I can make it, I now wonder if Rangi's few words were not better after all. Without a description the flying fish can be as exotic as imagination can make them. A kid in fifty years' time could think of a ship ploughing through oceans accompanied by flocks of fish of all colours, crowding and wing-beating about in the way that seagulls (of parrot colours) storm the home-going fishing boats.

Ever since war began I knew that I'd be a soldier, though no one else would hear of it. It's not that I'm against what my family has planned for me. It's not that I'm against the idea of studying law and nor am I ungrateful for what my family has done for me. Also I am fully aware of the responsibilities that they have placed on me, but there's time enough for all that. At seventeen I just didn't want to be a boy any longer and felt a need to break out of the family protection that has always coated me. Out there, outside the school gates, away from my family and my mountain, there was a whole world to see, a Battalion to belong to, a war to fight in. Since I knew I'd never be given family permission, and since I believed there were already enough school photos, enough sports cups, enough certificates to satisfy Ma, Pita, The Uncle, the family, I took permission for myself.

The day after Sports Day was the last day of the first term and instead of packing just what I needed for the holidays I packed all my belongings. It was quite usual for me to go back home and stay for a week with Uncle Willy in the school holidays, and then to continue on to Wellington to spend the second week with Ma.

But I wrote to Ma and told her that I wanted to spend all of the holidays back under our mountain with my uncle, as there were no other young men around to help the older people with their work now. It was true. Most of my cousins were already away at war. Others had left for the cities to find jobs and it was a hard time for the backhome people. Ma didn't need me in Wellington.

However, before I set out for Uncle Willy's, I went down to the bus depot, changed out of my uniform and went along to the army recruiting office to join up.

On arrival at Uncle Willy's I told him that I'd left school and wanted to stay with him until a position was found for me in Wellington, otherwise I'd be manpowered into war work. Near to the end of the holidays I wrote a letter to the school to explain that I wouldn't be returning. I forged my mother's signature on it. After that I waited for my call-up papers, and when they arrived told Uncle Willy I was returning to Wellington. Quite easy really. Ma believed I was back in school by then.

Of course everyone had to know what I'd done eventually, but it was several weeks before they found out. I wrote to Ma from camp but she never wrote back, so when on leave I always went to Uncle Willy's just to keep out of her way. I was thankful that big brother Pita was off to war by the time it was all known. Brother Rangi had returned to war zones also.

Pita and Rangi, being so much older than me, will never be able to think of me as anything other than a kid. One day soon I'll be joining them – but of course won't get a very good reception, especially from Pita. Their hopes for the future of our family have all been pinned on me.

Well, the future is the future. Now is now. I'm happy with the choice I made.

After many days with only ourselves and the American cruiser beating along in the centre of this vast, shifting circle bound by the horizon, we were joined by four destroyers. But before we crossed the equator the Americans and part of the destroyer escort left us, going off in another direction. We were supposed to be in dangerous waters.

We were all given a tot of rum on the day we crossed the equator, which we did at 3 p.m. on 24 July 1943 – as I have written on my souvenir card handed out to us by King Neptune. Some of the boys were hanging over the side watching out for this famous line!

Though some of our time on board is spent in drills and lectures there are other organised activities which help keep us interested as we make our way across mainly calm and empty seas.

Just about every night there has been a concert or entertainment of some description. These are put on by different troop sections or the Women's Auxiliary, and sometimes by the ship's personnel. We've put on several shows ourselves and sometimes a soloist or one of our quartets has taken part in a concert organised by other units. One of our boys is a pianist and he's always in demand.

A favourite sport on board is boxing for which I've taken out the lightweight title. A kid in fifty years' time might like to know that. I received one big shiner for my efforts.

The first time I attended a race meeting I won five shillings but came out losing every time after that. The racetrack is a long piece of canvas that has been marked out in sections. Once all the bets have been placed, each horse is forwarded along its track according to numbers rolled on a dice, continuing on amid all the shouting and barracking until winners and placings are decided. The little horses have been cast in metal and painted black, white or grey, or different shades of brown.

No more sleeping out on deck for fear of malaria, but despite everything I can truly say I'm having a good time on my way to join my Battalion and heading off to war.

Our first sight of land came when we spotted a group of three islands. We watched a flying boat land close to the main one, and it was a day later that we sighted coastland, presumably of Eastern Africa. I was surprised to see a mountain with snow on it, a reminder of my own mountain.

Thoughts of home?

But this doesn't mean I'm homesick. Far from it.

Eventually we arrived in the Gulf of Aden and called into the port to refuel and take on water. Looking out beyond the buildings of the port we could see houses of grey stone perched against steep hill faces.

No sooner had the boat stopped when natives were out in canoes trading fruit for money and cigarettes and other things. I saw at least two pairs of boots go overboard, as well as blankets, shirts and one ukelele. Chaps are going to return to their swags and wonder where their gear has gone.

We went on up the Red Sea passing by many islands. There were ships everywhere – dozens of cargo and coastal boats, as well as aircraft carriers and hospital ships. I've learned that since leaving Fremantle we've travelled nearly five thousand miles and expect to reach our destination, Suez, at some time tomorrow.

3

maadi

We sighted Tewfik, Port of Cairo, early on the morning of 5 August and anchored at mid-morning among ships of every description, going ashore on to a crowded waterfront where we just couldn't get used to people pushing themselves on to us to buy cigarettes and lollies, and fruit that didn't look too good. There were plenty of beggars too and they put you on the spot. Anyway we managed to have a good feed before boarding the train, beginning a slow journey with stops all along the way.

The first few miles of country were barren and dry – sandy, and dotted with clusters of mud houses that looked broken down and poor. But further on we were surprised to see how fertile the land was. Wheat seemed to be the main crop. Water was carried by canals throughout the whole district, and natives used either donkeys or oxen for work and transport. We soon became used to the vendors at the stations and had fun bargaining with them all along the way. The wogs are a lot of thieves, but in many instances the Maori beat them at their own game. We found it much cooler on shore than out at sea, especially as night came on when we passed through Cairo.

We arrived here in Maadi well after midnight and rose late in the morning. To my surprise and horror I walked right into Brother Pita. He pressed his nose to mine, but only because I am his brother, then without a word, turned his back and walked off. Brother Rangi, when I came across him not long afterwards, just laughed and called me a silly bugger.

I was unprepared to find myself encamped with my brothers, because although I thought I would meet up with them eventually, I imagined that at present they'd be away in the thick of battle somewhere. Rangi and I talked for a while about the people at home before we began duties. So I suppose it could have been much worse.

Most of the first day was spent making our tents comfortable and becoming familiar with our area. We looked around different huts and canteens and kept coming across boys we knew. There was plenty of cheek from the old hands who kept asking us if we'd bought ourselves a one-way ticket because they reckoned a two-way ticket was a waste of money.

I never would have imagined such a place, with the first impression being of a completely flat, bare landscape for miles and miles. As you become more accustomed to the view you notice the low rolling hummocks and the long plateaux. But it's all sand. I never could have imagined such a vastness of sand.

Nor could I have imagined the size of Maadi Camp. The hundreds of tents and huts, the row upon row of vehicles, the depots, the canteens and quarters make up a whole town covering many acres.

The Lowry Hut, in among all of this, has been provided by the New Zealand YMCA. It's a long brick building where you can buy food or relax with a drink. There's a swimming pool nearby, a good place to cool down in.

Our very own Maori Battalion mobile canteen is here too. It's a covered truck, called Te Rau Aroha, given as a special gift to the Maori Battalion by all the little kids of our backhome native schools. I remember kids and parents at home raising money for it in all sorts of ways – by holding concerts, running raffles and card nights, growing vegetables and making handcrafts for sale. Outside the stores they organised copper trails where people lined up their pennies and ha'pennies all along the edge of the footpath, from one verandah pole to the next, to the next.

When I saw the truck my thoughts kept returning to those little backhome snot-noses with their pennies, running off to school, some of whose names we can now see written on the inside walls and doors of the canteen. Their message to us has been painted up on the truck's canopy in two languages:

PRESENTED TO THE MAORI BATTALION
AS A TOKEN OF LOVE FROM THE CHILDREN
OF THE NATIVE SCHOOLS OF NEW ZEALAND

He tohu aroha na nga tamariki o nga kura maori
O niu tireni ki te ope whawhai o te iwi maori e tau
mai na i te pae o te pakanga i te mura o te ahi

My own backhome school, where I began my schooling when I was five, collected £20-1s-9d, and once when my family sent me backhome for the school holidays The Uncle gave me 2/- to give to them as our contribution. Altogether the schools raised £1000.

It was a thrill to see this result of their efforts and now to hear of some of the adventures the canteen has been involved in. Our mates of desert campaigns told us about Te Rau Aroha's wheels being immobilised in soft sand in the Sinai Desert and how, with enemy closing in, they all had to dig like blazes to get it out. They said it was captured in Minqar Qaim and managed a lucky escape, but only after all its goods had been ransacked. It survived a Luftwaffe attack too, bombs bursting all around it and completely wrecking most of the other vehicles in the convoy. Te Rau Aroha ended up bashed and battered with all of its tyres flat, but still mobile and with its wireless still going.

One of its most talked-about escapades was when it took part in a bayonet charge somewhere round Tripoli. There it was, the boys said, belting down a ridge in among all these mad Maori soldiers with their bayonets fixed, charging like stampeding bulls towards an enemy section. The van was shot up by a machine gunner, but with no harm done to its drivers and with the enemy eventually retreating.

It's been under fire on several occasions they say, as our man, Charlie YM, stops at nothing to serve men in battle, venturing to forward positions in order to deliver all sorts of goods from trench to trench. So the old truck has its fair share of dents, scars and bullet wounds and has been awarded its own wound stripes and battle stars too – something we're all proud of. It's part of home to us, part of our backhome families, and part of our own Battalion family now as well.

Charlie keeps the canteen well stocked with all kinds of sweets, chocolate, biscuits and drinks. The tinned goods include seafoods such as toheroa, mussels and oysters, and one of the favourite purchases in this weather is tinned peaches with New Zealand tinned cream that we always have at Christmas time at home. There's a supply of cigarettes and New Zealand tobacco as well as everything in the way of soaps, razors and toothbrushes – also books and stationery. The canteen is where we gather to yarn and sing and listen to the radio.

Reveille is at five-thirty every morning with breakfast at six and route marches and lectures right up to lunch. In the afternoons we have siesta time.

All the battalions have got teams together and we're practising for sports competitions. But though these competitions are taken very seriously, of more interest to me since my arrival have been discussions about the takeover of Sicily by the Allies, and what that might mean. All the German occupiers were sent packing out of Sicily, and not long afterwards, Mussolini was ousted from power. He got the boot! This all happened while we were making our way across the oceans. It all means something as far as our future is concerned. In the meantime our practices keep us occupied.

Sporting competitions are seen as a good way of bringing all of us new boys together as our Battalion is being built up. We're not the only reinforcement. Others have been marching in over three months, replacing those who went home on furlough or who didn't make it through the desert.

At the divisional swimming champs I won all my swims – heats and finals – just as I always did at school. I wouldn't mind if someone walloped me now and again, but never mind, the whole Battalion was there cheering and I was happy to do it for Twenty-eighth. Pita was watching, which pleased me more than I can say. Rangi has been the all-round champ several times himself, so I'm told, but he didn't enter this time. He left it all to me, he said afterwards. Anyway most of the swimming was won by the Twenty-eighth – eight out of nine competitions. Good, because Maori Battalion teams didn't fare too well in the sports contests earlier in the month, winning only the tug-o'-war. Some of the boys had to be restrained from getting in and helping the tug-o'-war team otherwise it would've been disqualified.

This is practically a new Battalion they say, though there are still some of the originals around, like my brother Rangi, who, apart from a two-month spell at home because of blindness, has been with Twenty-eighth since its beginning. There are such stories about him. I'm proud to be his brother. His blindness proved to be temporary and on the journey home his sight was already returning.

I'd been here almost a fortnight before Pita decided to break his silence. I had been avoiding him as much as possible, thinking that though he could choose not to speak to me there was nothing much else he could do. Here I was at last, on the other side of the world, not the first and not the last runaway off to fight in a war.

Back at the recruitment office all those months ago, I expected some sort of interrogation regarding my age, but there wasn't one. I believe they're taking anyone of any age now, because they're so desperate to fill the gaps. Maori Battalion casualties have been extremely high and replacements are needed. Unless you're medically unfit, and as long as you tell them, when asked for proof of age, that there is no record of your birth, you're certain to be allowed to join up. That's what I think. Anyway I'm happy with what I did, proud to be a member of the Maori Battalion and off on the biggest adventure of my life.

I expected a real ear-bashing from Pita, but all he wanted to tell me was that he'd heard the war was scaling down and that the Maori Battalion wouldn't be going any further.

We've all heard these rumours. The Maori politicians at home want us recalled, saying that our Battalion of volunteers has done enough already and that there have been too many losses from such a small population. Pita just seems relieved that I won't be involved in the fighting now that we'll all soon be on our way home. That's what he believes, but I really don't think there's any truth in it.

The locals, dressed in their long robes and close-fitting hats, come every day with their carts to the weighing stations, bringing fruit and vegetables heaped in big woven baskets. Or they bring eggs and other more delicate supplies in wooden crates which they carry on their shoulders. There are women wearing head-cloths and big dresses who sit round large wash basins washing and rinsing army clothes from daylight until dark. What a world there is to know about. The washerwomen remind me of the mothers backhome who take their washing down to the creek in summer time, soaping and rubbing and rinsing and yarning and spreading their clothes across the bushes to dry.

We've been getting into hard training in all this heat and dust. The sun boils down on to the parade ground and reflects off the sand right into your face, which doubles its intensity. The dust is so bad sometimes that you can barely see from one side of the parade ground to the other. This training is the most difficult of all physical things I've ever done so far and that includes all the stuff that I did out on the hills with Uncle Ju.

I'm quite happy about it all, pleased to be able to really test myself for the first time in my life, among the very best. It's so good to be here and to be part of such a great Battalion.

And I do believe my names give me the right to be here anyway, my full first name being Te Hokowhitu-a-Tu – The Many Fighting Men of Tumatauenga. Tumatauenga is the patron of war. The name was given to me by the grandmothers to honour my father and his war – my father being a member of the Pioneer Battalion of Maori soldiers of 1914–1918 which was known by the name. My saint's name, Bernard, was given by my mother and was the name I was known by while I was at boarding school. Saint Bernard is the patron of travellers and mountain climbers. So if it is correct that we are heading for the mountains of Italy I can feel well patronised by both my names. I can truly believe I made the right decision.

What it means (i.e. Germany being booted out of Sicily and Benito out of Italy) is that Italy has now signed an armistice and that the Eighth Army has crossed over into Italy. Since our New Zealand Division is part of the Eighth Army, the logic is that we'll be on the way to help out very soon. We haven't heard this officially, but that's where we're going I'd say – to Italy, Land of Pope and Glory.

Training is getting tougher every day, which to my mates and me is further evidence that we're heading off into action. Exercises take place out in the fields as well as among bush and around houses, and we've stepped up weapon training. Route marches include plenty of hill country. Good. Can't wait to catch up to the war.

Here's something odd and strange and unwanted as far as I'm concerned. Brother Pita came and sat with me last night while there was a bit of local brew going round, and at first began talking again about me returning home. Nothing has happened regarding the return of our Battalion, thank goodness for that, but it seems that some compromises have been suggested. I think there's been talk that younger brothers could be sent home in cases where there are more than two from the same family at war. There are three from our family but there are some families that have four sons away, and one I know of where there were five but three have died already. Pita was talking as though this was all about to happen, but I don't think so. He wants so much for this war to be over that

I feel sorry for him. If anyone should go home it should be him, after all he's the one with a wife and expected family.

After he'd given his opinion about these matters he sat quietly for a while. I thought I was in for a lecture, but much to my surprise and embarrassment, Pita, Big Brother, twelve years my senior, who has been more of a father than a brother to me, and who has never spoken to me in all my life except to correct or command me, began talking about personal matters, informing me about his life as though there were some things that needed explaining.

He talked about Jess too. It's none of my business. I'm not his confessor.

4

dream

Pita was a late joiner. He never wanted to go to war and told Ma he never would. But after a few years he found he couldn't not go, couldn't just sit at home waiting to get on with life – or couldn't just wait about for there to be the kind of life he wanted to get on with and not do anything about it. He had to get in and help end it, not just expect others to do it on his behalf.

To 'help end it' was the reason he gave Ma and the relatives, who all pleaded with him that one was enough from a family. The one they were referring to was his brother Rangi who had been one of the first to leave, and who had been away nearly three years by then.

'And one war is enough too,' his aunts and uncles told him. 'Think what the first one did to your father, think what it did to your ma. Think what it did to all of you.' But they couldn't prevent Pita from enlisting once he'd made up his mind.

There were other reasons he had for joining up, too. There was something in him, some wrong thing that hurt people or frightened them – something stuck in his works, pulling down inside him like a stiffened claw, which he needed to take to war. There was the mess of himself and what it did to dreams.

He needed to escape, and there was a war to escape to.

The girl, who started out as Pita's dream during the week that war was declared, came towards him down Molesworth Street as he made his way home after work one afternoon. This girl, who was wearing a blue coat with a velvet collar, a white beret with a silver pin through it, white gloves and brown shoes, had looked at him. A dream was all he wanted her to be.

The street lights were already on as she passed by. He saw how her brown hair tucked under the sides of the beret and hooked back behind her ears, noticed the thinness of her face, how pale her skin was under lightly rouged cheeks, and how she had brightened her mouth with lipstick. He didn't want his sisters wearing lipstick or any of that other stuff on their faces.

The girl's eyes were small and quick and dark brown, while her nose was little and pointed and made him feel like laughing. She became his dream, something to have in his life, something that was more than meatworks and making sure the family all had shoes, something more to think about than keeping his brother out of trouble.

Pita had other dreams too, ones that he knew he could make happen and that were already coming true. They were his dreams for Ma and the family. It was up to him to make them real. But the girl didn't have to be real. She could just be his dream. This girl wasn't for him, not even when the world was free.

A week later, when he and his sisters were on their way to the Club, he saw the girl again, carrying a flat satchel in one hand and a basket in the other. It seemed his sisters knew who she was.

'Her from the cake shop,' Sophie said as the girl passed by.

Sophie and Moana had gone ahead of him then, giggling into their hands about flour, icing sugar and raspberry jam. He knew they were referring to the girl's make-up. They were naming cakes and he was wild with them. He caught up to them and told them not to have such bloody bad manners, carrying on like that, all up and down the street. They shut up then and walked the rest of the way in silence. In fact they were so silent that he couldn't help thinking they might be inwardly laughing at him. His sisters had their secrets, conspired, made faces at each other when they thought he wasn't looking. They tiptoed round, pretended, said what they thought they should say when he was present, often making him feel that he was a man alone in a family.

Further up the street, opposite parliament, he came to the cake shop, its doors shut and screens in the windows.

Carrying what?

A music bag and a shopping basket.

In the basket was a white paper bag with twists in the top corners. In the paper bag, he thought, would be three or four of the cakes his sisters had mentioned: melting moments, butterfly cakes, vanilla slices, sponge drops, lamingtons, louise cake, fly cemeteries.

He didn't know how Sophie and Moana knew the girl was from the cake shop. All he knew was that when they first came to Wellington and their uncle-in-parliament had found jobs in the meatworks for himself and Rangi, his sisters had had time to absorb the city. They'd explored, window-shopped, learned the names of streets, found out where the tram stops were and which lines the numbered trams were taking. He didn't like the girls being round the streets when they should be at home helping Ma. Everything could go wrong.

Where to with her cakes?

To the tram stop? To catch a tram going where?

Or maybe she was off to the railway station to board a train to Johnsonville, the Hutt or Paekakariki. She was a girl alone, going home to a family with three? four? cakes in a paper bag. Sugar and raspberry make-up. It was something to wonder about.

He told his two sisters he didn't want them out roaming the streets, leaving Ma at home on her own, but to his annoyance Ma had sided with them, saying it couldn't hurt if they went out walking occasionally. It was different now Ma said, and told him he didn't have to worry about her being on her own once in a while.

She reminded him that she was never alone anyway, not since they'd joined the Club.

Still, he didn't like it. Sophie and Moana sounded different sometimes. Silly, kind of loose, and only tightened themselves up when they knew he was around, or that's the impression he had. If they weren't careful everything could go wrong. They could all go wrong. His sisters could be seized. Rangi could end up in the clink. They could all be murdered. Tuboy could escape from the family or be knocked down and sliced by trams. In spite of prayers, Mass on Sundays, their mother's rosaries and novenas, everything could blow up.

All their dreams.

He thought his sisters might smoke behind his back if they had money, might dress up like tarts with muck all over their faces, chase round after men. He couldn't tell what was in his sisters' minds.

What Ma said was true about life being different now and that she was never alone. Ever since they'd arrived in the city more than two years earlier, even before they'd joined the Club and Ma had become part of the Club's welfare committee, there was always someone at home.

Sometimes it was a neighbour that Ma had invited in, or their children who she looked after while their mothers were in hospital. It could be Chinee Boy from next door, or Maureen and Joey from across the road.

Sometimes there were relatives who came to stay for weeks or months until they were able to find work and accommodation of their own. Sometimes they were strangers, like the girl Mihiroa who his sisters had brought home from the railway station, a girl wrapped in a blanket who had made a journey from her home town and waited at the station for two days for a cousin who was supposed to meet her. Mihiroa stayed for a month, then one day when Pita and Rangi came home from work she'd gone. Not long after that he and his brother had given up their beds to a young couple who hadn't been allowed into the accommodation that had been arranged for them. On other occasions there'd be a girl Ma had found drunk in a shop doorway and brought in, and once a girl with a baby who'd been turned out by her family.

On arriving home from work each day Pita didn't know whose pair of shoes was likely to be found on the mat inside the door.

They'd been living in the city for almost a year when, on arriving home one afternoon, he saw a pair of men's shoes on the mat, polished and glossy. There was a grey hat on a chair in the hall.

That morning he'd given Ma a half crown so that his sisters could go and make the final payment on a wireless that they'd been paying off. The wireless was made of dark wood, almost square in shape, but scalloped at the top edge like the entrance to an important building. Covering the face of it, behind the fluted fretwork, was shiny fawn-coloured cloth woven through with gold thread in a diamond pattern which he was sure Ma and his sisters would exclaim over. He was hoping Sophie and Moana had managed to carry the wireless home safely and was looking forward to setting it up on the mantelpiece and turning it on. Now, as he went in, he was disappointed that there was a visitor.

Sitting at the table in the kitchen was a man dressed in a light grey suit, a Rinso and Reckitts Blue shirt, a perfectly knotted tie. He was spreading plum jam on home-baked bread and cutting it in a finicky way, pressing down on the slice with the tip of a finger and thumb, drawing the knife across to cut it into even pieces. He chewed, not letting a crumb drop, sipped tea as though doing so from fine china. But he put the cup down as Pita came in, standing to make his greetings.

'I was telling the good lady that I was in France, side by side with your late, brave father,' he said. 'In the fray together your father and I, and we were taken together, after the gassing in Messines, to the military hospital in England.'

When Fred finished eating he took a folded handkerchief from his pocket, wiped his fingertips with it then began talking about a club that he would like them to join.

'A home away from home for our people coming to the city,' he said, 'so our people can keep their customs and traditions, practise the songs and dances and arts of the Maori, learn from each other and be a comfort to each other in this new and different world.

'So dear family, it's a place for assembly and friendship, hospitality, comradeship and camaraderie, where we can all come together, where we can relax and learn and make ourselves at home. It's a place where we can welcome others of our race, befriend the lonely, care for the sick and needy. Therefore I have come to extend to you and your family, dear mother, my personal invitation to the Ngati Poneke Club, a place for people of all ages and denominations. The city can be unkind to those unfamiliar with its ways. I was a lost boy in the city myself once, sleeping rough at fourteen, not far from here, in the grounds of parliament, with my candle-box of belongings.

'Because, young Pita, many a young person is lured by the prospects and charm of the city only to find himself bereft and abandoned. It is from loneliness and want that many give in to the temptations of such a place. With no one to befriend them they seek out unworthy companions and become captives of the unscrupulous. They become the destitute, inhabiting the vilest of quarters. The evil, liquor, becomes their companion by day and by night, and with it comes immorality, and disease of both body and mind.

'Ah but these ones are not in the fortunate position such as yourselves, dear mother, with the close ties of family. They have come alone, or they are runaways. This evening at eight o'clock you would be welcomed with open arms.'

He stood to go, saying to Pita as he put on his shoes, 'Your father was a man of God, a brave man, affected much worse than I. Not only by the gassing but also by remnants sustained throughout. Yes, remnants throughout, my dear departed comrade. We were shipped home together. Brothers-in-arms, I've been telling the dear lady.'

5

moving

There was a terrible accident at our first transit camp, which was in a place called Burg el Arab, a hundred miles on from Maadi. Instead of travelling by transport the whole New Zealand Division marched the hundred miles – which we all thought showed we were being toughened up for something. And from the time of our arrival we were kept hard at it, the training including plenty of night exercises, which we reckoned was bound to have some significance for the future. We advanced from single unit manoeuvres to whole brigade operations, then on to full division exercises. Everything was really warming up.

As well as a step-up in training, sporting competitions continued to keep us interested. All the battalions had teams and I earned myself a new name while taking part in the sprint races.

At school I never had running shoes and always ran barefoot. Because of all the new gear I needed for school, especially in the way of shoes – already having rugby boots, tennis shoes, sandals and dress shoes – I just didn't want to ask the family for anything more.

Most of the Battalion runners wore tennis shoes or running shoes because the ground was so hot, but because the soles of my feet have not yet lost the hard layer of skin that builds up after years of going without shoes, I am always more comfortable without them. So I entered these sprints barefooted, and just as always, won all my races. So instead of Tu, or Tuboy, the boys began to call me Two Bare and Running Bare, which settled down after a while as Tu Bear. It's all right. I like the name. It's better than Tuboy.

By now it was obvious we were going somewhere soon. We had been given our inoculations and issued with battle dress – warm singlets and underpants, a leather jerkin and two pairs of boots. But despite all this activity, Burg el Arab will always be in our minds because of the tragedy that took place there.

One night we were having a really good go, practising an advance under a barrage of live ammo for the first time. It was all really exciting, with gun flashes lighting the sky and all the noise and explosions. Shells were screaming overhead, landing forward of where we were assembled, and we were all ready to move.

The next thing we knew the shells were falling short, right into our contingent. Men were dropping all around us and the artillery commander was shouting, 'Cease fire! Cease fire!'

Four were killed. One of the dead was cut clean in half. Several others, probably about ten, were wounded, one of them being a mate who came across on the boat with us. That was my first sight of men gunned down. It made me sick. Our poor Battalion. No one could say what went wrong, or no one would. We couldn't make sense of it.

Our next move was to another transit camp on the outskirts of Alexandria. Before being transported to the docks we were ordered to remove all forms of identification from our uniforms. We still wore our two identity discs round our necks of course, which wouldn't be removed unless we copped it. Well, if you cop it, one is removed, one goes with you. We call them our meat tickets. But these are not visible under our clothing. Nothing of what we were doing was allowed to be mentioned in letters home, which is still the case now. But I suppose it's okay for me to be writing about it here in my journal since there's no one to read it but me, that is unless there are a few ghosts looking over my shoulder. I wouldn't be surprised.

We soon found ourselves crowded aboard a boat called the *Nieuw Holland* and in convoy with *Llangibby Castle* and *Letitia*, crossing the Mediterranean – which I'd describe as inky, somewhere between Stephens radiant blue ink and Stephens blue-black. There was no doubt by then that we were off to Italy.

Our Battalion was among the last of the flights to leave, the New Zealand Division having begun its move ten days earlier. We carried so much on board – blankets, clothing for all weathers, dry rations and water cans, guns and ammo and tents – that it was difficult to get up the gangway without knocking each other overboard. We had our personal stuff as well, and there was no room to move in the sleeping quarters once we'd stowed our gear.

However, it was a smooth crossing and we felt we were being well looked after – in the water by destroyers, and by our planes from up above.

Last night we were chatting about what we carry about with us, what we wouldn't like to be without as we go on our way. With most it is photographs of wives, girlfriends and family; or maybe letters. Others carry their greenstone tiki or their Saint Christopher medals. There's more than one rabbit's foot, and there are ukeleles, mouth organs, song and prayer sheets, not to mention bibles. Some will not move anywhere without chapter and verse. Brother Pita has his rosary and a small scent bottle filled with holy water. As well there are rings and pins and favourite tobacco tins, or knitted scarves and socks. Denny has his pocket knife with which he carves out tiny wooden horses.

Some have more recent acquisitions that they treasure. Brother Rangi has a Luger that he takes everywhere with him. The German hand-guns are prized and said to be far superior to our own. Those who have them are not only keen to use them but also want to take them home as souvenirs.

The fountain pen that I write with was presented to me by Father John at our primary school prize-giving when I was awarded the parish scholarship that saw me off to boarding school.

At first I was happy to go away to school to get away from home, having some mistaken idea that I'd be moving out into the world. Well, as far as 'out into the world' is concerned I was better off round the streets of Wellington. The least I can say is that I was out from under the eye of Big Brother and The Uncle, though at school there were plenty of big brothers to keep an eye on me too. Never mind, I liked school on the whole, always enjoyed books and learning. And I've always liked the fountain pen, which is mottled grey and black with flecks of red here and there. I think it's the winking red speckles that bring it out of the ordinary. It has a gold nib, and a gold lever that lifts and presses down to suck in the blue-black ink. Blue-black is best because it lets words speak for themselves, that's what I think. Radiant blue gets in your eyes, tries to do the speaking. There's a gold clasp kept in place by a black screw-on cap. Brother Pita spent good money having my name engraved on it, and for me it's my pen that I would not like to be without as we journey on.

Well who knows where our keepsakes will end up, really?

Early in the morning, after four days on water, we were greatly relieved to see Italy in outline and were soon able to make out the white stone buildings of Taranto, some of them broken down by bombing. We disembarked from a gangway down the side of the ship on to landing barges to be ferried to the wharf, and if we thought the *Nieuw Holland* was crowded it was nothing to what it was like on the ferry. We were so tightly packed, and so hot, that I felt like stripping off and going overboard. On second thoughts one wouldn't want to swim because the water all round the harbour was full of wrecks and rubbish. It was thick and greasy.

We left our gear behind on the wharf for the trucks to bring, then marched through Taranto and on for about five miles to the village of Statte with its narrow cobblestone ways. All along the road people stopped and stared, wondering, I suppose, where these black boys hailed from. Who can blame them? We were sliding our eyes about too, trying to get a good look at them as well as at our surroundings.

All we found by way of a camp when we arrived were benches, timber and dunny seats stacked in an open space among olive trees and stone fences, so there was work to do. The cooks' gear hadn't arrived but we were looked after by Twenty-fifth Battalion who had encamped some days earlier. Luckily our packs came in time for us to pitch our bivvies before nightfall in the cooler climate.

The countryside reminds me of home with its green hills and paddocks, though the crops are different. Here in Statte we look out over olive and nut groves and rows of grape vines. There's a different light here, a kind of orange atmosphere. The sky could be a home sky, but it doesn't seem as high somehow. There's no silver. As at home we know the sea is not far away.

It's quite spooky how old the buildings are. Made of stone, some of them have been standing for more than a century, more than two or three in some cases. The houses, also made of stone, would never burn or rot or blow away like our wooden houses at home (or be knocked to pieces by a rampant father). It takes a war to do that kind of damage, of which there is evidence everywhere we go.

But there's talk it will soon be over, that the Allies will soon have it won. Not before I've had a crack at it I hope.

There are people about selling fruit and nuts and wine, and we're doing our best to communicate, attempting to pick up some of the language.

Plenty singsong at night.

Vino a volontà.

Also, plenty talk from Big Brother. Again.

Must be the vino.

The day after our arrival in Statte, our mobile canteen, shipped from Alexandria, arrived from Bari. That afternoon one of the local barbers set up shop under a tree nearby, and we sat about with our ukes and mouth organs, singing and waiting for haircuts. Now and again someone would attempt a conversation with the barber or one of his companions, whom I think were his brother and nephew. The brother and nephew had almonds for sale but seemed happy to sit with us after we'd bought what we wanted. They seemed to enjoy the singing. We were having some fun trying to understand each other and also we were trying to get them to sing for us.

After a while the boy's father spoke to his son, who stood, clasped his hands in front of him and began to sing. He was a boy of about twelve with a high, sweet voice. I lay there under the trees listening, and for some reason recalled a time back in the hills of home looking up at a bare sky. High up against the sky was a bird sweeping across, turning and sweeping across, all the time rising. And for the first time I felt a kind of homesickness creep through me. It was like a sound breathed through hollowed bone. I knew it wasn't that I wanted to be home, only that I wished the home people could be there with us listening to the boy. Their hearts would've expanded in their chests as mine did, their throats would've locked as mine did, causing tears to run from their eyes.

We wouldn't leave the little one alone, getting him to sing again and again, verse after verse, until we were able to join in:

Sul mare luccica l'astro d'argento
Placida è l'onda prospero è il vento
Venite all'agile, barchetta mia, Santa Lucia, Santa Lucia.

We've been singing the song ever since, and sometimes include it during practice in the choir that we've started up. Of course it sounds very different with all the harmonies we put into it. I don't think that's how the song is meant to be sung at all, feel certain that it's best sung solo by a young boy. Also I'm sure our pronunciation is not the best, but we enjoy the song all the same. We sent the family home loaded with goods from the canteen.

Our whole battalion assembled round a huge fire a few nights ago and recorded songs for the home crowd. Flat-out on ukes and banjos; mouth-organs going to town. It was a lovely night. But our last days in Statte have been wet and stormy, with lightning lashing blue whips around the sky and thunder striding and bellowing across it. We've been on the ends of our shovels, constantly clearing camp tracks and cleaning out the drains.

Route marches and practices around streets, in trees and fields have included plenty of night-time manoeuvres, much of it in the rain. We're hoping for a couple of sunny days so that we can dry out our gear before moving on.

6

hero

Pita's earliest memory of seeing his father was when he, at four years of age and Rangi two years younger, were taken on a train journey to visit him in Wellington hospital. The boys were not allowed into the ward, so Uncle Willy and Uncle Ju put them up on their shoulders, from where, through a window, they caught glimpses of this inert form of the man they were told was their father. The man, who had been gassed and shot and who had pieces of bullet in his spine and all through him, was a shape on a rack, a mound under white covers. The only visible part of him was his unmoving, bandaged head, which somehow looked as if it had been separated from the rest of him, as though it could, with a push, roll and smash on the floor.

Pita was two when his father left for war. Rangi had not been born by then. Neither of them remembered him. So prior to that hospital visit, their father had been just a story of a soldier leaving home on a wagon, then travelling by train and ship to a place called war, which was far away across the sea. In this war place there were guns and bombs and an enemy. From this place of war men from under their mountain had been reported missing, wounded and dead. But besides being known to them in story, the boys had evidence of their father's existence as a smiling man in soldier uniform in a photograph right there in the middle of the mantelpiece. There were several pictures in their family album which showed him too – a man on a doorstep at his uncle's house, a man on a horse with his sister sitting up behind him, a man drinking beer with his cousins, a man on a beach laughing and holding an octopus.

In those times there was wailing. Pita remembered the wailing as people gathered to cry for the dead. There were aunties taking breath deep into themselves before letting their heads and shoulders sink to their shrinking chests, as moans, as of cows dying, came out from in them. There were tears running down the faces of the grandfathers. Also there were people making long journeys to the hospital in order to visit those, like his father, who had been brought back in white ships.

'Little Father' was what everyone called Pita in those years, and for some of his aunties the name stuck to him well beyond those times. He was 'Little Father' who would grow up brave too, they promised him, even though it was his brother Rangi, the chatterer, the one always laughing and full of mischief, who had more of Dadda's ways.

At some time after the visit to the hospital, maybe it was months later, or maybe a year, their father came home to become part of a place in a room, which soon became like a dead space in their house and in their lives. It was a place in front of windows in the room that Ma had furnished with covered boxes and rag rugs. It was a room where old people were taken to rest while meals were prepared for them and where palliasses could be put down when visitors came to stay. It was a room which would be used when the priest came when it was their family's turn to hold monthly Mass.

Once their father was brought home from hospital the room could still be used for visitors, for waiting and sleeping, and for Mass, but on ordinary days it became a place with a presence now

– of a brave man, a soldier, a father, who seemed not to be any of those things at all.

Early in the mornings, even before their father was out of bed, the presence of him was in the room. There was the big empty armchair in front of the windows where he would sit later, the one Aunty Dinah's sons had carried in a week before he was brought home. There were cushions and a rug, and the dumpy that Ma had stuffed with rag and paper which she would lift their father's feet on to when she was settling him. To one side of the chair was a stool with father's medicines on it. On the other side were two boxes, draped with a cloth, where Ma put father's cup and plate, or where Uncle Willy could place a bottle of beer.

Even with the chair empty in the mornings Pita and his brother walked through the room without talking or hurrying, keeping their eyes away from this space where, later in the morning, the man who was a soldier, a hero and also their father, would sit. This man was nothing like the photograph on the mantelpiece with medals pinned into the wallpaper above it that were to do with bravery; nothing like the photograph in the album of the man in swimming togs with wet hair stuck down, laughing, holding up an octopus that he'd pulled from a rock-pool and turned inside-out so that it couldn't strangle him.

On returning from school, and before they'd changed out of their school clothes, Ma would send him and Rangi in to greet their father who would be sitting in the chair wearing the coloured jersey Aunty Dinah had knitted for him from ripped-out wool. Their father would sometimes lean towards them letting his head fall forward to where his shaking hands clawed together in front of his chest. Sometimes he would mumble something that resembled their names as though he had some memory of them.

Apart from that they seldom heard him speak, but they heard the grunting sounds that he made and the shouting and screaming that came from their parents' bedroom in the dark. Sometimes at night Uncle Willy would come from next door with a lamp to help Ma quieten him down.

Once a month, on the day before the priest came, Aunty Dinah and Cousin Ana would come and help Ma prepare the room for Mass. Uncle Willy and Uncle Ju would take father over to the verandah next door and keep him there all afternoon while the aunties swept and washed the floors, dusted the ledges and photographs and cleaned the windows. They'd drape the boxes with the Mass cloth and bring in flowers from Aunty Dinah's garden.

At Mass the next morning their father was a presence, like someone especially God-favoured, dressed in a white shirt and good brown trousers that Ma had bought from the jumble lady, the big chair pulled close to the priest by the altar of flowers and candles. He was like a suffering prize that they could all associate with in order to be especially favoured in the good books of heaven. It was always their father's privilege to be the first to receive the Body of Christ at Communion time, and Pita noticed that the Host placed by the freckled hand of the ginger priest on the tongue hanging out of their father's mouth – blue and spongy, like hua paua – was always whole and unbroken. It was the rest of them who received unto themselves half wafers of the Living Son, or sometimes quarters or fragments. Pita and Rangi would watch the white fingertips of the priest break the discs into halves during the consecration, marvelling that this could be achieved so perfectly. All the same they felt cheated. Halves and bits seemed not right, seemed like a delivery of purity of soul that was only half-pai, as though Father Vanderbeke was a thief.

'One eye, one arm, one leg,' Rangi whispered one morning during the Agnus Dei, and Uncle Willy who was sitting directly in front of them turned and said, 'And one arsehole.'

Pita and Rangi burst out laughing even though it was a sin to say bad things or think bad thoughts about hosts or priests. Because even though priests smoked and said 'bloody' they were close to God. They were God's very high-up servants. One look from Ma reminded them of that.

After Mass they all went out into the kitchen where food was set out on the table, and waited for Father to take off the vestments and pack them into his bag with the hosts and wine and candles.

Pita remembered that once when everything was ready they'd waited rather a long time for Father Van who was taking his time over a cigarette that one of the uncles had given him. When at last the priest came and stood in the kitchen doorway, Uncle Willy, still half pickled from the night before said, 'Come on you, Father. You fellas can do without a missus and a bob or two, but yiz can't do without breakfast.' And everyone had laughed down to the floor, back against the walls and up past the ceiling. Pita had seen the orangey plate of Father Van's teeth stuck up in the roof of his wide-open mouth. It looked like old fungus that he'd seen growing on the bark of Uncle Ju's plum trees.

Later when he helped father out to his bike with his bag, the priest said, 'Ah Pita . . . Ah Pita . . . "Thou art Pita, and upon this rock I will build my church."' Then he said what he always said as he was leaving, 'Pray for a vocation, young Pita.'

Gradually their father began to move, first his hands, then his arms, and after a time began to feed himself and hold his own cup. But sometimes he was low and brooding, not wanting what was put before him and not prepared to help himself. He'd send the covered boxes with the cup and plate on it crashing to the floor.

It was many weeks before he began to walk with the aid of sticks, no longer needing Ma to help him wash and dress, or to have Ma or Uncle Willy take him out to the dunny.

At night, after their father was in bed, Ma would kneel them all down in the sitting-room with the door open so that he could hear them say their prayers. Afterwards she'd push them towards the bedroom to kiss him goodnight.

One day, when they came home from school, their father was out walking in the sun, leaning on his sticks, his shoes scrunching on the gravel path. He was wearing just a singlet tucked into the top of his trousers and was being watched by aunties who were sitting on the step with their tobacco tins and tishy papers, giving him words of encouragement. As they sat and talked they rolled and smoked their racehorses – sleek thoroughbreds, each with a thin bit of tobacco tail hanging.

Their father began to say words too, speak sentences, but not to Pita and Rangi. Sometimes Uncle Willy would come and take him off on the rounds, visiting their relatives, and after a while he was able to go walking to the beach and paddocks on his own.

At other times he would go back into a low silence and speak only in noises, returning to the big chair for days at a time, hardly moving from there and seeming not to recognise anyone.

Also there were days or nights when he launched himself out of the chair to choke their mother, break their house to pieces, attempt to kill them all.

The first time it happened Pita woke in the night to the sound of their father smashing through the house, and not long afterwards his mother came to the bedroom door calling, 'Boy, get Uncle Willy. Quick. Out the window.'

So he'd gone out over the bedroom windowsill and run to Uncle Willy's place, only to find his uncle wasn't home. However Aunty Dinah came, bringing cousins Ana and Rexie. With Ma they managed to bring their father down on the kitchen floor, sitting on the arms and legs of this roaring, threshing man that would murder them all.

'Good boy,' Aunty Dinah said. 'You go and get Uncle Willy from up Juju's place. You go the long way round, Little Father, or you might fall in the water.'

But he didn't want to take the long way. He shuffled over the plank across the creek and hurried as quickly as he could through the swampy paddock that was holed by the feet of cows, and up the slope to the house where Uncle Willy and Uncle Ju were sitting on the verandah smoking in the dark. The dogs were barking and the two men stood to see who was coming.

'Uncle, Uncle. Come,' he called, and the two men left, running. The moon was sitting up there like a big white-face cow.

Aunty Janey came out of the house and took him into the wash-house, removed the long, muddy singlet that he was wearing, putting it in a bucket to soak, and helped him wash the bog off his legs. She put a big cardigan on him and took him home the long way.

By the time he and his aunt arrived the place was quiet, the house had been tidied, the glass cleared away and Uncle Ju and Uncle Willy were nailing sugar bags over the broken windows. The lamps had been lit, the fire stoked and Ana and Rexie were making tea for everyone. Their father was in bed asleep and Aunty Dinah was wiping Ma's face, smearing fat on her swellings and bruises. When he returned to bed Brother Rangi was still sleeping.

It was the first time this happened that remained in Pita's mind most clearly – waking to the shouting and smashing and his mother in the doorway; then going out of the window and afterwards sliding across the plank under the dark trees, stepping across the bog-holes watched by ghosts and a ghosty cow moon.

There were many times during the early years when he'd gone running for help while doors splintered, lamps toppled and pictures fell from their nails, as their father screamed and roared through the house, skin pulled tight across his face, his eyes protruding and his mouth stretched into a square hole as his lips pulled back from large, square teeth that were brown and broken. Those times blurred in memory.

Sometimes, by the time he returned with help, Ma had already taken their father down in a tackle, or somehow managed to wrestle him to the floor, hanging on hard with her arms clamped round his knees.

On thinking back it was difficult to remember that there had been quiet times, times when their father was 'good'. He couldn't remember those good times, though could recall his mother saying to those who asked, 'Good just now, thanks to Our Lord Jesus.'

7

free

When Pita was seven years old, he and Rangi came home from school one day to find Ma in bed with baby Sophie beside her. The aunties were outside wringing towels and clothes, pegging them out and swinging the line high with a wooden prop. Uncle Willy was out under the trees talking to their father while skinning and cutting up rabbits and putting pieces in a pot on the outside fire. Just that once he remembered hearing his father laugh like an ordinary man.

A year later sister Moana was born, and another four years after that Pita woke in the dark to the new cries of Little Brother, Tu. Pita was thirteen.

By then it was not only the space in front of the windows, or the best room itself that had become a dead place, a place that they would sneak by. Except when they had visitors, the whole house became a place of whispering and silence, a silence which was broken only by the noises coming from their father who now seemed to be the whole world.

While Rangi would go off and play up the creek with the other children Pita would not, for fear of what might happen to Ma while he was away. Even when Ma sent him out he would spend his time close to the house, usually at the woodpile cutting stove-lengths and kindling, afterwards remembering to put the axe away because everything like that had to be hidden from their father. Sometimes he'd play with the dog or just sit in the branches of the ngaio tree outside the kitchen window, listening.

It was when he was ten, and his uncles, who had previously not been able to get work, were given relief work digging ditches, that he began staying away from school. With his uncles away he was afraid of what might happen to Ma. He had new clothes that year – grey school shirt and shorts handed down to him from cousin Rexie. Ma patched and mended them, shifted the buttons on the shirt cuffs so that the sleeves wouldn't hang down, and she shortened an army belt for him, tightening it to keep the shorts from slipping.

He was pleased with the clothes but once at school all he could think of was that none of the uncles were home to help Ma, who could be bruised, cut by a piece of window, bleeding by a door, or dead. Sometimes he waited until playtime before running home. Sometimes he turned back at the school gates without even remembering that he'd done it, only finding himself on the tracks, heading homeward.

On other days he didn't reach school at all. He played on the beach until the other kids had gone, then made his way back up to the house to sit in the ngaio tree, listening. Often in the afternoons he went over to Aunty Dinah's place because he knew she wouldn't ask questions. She'd only say, 'Ah what to do without you, Little Father?' and give him something to eat. Because she went over to check on Ma and the state of their father each morning once the workers and school children had left, Aunty Dinah was able to give her thoughts, 'Good today, I think so,' or, 'Boiling up to something, I think so. I told your Ma get herself outside, or come over my place.' On those 'boiling up' days Aunty Dinah always took baby Tu home with her.

Their father spent time outside on the good days, sometimes

walking as far as the beach, or calling in to visit at one of the houses on the beach front. One day Pita watched him take a spade out back to where they dug their rubbish holes. He watched his father thrust the spade into the ground and leave it upright there. Sometimes his father looked up into trees, squinting even when there was no strong sunlight, drawing his top lip above his teeth making him look thoughtful, as though considering something serious to do with the tree. He'd watch him shake a branch as though testing it, and watch as he turned, put his hands in his pockets and walked away. Pita saw all of this from his tree. Once his father looked up to where Pita was sitting, saw him there, shook his head and went inside.

The family all learned to read the bad-day signs – the gone-away look of the man, the muttering which they knew would become louder and louder until it was a roaring then a screaming, a rushing at walls and doors and windows with anything that was at hand. But everything had been hidden away by then except for father's own walking stick.

Ma and Aunty Dinah needed Pita's help on those bad days. When trouble started Pita would rush in, tackling his father round the knees, making sure of it. As he did this Ma and Aunty Dinah would grab an arm and shoulder each, tipping the man forward. They'd hold hard as he rolled and struggled, howled and roared. Sometimes the man would beat them off and they'd come at him again, getting him down, pinning him there, pushing his arms up his back the way they had seen Willy and Juju do.

After what always seemed a long time the yelling and crashing would stop and they could let go. The man would get up and go and lie on his bed. On those days Ma never said anything to Pita about being away from school, or asked why he happened to be home.

There came a time during the years when Tu was a baby that their father's 'breakouts', which was what Ma called them, were less frequent. Sometimes their father seemed to know them. He spoke to Pita and Rangi and their little sisters sometimes, though none of them could ever respond to him because they didn't know how.

Or perhaps it was that Ma came to know when there was a bad turn coming on and was able to get enough people around to restrain the man. Sometimes when someone went next door for Uncle Willy, their uncle would say, 'Ha, the old man gunna blow.' He was always 'the old man'. Pita didn't realise until their father's death that he was ten years younger than this brother-in-law who referred to him as 'old man'.

They all shielded little Tu from their father's breakouts. At the first sign of trouble their young brother was taken over to Aunty Dinah's, away from the breaking and shouting. If it happened at night when Tu was already asleep, Sophie and Moana would carry him out through the window and take him next door until their father was subdued, or else his sisters and Tu would all spend the night there with older cousins Ana and Rexie.

As Tu grew he spent more and more time with his uncles, sometimes at home with them, sometimes up the creek where they set their eel traps or cut their firewood. Sometimes they'd take him far back into the hills hunting, where they would stay for three or four days.

'It isn't how we lived before,' Ma would say. 'It isn't what we believed it would be like once the world was free.' Ma often spoke of sending her youngest to boarding school, just so he could know another life.

When they grew older Pita and Rangi were easily able to overcome and hold their father down while Ma went to fetch her brother. Uncle Willy was the one who could most easily calm him. Once, at an especially bad time, Rangi came with an uppercut to their father's jaw that dropped him. And their mother, looking down at this man, her husband, laid out in the kitchen with not even enough space left to walk round him, said, 'Just because he come home from war don't mean he never died there, your poor father.'

Pita was twenty and Tu was seven when their father freed them all.

Jobs were difficult to find but Pita and Rangi never thought of leaving Ma and going away to get work as others had. One of them would stay round the house fetching water and keeping the wood pile stacked, while the other worked out back in the gardens.

One afternoon Pita was out digging potatoes with his uncles and cousins when Rangi came running, calling out to tell them their father was dead. He heard the words that his brother said but didn't understand them at first. He set off at a run and was almost home before he realised that he was on his way back, not to a mad, raging father who he would take down in a tackle, but to a still, silent, dead one. For the rest of the way home he prayed that it was true.

People had already gathered by the time he arrived. His father had been laid out on the bed, pillow removed, body straightened, arms placed by his sides and eyelids closed before he stiffened. He looked not a lot different, except for lack of bandages, from when Pita had caught glimpses of him, from a position up on Uncle Willy's shoulders, through a hospital window seventeen years earlier.

'Father's at peace,' his aunties said. 'Gone to Our Lord.'

His mother's face was pale as she reached out her arms to him.

'He's free,' she said.

Peace and freedom. Not their father's but their own.

Pita felt tears running. There was an air of gratitude in the room.

During the following days of mourning the eulogies and prayers were mostly to do with freedom of their father from his torments. Pita waited for it all to be over.

At the graveside he heard Ma's breath leave her in a slow sigh as their father was let down into the ground, and he sat with her while Rangi and their uncles shovelled the dirt in the hole.

The uncles, as they shovelled, were wisecracking about this mate they called Jimmy, the mad old bugger who thought he could take on a whole enemy on his own. The spades lifted and piled, lifted and piled, then hit down, patted down, shuffled the dirt and smoothed it.

'Take that, Brother. Don't come looking for us, see.' Pat, pat.

'Won't get outta this one Sister, our mate here.'

Ma allowed herself to smile and be tired after the three days and nights without eating, and with only snatches of sleep.

Nights and days, many years of nights and days, and now those nights and days and years were floating out of her on long flowing breaths as she felt herself lifted by the elbows to be walked to her house for the cleansing. After the house rituals they all returned to the marae for the welcome to the new day, and to the talk, the songs, the feasting that belonged to the living.

It was at his father's death ceremonies that Pita came to realise that this old man, their father, was just thirty-nine and was the youngest of his generation of brothers and cousins.

How strange their house seemed after everyone had gone home. In it their mother mourned, slept, sat waiting, looked for work to do. Then, a little at a time, she began bringing out photographs, crockery, holy pictures and ornaments that had been wrapped in newspaper and put away under beds and in wardrobes. She mended the statue of Mary and put it on the mantelpiece in the front room. It was as if she had upturned the palms of her hands and pushed twenty years off to the moon. They were all pleased to see again these objects they'd almost forgotten about. Even the medals that their father had clawed from off the wall were polished and put back in place with the soldier photograph – which seemed to have new meaning now. It was as though their father was now able to be the father he had never been to them once he came home, that is, the man in the photographs.

It was as though they had stepped out of a time of standing and trembling in a thunderous place. Now perhaps other steps could be taken.

After a while Pita began to realise that it would be all right for him and Rangi to go away and look for work now. They could find jobs, save and make a better life for them all, get money together for the future.

There was a future. Ma had begun to talk about it.

But after a time of trying to make the place her own again, it was Ma who decided they should all leave.

'Too many sad memories,' she said. 'No work for the family and no college for the little one when he's old enough. There's no money to get the land going and no future for us here. We're going nowhere.' Then she told them she'd written a letter to her uncle who worked in parliament asking him to find them a house in Wellington. 'We want our Tuboy to go to a good college, have a good job, get clean work with good pay like our uncle in parliament,' she said.

Tu, who had been sheltered from rage, was their hope for the future.

8

rain

The road we started out on was chock-a-block with traffic, and though at first the way forward was over flat or partially rolling countryside, the route soon became steep and winding. Signs of war were all about us. The cratered roads and the shattered bridges were made passable only by continuous filling and mending, and incessant rain meant that the whole way was through tracks deep in mud.

Mud soldiers we were, looking for a war. Somewhere up the leg of this boot was the Eighth Army waiting for Twenty-eighth to come and join it, a war waiting for the Maori Battalion to come and fight in it – Maori Battalion staunch and true.

Everywhere we went there were shell-damaged houses, and as we passed through one of the villages we saw that there wasn't a wall or chimney left standing. What had been a courtyard had become a mess of smashed marble fonts and memorials and broken angels. There were a few people picking through the rubble, but where had the rest of them gone I wondered. I couldn't think what it was like for people trying to rebuild their homes and their lives.

On we went. Rain and more rain, and mud galore.

In Lucera we spent two more days in the wet – eating wet, sleeping wet and unable to get rid of mud. But there were compensations. What my stomach remembers about our days in Lucera is the good feed of pork that we had.

I think my brothers were surprised at how I could take down a pig and deal with it, perhaps forgetting that I'd spent many a school holiday on backhome ridges and in the valleys hunting with Uncles Willy and Ju. The bush pigs of home are tough and cunning, ridge-backed, mean when cornered, requiring good dogs to bail them and take them by the ears so that the man can go in with his knife. At certain times of the year we'd be on the lookout for weaners to take home and fatten so people wouldn't go hungry at Christmas. I thought of this, thought of the backhome people as we filled our stomachs.

These Italian pigs are different animals however. Poor pigs. They were lost, lonely, the boys said, war orphans gone bush. Whether this was all true or not, whether they were lost or orphaned or not, we found them. They were out of condition but tasted good all the same – yum yum, pig's bum – and would have tasted all the better with a side dish of chicken, which we almost had, but this was not to be.

Tommy and Matene went out hunting chickens before dusk one evening in light rain. They'd seen the chooks earlier in the day all pecking about in a yard two or three miles away. Going in as close as they thought possible without being seen, they gave a sweeping blast with a tommy gun and ran in to pick up their catch. The chooks were running, screeching, squawking, and there were feathers flying everywhere. The only trouble was that not one of them was dead. Ha ha. The boys scrammed out of there, returning to camp out of breath, wet and stuck all over with feathers

That was in Lucera.

A few days later we took to the road again as the rain continued, making our progress slow, slow, slow, with trucks and vehicles sliding off the verges, bogging down in the soaked fields with wheels spinning. The route was even steeper now, narrower and more winding, and the military police trying to unravel the knots of tanks, trucks, artillery and service vehicles were having a hell of a time. Man against Tawhirimatea. It was an uneven battle.

Here and there we went, mud men, helping get wheels out of the bog and vehicles back on the road. We were horses, dragging trucks through mud by long ropes, ending up pretty stiff and sore and with another sleepless night ahead of us, another night in rain with clothes, tents, blankets, everything, soaked.

Choc and I worked at keeping water from our bivvy and our gear, and at finding a place dry enough to sleep in, but the rain beat all of us in the end.

'At home,' Choc said, 'sitting by a fire having a feed of brisket and watercress, beats this, you reckon?' We were pulling off soaked boots and peeling off socks. Out on the slopes others were fooling about in the wet because there was little else they could do. There was no arguing with this god of the elements.

'Only if there's doughboys,' I said as we plunged out into the wet and dark to join them.

By morning the sun was out, a watery sun without much heat in it. We spent the day hanging out clothes, drying everything and making up for lost sleep. And the following day, joining the traffic, again in heavy rain, progress was so slow that it took from early morning until dark to travel the seven miles to our next stop. This was on the banks of the Sinello River where we spent another couple of wet and uncomfortable nights.

And we still hadn't found this war.

The next day we moved on until finally arriving here on the southern slopes overlooking the Sangro River. Below us is a sweeping valley with cultivations across the flats continuing all the way to the wide riverbed. Beyond the river is a scattering of houses, dark green groves, and a cat's cradle of white roads which lead up to where we've been told Jerry is backed up in the low hillsides. To the left are layer upon layer of hills rising, until, way beyond, they become a continuum of snow-dusted mountains. As we look out many of us are reminded of home, though my own backhome mountain is a lone one.

So here we are on the other side of the world looked down upon by other men's mountains. I wonder what these other mountains and these other men think of these intruders? We're close to the battlefront now and some divisions are already patrolling across the river.

The Sangro is a mean river if all we hear is true. Waters, nosing along over a stony bed in dry weather, can deepen in a day and take off like a pack of mad dogs once the rains begin, bringing down with them snow from the many peaks.

In the easterly direction the river runs towards the coast. Somewhere, though we are unable to see it, is the sea. It's from this direction that we hear the sounds of war, and from our position we are able to watch the constant passing of planes across the sky as they come in waves to bomb and strafe enemy posts. That's more like it.

So, as we of the Maori Battalion settle into our new site, others of the New Zealand Division have been clearing ahead and have already driven Jerry back behind the river. As days go by conditions worsen. The water rises. It's fast and cold, and the men who have to patrol across in the dark, sometimes have to form human chains in water up to their necks in order to get across. Sometimes they use ropes or poles to support themselves, but on some nights and in some places they have been unable to cross at all.

When they do make it across, cold and loaded down with wet clothing, they go on to examine the way forward. Their job is to clear the way of mines and root out Jerry from trouble spots in preparation for an assault.

The assault is what we're waiting for.

This is the river that we want to have a crack at, the type of action that we're eager to take part in as we stand in reserve. But in the meantime we keep up the training and route marches, finding that the broken down *case* that surround us provide good targets for practice with anti-tank guns.

Also there are other distractions that help fill our days.

There was great excitement last night when our mud-caked,

bedraggled Te Rau Aroha arrived. What a noise when we saw it limping towards us. There were shouts and cheers and we all broke into a loud haka of welcome: 'Toia mai, Te Waka' – 'Drag forth the canoe, drag it forth.' There were several haka. Companies from the different home areas vied with each other, one haka finishing and another starting up, drowning out the sounds of war.

I bought cabin bread, Minties, a bottle of ink, two squares of blotting paper, tobacco and cigarette papers, and I borrowed a book, *How Green Was My Valley*. I also purchased razor blades as all the blades I had were rusty and I had to throw them away. I reckon there's enough whisker on my face to warrant another shave. We congregated at our canteen, and later that night, tucked away with the mobile cinema and the generator truck under the shelter of a hillside so that no lights would show, we had an evening out at the pictures. The main feature was *There Ain't No Justice*.

The next day a whole lot of donkeys tip-tapped into camp, all part of the plan no doubt. The cooks reckon they'll put them on the menu if we run low on supplies.

In the dark hours of the following morning we awoke to the sounds of barrage fire and left our beds to watch the quick red blooming of the far slopes as the strike across the Sangro began.

9

angel

'You carry your uncle's name,' Pita heard his mother say again, as she pulled Tu from under the slatted seat where his tooth had gone. 'It's because of him,' she was saying into the face of Little Brother with blood dripping from his mouth. Ma squashed him back into the seat beside her, while Sophie went to get water in a paper pouch from an earthenware jar at the end of the carriage. 'Your uncle in parliament.'

Pita understood Ma's message was not only for Tu but for all of them – his sisters, Rangi and him, and also for herself. It was unlike Ma to worry about what others thought of them because it was how they all measured up in the eyes of God that Ma really cared about. Though Pita thought it was true about having to live up to the uncle's name they bore, he thought Ma shouldn't be concerned. They weren't going to let her or the uncle down in this unknown place among unknown people. Pita was going to see to that.

He'd never been anywhere before where he was unknown, where he knew no one. Here was a train full of people, all unknown. Out on the platform at the stop for refreshments he'd recognised no one, and he and his brother had stood unseen at the refreshment counter until Rangi, in a loud voice, had demanded tea and sandwiches. Always hot-under-the-collar, that was Brother Rangi. Rangi couldn't wait, even for a few minutes.

His mother dipped the edge of her handkerchief into the pocket of water, dabbing and wiping Tu's mouth and chin with it. Then she began cleaning blood spots from the jersey that Aunty Dinah had knitted for Tu from pulled-out wool from their father's pullover of pulled-out wool.

They had all needed new clothes – clothes, not new – in which to bring themselves to the city, clothes which would help them belong in this new place, clothes in which to present themselves to this uncle who worked in parliament. These skirts, blouses and trousers had been handed on from aunts, uncles and cousins, or sometimes mended or remade from what they had been given. Sports coats and shirts for himself and Rangi had been sorted from the jumble lady's bundles during her recent visit.

Most difficult of all had been to find shoes for everyone. With the exception of Ma, who had a pair of good shoes which she wrapped in newspaper and put away in a box for special occasions, none of them had had shoes before. However, The Uncle had sent shoes for Pita and Rangi. Among the jumble Ma had found sandals for Sophie and Moana, and a pair of over-sized tennis shoes for Tu.

Now the difficulty was in keeping these clothes clean in all the soot and dirt of the train. Ma was tipping the remainder of the water into Tu's mouth and telling him to swish it around and swallow.

'Swallow, swallow,' she whispered.

But instead of swallowing, young Tu leaned and emptied his mouthful into one of the spittoons set into the middle of the floor in the aisle of the carriage. They'd earlier watched one gentleman spit a gob of tobacco there and another knock black spiders into it from out of his pipe.

Rangi thought that in the city there might be plenty of pretty girls, and Pita thought about that too sometimes – film star girls, in pretty dresses, film star stockings and diamond shoes. Dream girls.

Ma was good-looking, he thought. She was still young and seemed different now. Her face was different, smoother. But maybe all their faces were different now? The coat she had on was short in the sleeves and tight across the back and shoulders. It wouldn't button up, and the headscarf that Aunty Dinah had given her was old and faded. However, The Uncle had written to Ma about work that he and Rangi might get. When they had work Ma would have everything she needed. His sisters, huddled under a blanket on the adjacent seat, needed coats. They'd all have what they wanted once he and his brother found work.

Sophie put the blanket aside, bending and looking at the smutty floor. She reached down, then held up the tooth for Tu to see. Tu stood and took the tooth from his sister, holding it up to the light, spreading his legs in the aisle to keep his balance as the train sped along.

'Give it to me,' Ma said, taking the tooth and putting it into a spare paper cup which she folded and put into the pocket of the too-tight coat. 'And be good,' she said, by which she meant she didn't want Tu standing spread-legged in the aisle, rocking backwards and forwards and holding the tooth up for everyone in the carriage to see. There was a child looking down at them from the luggage rack where she was netted along with bags and parcels.

Pita gave Tu a tap on the arm, pointing to the seat beside him, and Tu sat, rocking back and forth with the motion of the train.

'Sit still,' he said.

Earlier, he and Rangi had gone out to stand for a while in the space at the end of the carriage. It was cold out there. The wind was flattening the darkened grasses beside the railway line and bending the trees. They watched two people opening a farm gate, lifting it outwards and taking long steps through black mud, and while they were standing there watching, the carriage door flew open and Tu charged out. He gripped the handrails between the two cars and swung himself – a piece of straw – above the shifting and grinding metal plates that bridged the big iron couplings joining the carriages, the wind whipping at his clothing, a large smile on his face and him ready to fly into the chop of train wheels.

They grabbed hold of him, took him inside and sat him down by Ma. He needed watching.

'You got your uncle's name, you got to be good,' Ma said then.

Pita agreed that this little brother of theirs did have to be good, did have to know how to sit still and not have everyone staring. But although Pita couldn't see Rangi's face he thought his brother was probably blowing out his cheeks, letting air vibrate out through his lips and wishing they'd all leave the kid alone. That was him. That was Brother Rangi.

But people would always stare anyway because Little Brother had such black curls, such a wide head, such perfectly curved eyebrows and such lit-up eyes. It was the face of an angel people said, which didn't mean Little Brother knew how to behave.

Anyway Pita had given Tuboy's hair a good trim for the journey, left a few curls on the top of his head and that was all. The aunties thought he'd gone too far with the haircut, but agreed it would last for a good long while. Ma was waiting for the cubicle at the end of the carriage to be free so that she could go and tidy herself. In less than an hour they'd be in Wellington.

Their first view of the city was of heavy sky dropped over the purple water of the harbour, the dark shapes of hills showing through it. There were smudges that were ships and sheds and unfinished buildings. The train slowed, laying back white smoke, sounding its whistle and creaking along the tracks past the dirty sheds, over oily, broken rock, to where the yards began. This was the end of the line.

They made their way along the platform in the crowd, Pita and Rangi with the large cases, Moana holding on to Tu, and Ma and Sophie ahead carrying packages. Ma stopped and turned every now and again in an attempt to keep them all together. All the time there were people rushing past them without a word, without a glance, until they were the only ones left on the platform.

'Chased by the devil,' Rangi said of the hurrying people, and laughed a loud laugh. It was cold. The shoes were damn tight. There was a different wind blowing.

'Our house, our house,' Tu said as they came into the station concourse. The circle of his face shone where Ma had cleaned the sooty marks away with her wet handkerchief.

'Sh, sh. It's the railway station, sh, sh,' Ma said.

Most of the people from the train had dispersed. Workers with their dinner tins made their way to the streets. There was a woman in a thin dress pushing an empty pram, a boy coming in with morning papers in a canvas bag that was pulling his shoulder down, two men in sooty clothes and greasy felt hats sweeping with big brooms, and other people on seats waiting with bags and bundles.

Standing to greet them was the uncle-from-parliament wearing a warm coat, and a hat which he removed as he came forward. He walked them out into the city where trams and vans went by, and where they were among people crossing roads and heading along the footpaths under shop verandahs. They continued on past large buildings and the houses of parliament, to a street of tall houses where they stopped by a pathway leading up to one of them. It had white paint bubbling and peeling on its walls, and an orange front door. There were four large windows, two up and two down.

'Our house, our house,' Tuboy said, running up the path as The Uncle took the key from his pocket. Pita, who knew Brother Tu shouldn't be rushing ahead of The Uncle like that, pulled him back off the doorstep while The Uncle unlocked the door.

The Uncle led them, in a smell of gas, through the downstairs rooms, switching on lights, turning on taps, and saying in a voice that resounded in the almost empty rooms, 'Let there be light and there was light,' and 'Let there be water and there was water.'

There was a small, dark kitchen with a wooden bench under one little window, and cupboards and shelves and a gas stove. On the wall in the bathroom was a water tank from where a flat pipe led down to a high bath. Pipes, painted the same cream colour as the walls, brought water to taps over the basin, hot and cold.

From the bedrooms upstairs they could look down on roads where traffic went by, and on to footpaths where people walked. They could see Chinee Boy toddling about in the yard next door while his mother filled a coal bucket from under a tin shelter. Trams rattled past. Out over the city they could see past the houses to the Basilica of the Sacred Heart, the houses of parliament, the government buildings, and beyond the buildings to a glimpse of the sea. Ma was wiping her eyes, thanking God, thanking The Uncle, as they followed him from room to room.

'The rent's due once a fortnight,' The Uncle said, 'but it's paid up for two weeks. You have two weeks. There's money needed for your coal and electricity, coins for the gas. I know your widow's pension won't go far. I know a Maori woman whose man has died gets only half the pension of a Pakeha widow, but don't you go short, Ora. If you're short to start with, you come to me.'

'Oh Uncle, you done enough already,' Ma said. 'All thanks to you. And to Our Lord. We won't let you down.'

'You boys get off to the meatworks in the morning,' The Uncle said. 'The season's started already. They've got sheep and lambs in the yards and they begin the kill tomorrow. It'll do the boys for now,' he said to Ma, 'until they can get something more regular.'

Pita went down and took Tu off the banister, feeling the same excitement as he knew his young brother felt at having such a fine house to live in. Ma was right. God and The Uncle had been good to them. They would unpack their things, get their new house in order and just hope that in the morning he and Rangi would be able to sign up for work. Ma was right, they'd had enough help from The Uncle. It was all up to them now, up to him.

Pita and Rangi went to the meatworks the next day and were given work in the fellmongery stacking pelts. On some days they were sent to the pulling-room where they removed wool from skins and prepared them for drying. Work of this kind was not well paid, but halfway through the season when there was sickness affecting several of the meat workers, one of the bosses came in and asked if any of them could use a knife. Rangi volunteered and was soon earning better money as a slaughterman, a job he would be able to return to each year now that he'd had a chance to show what he could do.

At the end of each season Pita and Rangi tried for more permanent jobs but they were difficult to get, so they found whatever temporary work they could in the soap factory, or shovelling coal, or loading goods at the railway sidings and the wharf, until the killing season started again.

There was talk of war.

10

road

We started out in trucks, joining a mile-long queue at a bridge that has been built across the Sangro. It's a good bridge, strong enough and high enough for traffic, but the ground coming on to it was nothing but a quagmire, and each vehicle that attempted to pass through made it even worse.

Hold-ups on the other side, where the ground was equally as soft and marshy, meant that even the lightest vehicles were caught up. Heavy trucks had to be winched while others were towed through the mire. It was a mess.

After some hours we became sick of waiting, so left our trucks and waded across the river. It's a greedy, cold river this Sangro, but even so we were pleased to get out of the vehicles and move on, warming up as we marched forward to a place that has been named Point 208. We spent the night there.

Another move onward the next day found us set up across a gully overlooking a stream from where we could see across to the town of Orsogna, perched on the highest of all the ridges which rise sharply from deep, narrow gorges taking the flow down from the mountains. Seen from where we were, Orsogna was a line of shadowy buildings extending the length of the cliff-top. At the centre, a church tower, thin as a needle, pushed itself up against a sombre skyline. What a place to build a town, but I know the reasons will be to do with history and with needing a position which can't be overrun by an enemy – just as with our old hilltop pa sites at home, which were once terraced and fortified and impenetrable. Now Orsogna has become occupied by enemy invaders, and the New Zealand Army and the Maori Battalion have become part of its history too.

Orsogna is where Jerry is making a stand. We have to remove him from there so that we can get ourselves on the road that runs out to the coast, opening the way to Rome. Just as with the old sites at home we realised that all approaches must be visible from Orsogna and that for those battalions who had the job of taking over the town there was no easy way in.

And visible is what we were too, as we waited across our gully. There was no place to hide anywhere in the surrounds of such a position.

When the time came the Maori Battalion was to go up by a roundabout route and hold north of Orsogna while Jerry was sacked out of the town from the south. That was the plan. Once this was done the way would be clear for tanks and guns to come through and forward to where we were holding, and we'd all move on together. This is what we understood as we waited to be called into action. From our possie the 'new chums' among us watched battles already taking place among the hills and slopes all around, while the 'old chums' went out and about, returning with chooks and cabbages, and cooked them up. No need to eat donkey with these men around. Good thing. All the time, when it was not actually raining, there was rain in the air.

In the first stage of our move into battle we were taken by truck to a place called Hellfire Corner, from there marching on to a valley behind where Twenty-fourth and Twenty-fifth Battalions were holding a ridge called San Felice. We made ourselves comfortable in haystacks and among the shelter of trees, feeling all tuned up because we were waiting to go into our first piece of action – we new boys, that is. Most of the old hands went to sleep while enemy shells broke up the landscape all about us and planes passed continually overhead. These were our own planes, ready for business.

Our artillery opened up at last, and half an hour later we were on our way loaded with packs and ammunition – as much ammunition as we could decorate ourselves with because we had to carry it all, having been informed that the terrain we would travel was not suitable for ammo carriers, or for anything at all with wheels.

On our way to the road Jerry shelling had us diving into drains and ditches, or anywhere where we could keep ourselves out of trouble. There we would wait, moving on during pauses in fire, and in this way eventually arrived without coming to any harm. At the road we saw that our tanks were assembled ready to make their way up to support us once the way through Orsogna was opened up for them. It was good to feel the power of tanks behind us as we turned off and began to climb again.

Over the top of San Felice we went, ducking and diving in all directions as shellfire pounded the slopes. Down the other side we scooted with our loads, past smashed houses and olive trees, across flat land and through a stream called the Moro. Once through we began a rocky, slippery climb which would get us to our start line.

Barefoot and unencumbered as in the hills and spurs of home it still wouldn't have been an easy ascent, but with weapons, loads of ammo and the weight of boots, and with shells landing and chips of rock flying, this climb was a real humdinger.

And where was this start line?

One rise led to another valley, another valley to another elevation. Down again, up again, while our artillery kept up its rumble and our planes swept overhead. We could hear them bombing hell out of Orsogna.

At the start line we assembled into our companies, one to move right, one going centre and ourselves keeping left – the bad side we soon found out – to tackle this final escarpment which was named Pascuccio.

Pascuccio. What a way.

It was a cliff face that we had before us, though it was covered in beheaded bushes and there were the narrowest of bombed and broken tracks skewing upwards.

'All right little popgun soldiers, up we go,' Rangi said. And yes, you could feel pretty small looking all that way up. Looking up brought out a whistle or two.

Rain began and smoke from artillery fire seeped around us as we made our way up over landslides, bare rock and oozing clay, all damaged by shell. With Jerry Spandaus opening up, tracers whistling, mortar landing all about us, splinters and rubbish flying everywhere, we edged ourselves by shelves and ledges and over-hangs, crossing deep gouges and hollows while the whole hillside trembled. There were chooks squawking and scattering all over the place too – skinny and half naked. As we climbed the rain became heavier and we soon noticed that our planes had gone.

But we hadn't yet come to the worst of it, for near the top was a sheer climb that had us wiggling our eyebrows and popping our eyes open at each other, telling ourselves that the joke was on us. Anyway up we went, popgun soldiers and our pounds of lead, dragging ourselves up by gripping whatever vegetation would hold, then at last over the top we came, but right on to an enemy post.

Fortunately Jerry wasn't expecting a visit from behind as he was concentrating his attention on the road beyond. There was an almighty scrap after which several of them lay dead, one by my own hand – the first, but not the last that night.

What a job. We lost two of our mates there too. That was only the beginning.

We moved on to the Orsogna road, some of our company remaining there while the rest of us ran through fields of smashed grapes and flattened corn, to explore down past a railway line – testing the temperature of the water, so to speak.

The water? It was hot.

So finding ourselves under fire from houses down there, and with injuries mounting, we hurried back as darkness came, to where we were to set up our defensive in a walled cemetery, a place none of us was happy to be in. No one wanted to dig there with all those bones in the ground. It seemed like asking for trouble.

Bootleg, who had a deep graze on his leg, wouldn't lie down to have it bandaged in case one of those old Italian spooks came and sat on him and wouldn't let him up again. They might take him off to Eyetie heaven he said, off on some funny road and he wouldn't know what the bloody hell they were all gabbing about in their bloody spaghetti lingo. He stood, leaning on his shovel while his pals fixed him up. There was plenty of bandaging going on. No one was keen to let his blood drip in a place like that. Who can blame us?

So far we'd kept the enemy at bay and arrived at the place where we were supposed to be, but we could tell by the clamour on the other side of the wall that counter-attacks were already underway. We knew that the rest of our company – because they hadn't yet rejoined us – must be having a rough time out there on the road. Despite this, the general opinion seemed to be that it would be better to die out there where the action was rather than behind solid walls messing with ghosts – especially at night when these kehua were likely to be out roaming, stealing a man's spirit and leaving him spooked, with his eyes rolling.

Well, in the end, old bones or not, ghosts or not, we made our trenches deep enough and wide enough to keep us out of sight because it wasn't long before there was all hell going on outside the walls. But what a place. What a situation to be in.

Never mind, we thought, before morning Orsogna would be overrun. Soon after that our tanks would arrive and off we'd go on our way to Ortona, Pescara, Ancona, San Marino.

Names, names.

Somewhere was Rome.

Tanks came, but not ours and not from the expected direction. We soon realised that what we thought was our own armour arriving were Jerry tanks clinking and grinding down on us, accompanied by their mortars, their artillery and their infantry. Bullets hammered the walls of the cemetery with enough commotion to wake the dead, and as this massive counter-attack continued we found ourselves blocked on all sides. The enemy had held fast in the town of Orsogna and our armour had been halted.

All we could do was attempt to fight our way out of the position we were in, getting ourselves out of the cemetery and back across the road to the cliff edge, otherwise we'd soon be meat in vegetables, stretched out flat like all of those dead Eyeties in their walled resting place.

Jerry was everywhere. His tanks were crowding in, one on fire lighting up the middle of the road as we ran out charging with our bayonets, which was all we could do. It was a fight close in, where you had to be first, or dead. It was a scrap where we left a sprawl of cut-down enemy, adding to other dead and dying men, both enemy and friend, who were already littering the fire-lit road as we battled across it.

Once on the other side, we were joined by what remained of our company, digging in below the roadside where we kept our heads down, being constantly pounded with mortar and artillery and wondering how much longer our ammunition supplies were going to last.

In the meantime we'd given up hope of our own tanks arriving as enemy tanks continued to mass down the road. This was a full scale hit-back, and though we'd been told that carrying parties were attempting to bring anti-tank guns up the bluffs, we knew what a difficult way it was, how impossible it would be in the dark.

Before the ammo ran out the mules arrived up on the spur with new supplies and it wasn't long afterwards that Brother Rangi left his trench, going out on his own with a load of grenades towards one of the forward enemy tanks which was beating its way along. In among all the other sounds – of gunfire, explosions, the yells and screams of men – we heard the deep thump and crack of metal as he unloaded the grenades into the tank's tracks and demobilised it. It was the kind of action Rangi was known for. He lobbed another into the hatch as men attempted to escape, and there was a deep explosion. We saw the flames shooting upwards and the debris flying in the light of fire as he returned, loading up with more bombs before going out again.

One man's actions were not enough, of course. Without tanks or big guns we had no answers. Here we were bound on three sides. We remained dug in, finding targets wherever we could, but with enemy left, right and beyond, daylight was certain to see us dead meat in a bloody sandwich if we didn't move from there. In the early hours of the morning orders came for us to withdraw.

So we made ourselves scarce, some of us with extra picks, shovels and rifles to carry, while others struggled down under escort with the wounded on stretchers. But by then Jerry had occupied some of our retreat line as well, and men fell – from a barrage coming from behind a wall, from stray fire in the dark from behind a tree, from rock splinters and flying debris.

The extra gear had to be abandoned. We had to judge where the fire was coming from and make our way from one *casa*, one hideout to another, doing what we could with our guns and our blades. Some job in the dark. I really don't know how I come to be still alive.

From a distance the enemy are men without faces though they have a certain height and width. When you see a man fall you're not sure whether or not it was your bullet or someone else's that dropped him, so his death does not feel so real to you.

In close the enemy are men also without faces, but close in there is no long shot, there is no width or height to a man, only a point that you know has a certain depth to it and a certain density. It's the point, the depth, the density that need to be understood so that the thrust, the slash, may have its effect. It's what has to be done so that you can keep on living. It's what you must do again and again. It's real. In your own heart you have to be as resilient as your blade. What a job it is.

On the way back, once clear of the enemy and nearing daylight, and much to the amusement of some of the old boys, I emptied my trembling gut into a drain and I wasn't the only one. That's all right. Sometimes there's nothing like a good spew. We arrived back at our bivvy area wisecracking and laughing, which helps get rid of the shakes and makes you remember that you could do with a good feed and a sleep. There was a hot meal waiting for us, for which we were grateful. But there was an over-supply of food since so many of us had been left behind on the roads and ridges and there weren't enough returning to have breakfast.

Since that time we've had some fun imitating ourselves and each other tipping and toeing up the precipices, slipping and sliding, or having to hang on or make a run for it loaded with all our ammo.

Pascu-u-u-cci-o-o-o.

And because of our uncomfortable time spent among the dead – the long dead, I mean, the dead ones already buried – we began talking about kehua we had encountered. These were ghosts that we'd seen ourselves, perhaps heard knocking or calling, or ones we'd been told about. There were ghosts in the form of birds that Tommy told us of, which had eyes like onions and hung upside-down in trees outside an uncle's house – all the work of an ugly woman who had covered the uncle in curses because he'd insulted her. There were stories of apparitions at the time of death, of speaking lizards and squeaking owls; of men with bird's feet, wearing long cloaks, who came out of the mists to entice people deep into mountain forests where they became part of the bird-people tribe. Though the stolen ones were never seen again, sometimes you could hear their lonely singing.

It's funny. Thinking about it now, though I don't suppose it's really so, it could seem as if the most frightening aspect of the whole night was a few hours spent among the buried bones of old dead Italians.

So how do I feel now that there is time to sit and write, recalling some of what happened during the twenty hours of my first encounter with the enemy? My main feeling now, overriding other feelings, is one of pride. Not because I have killed men, though I'm not trying to pretend the lives of those enemy soldiers meant anything to me. They were the objectives, their deaths a necessity. But can you do-in a man just as you do-in a pig or a bullock? No. Not this little soldier anyway.

But I feel all right. I feel okay because I was able to do what I was meant to do. I didn't fall short of doing the job I set out to do, and it's as though I've now passed a test, become a true soldier justified in his existence at the front. It's as though I've now earned membership of my Battalion, having done some of what Twenty-eighth is known for. And for once in my life I feel that I've been truly challenged, and that I haven't failed – even though in sleep there are bones knocking at the sides of my house as though trying to break through its walls.

Even in my waking hours there are sounds in my head of a blade withdrawn with a squealing sound, accompanied by screams and the noise as of a moaning animal being pulled from the bog by horse and chain. These are the worst sounds I've heard in all the sounds of war so far.

'You don't risk your life,' Rangi said.
'Look who's talking,' I replied.

Despite our stiff climb up Pascuccio we found ourselves in a hollow overlooked from two sides by enemy high points. Because our tanks could not be brought through Orsogna we were left high and dry and were forced to retreat, having to give up our hard-won positions on the road.

In other respects 'high and dry' is not the right expression. Really it was the enemy who were high and dry. High in their hilltop town, secure in their fortifications and lookout advantages. They were dry in their solid unreachable buildings with their booby-trapped entrances and mined doorways.

So though I believe we did all that was asked of us, maybe we were beaten from the start by rock and ridges, and by rain which caused the cancellation of our planes. It was rain too, though also the strength of an all-seeing enemy, that ensured our tanks never arrived.

Still I am a soldier, a proud man of the Maori Battalion, ake ake kia kaha. There'll be another day soon that will find us on our way to Rome and to victory.

In the meantime we rest up in reserve, waiting to have another go at Jerry. As we wait we learn that bulldozers have been brought in to make a way for tanks to reach the cemetery area by a different route. We'll be returning there presently to provide protection and to assist our armour forward.

Further reinforcements have come across from Maadi to join us. We're not the new boys any more.

11

mea culpa

There was familiar sound coming from behind a wall – a song, voices flowing over and under like plaited water. Someone was playing a piano. The sound halted the family for a moment as they climbed the stairs of the *Evening Post* building to the studio at the top. It put away the sheen of roads and pavements, the cold of concrete and glass, the clanking trams, the horns and sirens and the pinching shoes. It walked them barefoot up creek tracks in a damp and marshy dark that had the feeling of people going through. It sat them beside fires, by sugarbag windows, by lamplight, by Uncle Willy and his banjo.

Pita heard Ma's breath leave her as they made their way up, and it reminded him of the sigh that had come from her as they'd sat together when his father was let down into the ground. Later, on that day of his father's burial, when they arrived back at the marae, the songs for the living were sung. Now here was one of the same songs bringing them forwards and plaiting them into it as they entered the room: 'Haere mai ra, ki ahau nei ra' – 'Come, you are welcome'.

Come.

And walking in on a song, with their sixpences and Ma's long out-breathing, it was as if he remembered who he was now as the words reached out and gathered them. It was like a homecoming even though his feet stood in a different place, a place Pita had been trying to make his home for more than a year. For the whole of that year it was as though he'd been immobilised. Now he could feel himself being warmed and brought back into action. It was as though his heart had suddenly begun beating in time with the city and now he could begin to be himself again.

It was a relief.

It made him feel kind.

Inside the room with its polished wooden floor and its chairs backed up against the walls, was a group of about thirty young people and a few elders, all standing in rows being conducted in their singing by a man wearing silver-legged glasses. He was holding a pencil.

As they came inside to sit and wait, the pencil, held between finger and thumb, was writing the voices down, writing the song to a close 'He aroha tino nui, haere mai' – 'Abounding is my love, so come' – a song written away into air. Pita was holding his breath.

During the supper break and the welcome to them, Kingi, with the light reflecting off the glasses so that his eyes looked like headlamps, told them that the group was practising for a fundraising concert to be put on in the Town Hall later that week. The money they raised would enable them to donate to a new meeting house up country.

'We mustn't forget those living up country, our home people,' Kingi said, 'otherwise they might leave us in this city when we die, might forget to come for us.' Kingi had long soft cheeks that creased and flapped and gathered in folds like flags, skin as black as flax pods. 'New voices will be a welcome addition, add strength to our singing,' he said. 'We've been in such demand round our city that we've begun to think our engagements will never end.'

Our city?

It was a new thought.

'I daresay many of the songs will be familiar,' Kingi said after supper when the family joined the group for the programme of action songs, poi and haka. It was true. They knew most of the items already, but this was different from being backhome round the cooking fires. Now they were in formation – four lines of girls, two lines of boys – practising to get their actions in unison while Kingi went along with his hand behind his ear listening for anyone who might be off key.

So the studio where the Ngati Poneke practices were held became the family's place to assemble every Monday. Each week their nights and weekends became more and more taken up with concerts and club activities, and their house became a place where Club friends could come before practice, especially for those living too far away to go home for tea. They would bring fish and chips or a loaf of bread and Ma would make tea in a big pot for them.

For Pita, belonging to the Club was like an end to starvation, somewhere to go where he didn't need to feel so backward, so ignorant, so up-in-a-tree. Up until then, outside of home, it was as though he'd had nothing to say to anyone, no conversation at all. At work he was unable to tell whether workmates were kidding or deliberately offending by remarks they made, or whether they could be laughing at his expense. Sometimes he was aware that he was being treated like a child but didn't know what to do about it.

Out in the town he found it difficult to be among people who rushed ahead of others on the path and stepped past the elderly. But then again he felt too slow on the footpaths, as if he was blocking the way. In churches and theatres he always went to back seats, afraid he could be taking up spaces belonging to others, or places that others may want. He didn't know if there was special seating or not. So, even though he believed there were rules and he was afraid of breaking them, he didn't know what those rules were, which made him always careful. Outside of home and outside of the Club he kept himself quiet, being afraid of making mistakes, of breaking codes. It was as though his voice had gone.

They'd been Club members for a year, attending practices and taking part in fundraising and concerts, when war began and Brother Rangi enlisted and left home.

Soon afterwards the girl-at-the-end-of-the-line came to live with them. This was Ani Rose who the boys liked to tease because she was so small, and because teasing her was always worthwhile. Having the smallest stature of all the Club girls meant that Ani Rose was always at one end of the front row in their concert line-ups.

'End carriage,' they'd say as she took her place.

'Standing in a hole, you Ani Rose?'

'A bit missing off one end you think, Ani Rose?'

But she was smart, Pita thought, a match for any of them no matter how small she was.

'Might be you with a bit missing off one end, so you watch out,' she'd say, swinging a poi at them and flicking it so that it hit with a loud crack on the back of her hand. A few moments later she'd be leading them into their first song.

When they first joined the Club, Ani Rose had a room in the city and worked at the Levis factory as a machinist. On Sundays she attended Mass with them at the Basilica, and afterwards came home to spend time with Ma and his sisters. During winter Ani Rose had been sick and Ma insisted she give up her cold room down town and come and live with them.

Even before war was declared there'd been discussions, in the build-up to it, about the formation of a Maori Infantry. It was the talk of the Club at Monday night practices. It was the talk at home when visitors came, and there were arguments up and down the country about whether their men should go to war or not.

'It's not our war,' some would say.

'We've already given men to one war on the other side of the world. That's enough.'

However these were small voices on the whole. When the formation of the new Battalion was announced the news was greeted with general excitement. It was what many had been waiting to hear and men were queuing up to join. The night that the recruiting officers came to the Club, the number of its men was cut by half and Rangi was among the first to enlist.

Though Ma was against it, Pita was relieved Rangi was going. Rangi was spending too much of his spare time at certain addresses round town which were known as party houses, and where there was often trouble. Pita had gone with Rangi one Friday after work, but once was enough for Pita. It was like swallowing dreams. The drinking went on all night and by the end of it all their money had gone down their throats, so he never went again. Rangi continued to go, but would give Pita money to look after before he headed off.

At first he did.

What began as one night out in a week became two nights, with Rangi arriving home in the early hours of Sunday and stumbling into bed. In the morning he would turn up to Mass red-eyed and smelling of drink, there only because Ma had insisted.

'Your father was always at Mass, Mass and confession, no matter how he was in himself,' Ma said. There were a few things Rangi could've said to that, about their father, but he didn't. Pita wished Ma wouldn't bother about getting Rangi up on Sundays, and one morning he told his brother that if he couldn't come decent to Mass he shouldn't come at all. Rangi hadn't been back at Mass since, which upset Ma even further.

There were girls round town that Rangi told Pita about too.

'Come on, man,' he said. 'They're looking for it. What's the harm?'

'Plenty. Plenty of harm,' according to Pita. 'You wouldn't want our sisters behaving like that.'

'Well, course not.'

'The next thing bringing home a baby for Ma to look after.'

'Course not. Only a bit of fun.'

'Fun's not what we're put on earth for.'

'Why not? What else?'

'You let the family down, that's what. And God. What about God and mortal sin, heaven and hell? You make your act of contrition and you just forget about it the next day, or what?'

'You still do that?' Rangi asked as though really surprised. 'Brother you don't want to go thumping yourself, *mea culpa*, all that. There's enough'll thump us without ourselves thumping us.'

Once Rangi stopped going to Mass, Pita wouldn't see him all weekend, not until he went to work on Monday where he'd find his brother as good-humoured and as hardworking as he always was. But Pita was afraid his brother was heading for trouble, that one day he'd end up in the lock-up and what would that do to the family? What would that do to Ma?

One night Rangi turned up at Club practice after being out drinking with friends after work. He walked in late and half primed, so Ma turned him at the door and sent him home. Later that night she reminded Rangi that they carried their uncle's name, the uncle who had helped them, who had an important job and couldn't have members of his family harming his reputation.

'Weekends are bad enough,' she said. 'Now it's week nights. You'll get yourself in trouble being round the streets like that, or in those no-good places you go to.'

'Where else is there?' Rangi asked. 'Not allowed a drink in the Club. Why not? What's all this Club about anyway? Who's it for?'

'All of us,' Ma said. 'It's for all of us but you got to get there decent. Got to set yourself up high.'

'And not allowed in the pubs with the Pakeha and the Chinaman. Why only the Pakeha and the Chinaman? Why can't the Maori boy go to the pub for a drink after work too?'

'Well it's the law,' Ma said. But she stopped at that, said good-night to them all and went to bed.

So even though Ma was against either of them going to war, Pita was glad Rangi had joined up so that the army could look after him, keep him out of trouble. Maybe they'd knock some sense into him while the rest of them got on with their lives. That's how he felt at first.

12

snow

Two days before Christmas we were given new orders which found us on the march, again through mud and water and once more making a difficult climb, this time by a different face, bringing us to a position not far from our former cemetery possie. This time we knew our tanks were standing by in the cemetery and what a kick we got out of spotting them winding forward from among the trees as we ran to form up behind them. But we were hardly on the road before the first of them was hit.

What a road it was we'd been set upon. Even before we came to it we could hear the rumpus, and as we came near could see that it was being blown to pieces, with shells bursting all over it and bits of rock and road and shrapnel flying. Airborne shells exploded above and red-hot metal rained down. All this time big guns were blasting away at our tanks which were breaking up and bursting into flame one after another. The whole earth shook. To add to all of this, there was constant hammering fire coming from the direction of Orsogna.

So there we were once again with our tanks out of action. There we were once more scooting for cover, flattening ourselves in the already flattened vegetation with debris falling and bushes on fire. Fire everywhere. And I remember thinking as we lay there squeezed together in a bunch, that if you move even slightly, among bushes or grass or anything leafy, the leaves will tell on you. They'll tell where you are. What a thing to think about, because who out there would be watching a leaf twitch when there were much bigger matters to be concerned with.

Anyway, in the middle of it all, our CO, who was flattened there with us in the flattened vines, turned his bleeding head, pressing the side of his face into the shaking ground to speak to us.

'Let's have a party,' he said.

Someone started singing in a kind of a whisper 'Show Me the Way to Go Home' because of it being a favourite party song back home. 'I'm Tired and I Want to Go to Bed.'

After a while we had to clear out of there and men were dropping all over the place, among them Cousin Tama and Roddy from the Club who'd only just come in with the latest reinforcements.

We've sung the old party song a few times since being settled back here on Cemetery Ridge. Some of the boys feel real meaning attached to the words. Not me. I'm not ready to go home yet, though looking out over these spurs reminds me of home, and during these cold hours of waiting I recall a particular hot summer day out on the hill-slopes with Uncles Willy and Ju. We were getting firewood. I think about the influence that such days and times may have had on my life as a soldier.

We were high in the hills where there was a suitable stand of manuka, and we had cut two loads which we trimmed and stacked, securing the first load with chains ready for the horse to pull. I was about ten years old and Ma had sent me backhome for the school holidays.

With Uncle Willy behind us watching the load, I guided the horse. Uncle Ju was ahead, using a long trimmed stick to assist him on his way down the track and also to hold aside brush and branches as horse and load went through.

We hadn't eaten since early morning, so when we reached the flats my uncles sent me down to the river to catch an eel or two while they unhitched the first load. I went along the river banks and soon found a couple of holes from which I pulled two medium-sized eels, throwing them up on to the bank and rolling them in the dry grass to clean off the coating of slime. We made a small fire and put the eels in the embers to cook. While we were waiting we stripped off and went into the river to cool down.

As we came out of the water Uncle Ju picked up his stick and began stepping with it, holding it upright and close to his body like a taiaha. He stepped high up on his toes with his leg muscles tightening into balls.

'Watch this, watch your uncle,' Uncle Willy said.

Uncle Ju began a series of movements with the piece of manuka, using his hands and wrists to quiver it, manipulating it along his arms and all about his body in ways which, at the time, seemed quite magical. Drops of water flew off him as he paced and pranced. They glittered in sunlight.

He went out over a wider and wider area – fast steps, slow steps; high and low; running on the spot; moving forward and moving back; moving in circles small and wide. And as I continued to watch, it seemed to me that Uncle Ju had become a bird. Everything about him and everything he did – from the way he stepped, the way he moved his head, the way he widened his watching eyes, the way the stick flicked and flickered – made him birdlike, even though Uncle Ju is a rounded, well-built man.

When he finished he tossed the stick to me and said, 'Here, son, have a go,' and that was when Uncle Ju began instructing me in the arts of the taiaha.

I always looked forward to school holidays when I could return to my mountain and to my uncles who taught me many things about life and survival, and I looked forward to learning more of these skills of weaponry that came from the olden times.

We've had some tussles out in these other men's hilltops, and also many losses. But we made a few gains as well. After that first disastrous day we managed to clear a way for tanks to move ahead, as we had been sent out to do. After that our task was to hold where we were, fighting off all enemy approaches.

It was very cold. Rain began again and we couldn't keep the water out of the slitties, so we were fighting, eating, sleeping wet most of the time. But a hot meal arrived by mule train once each night before daylight, which always seemed like a miracle. From time to time we were able to supplement these meals with poultry – chooks left behind by fleeing civilians – which we cooked up in our little tin boilers. Also we had mail and parcels from home delivered by mule as well, which helped to keep out the cold and the wet.

Parcels included all sorts of good things, such as oysters, chocolate, whitebait fritters, tinned pears, and fruit cakes or puddings that had been baked in Edmonds baking powder tins. I remember that while I was waiting backhome for my call-up papers I watched Aunty Dinah and Aunty Janey making these cakes and puddings for the food parcels. I also remember the men butchering a couple of Uncle Ju's beasts and lighting the outdoor fires to cook the meat, preserving it in fat in kerosene tins for the soldiers. It was food preserved in this way that was now being delivered to us, whether meat, fish, shellfish or mutton-bird.

Aunty Dinah taught the girls to knit garments for comfort parcels too. She didn't have enough knitting needles for everyone so I helped Uncle Willy make a few sets for them from number eight fencing wire. They knitted scarves, socks and balaclavas whenever they could get wool. Just the job for conditions like these.

'Give your bayonet a wipe before you cut into the pudding,' said Bootleg out on the cold wet hill-slopes.

But those days of waiting were bad times for the home people. Every day there was news of death. People were crying every day. Every day, in one meeting house or another under our mountain, in our village, or in a village nearby, there would be a soldier photograph displayed in a meeting house. Sometimes there would be two or three at once. People would gather, wailing and crying, and I recall how bewildered everyone was. Death in far-off lands, death without a body, was a death not fully believed. There was only a photograph as a reminder, only a photograph to touch, to stroke while the death ceremonies took place, and no burial to bring about conclusion. Every day people were on the move, gathering at one marae or another to mourn.

I saw all of this, took part in all of this, fully understanding that one day people could be gathering under the verandahs for me.

Never mind. Here I am. So far, so good.

Christmas Day found us still wet and freezing and under fire out on our ridge, and thinking back to just over a month before, when on a warm night under a clear sky in Taranto, beneath stands of cypress trees and overlooking a moonlit valley, we gathered round a bonfire to record our Christmas messages.

On Christmas morning, in the warmth of summer, our families would have listened to the broadcast, hearing from our leaders and padres that we were all okay, that we had adapted well to the colder weather in this land of rivers and mountains and were well equipped for what lay ahead. They would have pictured us all together by the blaze of a warm campfire, not knowing of our true situation out in the hilltops. Good thing.

Two days after Christmas we were relieved by another battalion and returned here to Castelfrentano where we enjoyed Christmas dinner a couple of days later. We had pork, chicken, mutton-birds, pumpkin, potatoes, cabbage and steam pudding cooked in the hangi. All of this we washed down with wine, beer and liqueurs, spending the rest of the day and night being drunk and having a real party, a good old singsong. Bootleg took snaps of us all with a flash-looking camera that he acquired in Taranto in exchange for boots and blankets.

Wherever I may roam,
On land or sea or foam,
You will always hear me singing this song,
Show me the way to go home.

But not me, not yet.

We woke on the first day of January 1944 to a real dead dark – the darkest dark I've ever experienced. We were warm in our beds, Choc and I, in this dark darkness, but everything was moving. There were sounds that seemed far away, of blurry voices and blurry laughter. And with everything sounding so fuzzy I wondered if I'd gone deaf as some of the boys had because of all the blasting up on the ridges.

There was an earthquake going on, I thought, or perhaps we were being attacked.

Before we could wake properly and get out of our blankets we saw a slit of grey daylight which suddenly widened, and in through that gap in the dark came a shovelful of snow. But we didn't realise at the time that this cold mess that had landed on us was snow. We couldn't realise it because neither Choc nor I had ever been in snow, and had seen it only as a far-off white hat on our home mountain. Voices and laughter were disappearing without the sound of footsteps.

Once outside we could see the land was covered in white and we realised we had slept through a blizzard. The tents we'd been sleeping in were completely covered too, and some had collapsed under the weight of the snow.

After our eyes stopped goggling at this sight, this land of snow, we put on coats and boots and went off, treading, sinking, falling, laughing, getting the feel of this new thing – this snow. We took our shovels with us, catching up with the others to assist them in this cold reveille.

A few days later we were wedged back into place on Cemetery Ridge, looking out from our broken shelters over a battlefield that was completely white. It was a hard time, an edgy time, especially at night – which was the time for visitors, with the enemy patrolling in their white snow suits, coming at us from behind gunfire and hand grenades. It was a time of stalking and close encounter. It was a nervy time of being out in the dark in snowbound trenches, eyes toiling across white silence, where shadows could be those cast by a slice of moonlight on trees, or where shadows or trees could be men. There could be a movement of those shadows, a change in the contours of snow that might be from an air flurry or a movement of enemy, but which could also be an imagined change. It could be a mirage or a transposition from a ridge beyond, or from another time or place. It could be a change made up from our own jittery fabrications.

It could be the patupaiarehe with their white skins, red hair and green eyes, come to steal us away and marry us.

'Where is this backhome boy now?' I kept asking myself, and sometimes when it was particularly quiet and I was waiting to go out into the trenches, and thinking about where I was and how I came to be there, a feeling of unreality would come over me. I felt as though I had become part of a picture or a Christmas card, or a story of woodcutters and princes in a book once read. Here I was in the once-upon-a-time, in some make-believe place.

The reality of two-hour patrol in the snow soon put paid to those imaginings. Out on a snowy ridge, as shadows come closer, the white becomes the iced white of your eyes – eyes which have become chiselled and blind like the stone eyes of statues. Out on a snowy ridge, sometimes the shadows leap and cry out as you cover them with fire, then for a time there is just the silence of snow. You become unsure. It is only once daylight arrives that you know for certain that the shadows were shadows of real men.

In a snow-covered field death is contorted, limbs are angled or unjointed, torsos are splayed or crumpled or torn apart. Eyes are the frozen eyes of statues. Men are marble, broken angels.

13

manpower

One night at the club, after Rangi went into training camp, Sophie brought one of their friends to talk to Pita about work at the Woollen Mills where they made cloth for army uniforms. Pauline, who had been working there for three months by then, offered to take Sophie and Moana to apply for jobs. Now that it was war time there was work for everyone she told Pita, and she reminded him that everyone was expected to take part in the war effort.

'Essential industry, that's what everyone's talking about,' Pauline said. 'Sophie and Moana are bound to get manpowered sooner or later. But don't you worry, I'll look after your sisters.'

When they first settled in Wellington his sisters had wanted to go out and look for work but he didn't allow it. He believed they were needed at home, even though Ma had pointed out that it wasn't like backhome where there was always so much to do, growing food, getting wood, carrying water, and where there was no paid work anyway. Here in the city it was money they needed. Still he didn't approve. It wasn't right. He and Rangi could look after the family without the girls having to get jobs. He knew his sisters were disappointed with his decision, though they said nothing. They were silent around him, making him feel as though he was somehow in the wrong.

'Just till we get something else,' Sophie said now, her hands clasped in front of her, her eyes looking into him.

Something else? This meant they believed he'd think the woollen mills an unsuitable place.

'Something closer,' Moana said.

What was it about him that made his sisters so shaky, afraid to breathe?

'And now Rangi's away . . .'

He didn't need it pointed out to him that there was less money coming in now that Rangi had left. But Rangi usually wasted most of his wage anyway. He thought of reminding his sisters of that but he didn't.

'Not you,' he said to Moana, louder than he meant. 'Someone has to stay home with Ma.'

But by disallowing Moana it seemed he was giving permission to Sophie, who continued to watch him while reaching out a hand to Moana who by now was in tears. Work at the mills, work anywhere, wasn't what he wanted for his sisters. Now he felt manipulated. Moana was still sniffling when they arrived home.

'You got to go to work too, with your sister,' he said, more roughly than he intended. 'You got to keep your sister company on the train,' and Sophie and Moana came and threw their arms around him. He was mad with all this crying.

'Wash your face,' he told Moana. 'You didn't have to be stupid, bawling in front of everyone at the Club.'

Pita didn't know what it was about him that made people cry, but also didn't know why his sisters were so anxious to get out and work when there was no need. After all, he gave them money. He'd bought them a wireless on lay-by and there were just ten shillings left to pay on a sewing machine. It was difficult to know what was in his sisters' minds.

A month after Rangi left for training camp the killing season began at the works and when Pita returned there, after having spent the off-season on the conveyer belt at the pickle and jam factory, he was asked to go into the abattoir instead of his usual place in the cool stores and freezers. There was a shortage of slaughtermen now that men were leaving. Gone off to slaughter a few Germans instead, everyone said. Every few days, as the younger men enlisted, he found himself moved to more skilled work with older men.

It wasn't the kind of job he enjoyed. Rangi was the one who was good at that sort of work, he thought. Beef or mutton on a hook and a knife in his hand, his brother separated and dragged the skins down, made the cuts, tumbled the innards out, boning and quartering – quick and hard and sharp like one of his knives. It was all work to Rangi. Sweat was what he liked. War was what he liked. Blood and guts, the stink of boiling offal, were nothing. Rangi, singing and joking as he worked, somehow made it all seem clean.

But Pita liked being there with the older men. Ned, on the next hook, with his big hands and rolling wrists, was a patient teacher who helped him keep pace. Also he was thankful for the work because the money was good while the season lasted, even though it was really permanent work that he wanted. Work between seasons in the canning factories, or cutting out gorse or shovelling coal, was hard to get sometimes. What he really wanted was something steadier with more future in it, the future that Ma talked about.

It was one morning after they changed from sheep carcasses to beef that Pita let his knife slip as he was trying to step up his pace while trimming a cavity. There was so much stain on his hands that he didn't realise at first that he'd injured himself, only wondered why his knife had dropped to the floor and why, when he reached down, he was unable pick it up again.

'Boy, y' thumb's nearly off,' Ned said, and called Colin the supervisor, who then took him to the hospital for stitches and bandaging.

On some days during winter, while he was working at the cannery, Pita would take a tram and go home during the dinner break. On the way up Molesworth Street he would look in through the doorway of the cake shop and catch sight of the girl. She would be wearing a pink smock, and a triangle of cloth on her head which caught her hair back behind her ears. She'd be busy with lunch-time customers, smiling, her lips just parted, and her eyes, squeezed by the smile, almost disappearing. It was only a glimpse as he hurried home to have a meal that Ma would have ready for him before the rush back to work in time for the whistle. In the afternoon, in the noise and monotony of the factory as he loaded tins on to the conveyor belt, he could think about the disappearing eyes.

Also, on Club nights he watched out for her as she made her way home with her basket and bag, wondering where it was that she went after work on a Monday that made her late going home. He knew that she noticed him.

The girl was not for him, not even when the world was free.

One night at home when they were all sitting at the tea table, sister Moana said that Jess at the cake shop had asked her his name.

'What were you doing down the cake shop gassing about our family?' was what he said. 'Where did you get money for cakes?'

'I sent her for coffee buns,' Ma said. 'Your uncle was visiting.'

If he could be different, more like Brother Rangi, he could've had them all laughing instead of all shut up and his sister feeling bad. And maybe, if he'd been different, he could've found out from Moana more about the girl who had become his dream. What else had the girl said? He was sorry for the silence he caused.

'Got her eye on you,' Rangi said. He was home on leave at the time, and as he spoke he smacked Pita with an elbow while his sisters and Tuboy and Ma all swished their eyes over him to see how he was taking this crack from his brother.

He stood up from the table to help himself to more food from the pot and knew his sisters would be shifting their eyebrows at each other while his back was turned. Tuboy was scoffing food like a pig and he just wished Ma would tell him to mind his manners.

Everything could go wrong if they didn't all hold on.

Jess?

If he were someone different he could've asked how Moana found out her name, whether she'd overheard someone say it or whether the girl had told Moana herself. He didn't think she would do that. You just didn't go telling your name to strangers.

On the day that he made his way home from hospital, with his hand bandaged and his arm in a sling, he paused by the cake shop window. The girl Jess had her back to him as she rearranged goods on the shelves after the rush at lunchtime. The older woman behind the counter was wiping down trays. He decided that he'd go home and clean up, then come back and buy a cream sponge for Ma.

'Pita, Son, what happened to you?' Ma said when he walked in. Ma, and Aunty Puti from the Club, had the table spread with goods for a bazaar. There were pot-holders, aprons, peg bags and oven cloths, all cut from sugar bags, which they'd edged with scraps of material left over from dresses. The two women came towards him looking into his face.

'Took my thumb for a beef kidney Ma,' he said.

'Sit down, son. You look like . . .'

'Don't you black out on us young Pita,' Aunty Puti said.

He sat long enough to satisfy them and to drink the tea Ma made for him, then he went to light the califont to heat enough water so that he could kneel in the bath and give himself an all-over wash. He dressed in the shirt and tie, the green pullover and grey slacks that he would wear to the Club that evening, and went out on to the street.

'You look as though you've been to war already,' the older woman said as he went into the cake shop. He didn't know what to say, wondered if the woman was telling him he should be enlisting. The girl was handing a bag of buns to a man, wishing him good afternoon, putting change in his hand.

'What can I do for you?' the woman asked. He decided he needed two sponges rather than one. Aunty Puti was at home and since it was Club night there would be others calling in who hadn't had time for a meal. He gave his order, not looking at the girl, not expecting her to speak, and he was wondering, now that he'd ordered the sponges, how he was going to carry them home one-handed without squashing them. But the woman was putting them in boxes, one on top of the other, tying the boxes together and making a string handle.

'What happened?' the girl asked.

'Nothing,' he said, 'a few stitches.'

He paid for the sponges and left.

During his time at the freezing works and while working at his between-seasons jobs, he'd often thought about finding work with better prospects. But because of long hours and overtime whenever he could get it, there hadn't been time to look for anything else. Now he decided that he didn't want to go back to the meatworks, and since he was off work with his injured hand there was an opportunity to look for something better, a job for life. The Post Office, Native Affairs or the Railways, the uncle-from-parliament advised. A government position would mean security with opportunities for promotion. It was what Pita wanted, having had enough of seasonal and irregular work.

He found that there were positions available at the Post Office and Native Affairs, more and more places every day, but they were advertising for clerical workers. He felt he hadn't had enough schooling to apply for those. No, an office wasn't the place for him. One day Tuboy might have a job like that once he was educated.

At the Railways the foreman told him there were job vacancies.

'Can you push a broom, boy?' he asked. 'Come back when you're hand's better and you can probably get a job pushing a broom.'

Pushing a broom? He felt demeaned by the suggestion, but he called in to see his uncle and spoke to him about it.

'A boy's job,' his uncle said, 'or a job for an old man. It's because they don't want to pay you too much.' Then his uncle hesitated for a long time before he said, 'If you want to try it you could work yourself on from there if they let you. You have to prove your worth. If you want to take this job you'll have to be the best sweeper they've ever seen. You'll have to be prepared to fill in other positions if the opportunity comes along and you'll have to be just the very best. So good that they can't deny you. That's how it is. The brown man has to be twice as good as the white man in order to be equal.'

It was late afternoon when he left his uncle's office so he decided to walk round town for a while then go and sit in the grounds of parliament until it was time for the girl, who now had a name, to finish work. He would see her walk by on the way to the tram stop or the railway station. But he decided he'd stay on the other side of the road so that she wouldn't talk to him. If she looked across and saw him he could wave and walk on home.

14

ol' man

It's a tough country and a tough enemy. We were not able to make it to Rome via Orsogna and the whole of the New Zealand Division was pulled out. Once we were brought back from the ridges we began a move to the south-west.

Well, no one was sorry to leave those snowy hills and muddy river flats behind. There's more than one way to Rome. We were pleased when we heard that we were heading for a rest area in a place called San Severo.

Plenty vino, plenty singsong, plenty pretty girl, we thought. But once again, as we were preparing to go, we were ordered to remove all identification. If it was a rest area we were going to, why the secrecy?

We journeyed through the first night, heading south, and the next day came to San Severo, which looked so inviting and peaceful with its clusters of houses, its open fields and its rows of vines. But this was no holiday we were going on after all. We passed right through the town without stopping. No vino, no singsong, no Maria to see.

Everywhere we went we saw civilians on the roads and verges with their carts and bundles. They were mainly women, children and old people, made homeless by war, who wandered the roads and fields. They were ragged and hungry, sleeping in caves and ruins.

One night, while we were having tea by the roadside, an old man and two little girls came by. They started out across the paddock, probably going to find shelter for the night.

'Grandfather come. *Venite*,' we called. He stopped, looked our way, then began to walk on again.

'*Venite*, Grandfather, come eat.' We made eating motions with our hands to make ourselves understood. He came towards us, ushering the two children in front of him. The girls were thin and mud-caked, their clothes were torn and their feet were wrapped in rags. We sat them down and shared out our food, and when they'd eaten we gave them socks and blankets, food and cigarettes as they stood to go.

'Where are you going, Grandfather?' we asked. He must have understood us.

'*A Taranto*,' he replied. Then he asked, '*Voi dove andate, soldati?*'

We took a guess. 'To Rome,' we said.

He spread his arms out from his sides with his palms open towards us, smiling and showing four or five teeth. '*Ah, che bella Roma*,' he said. He lifted one of his hands close to his face and spread his fingers. His face was like something from dirt, something from mountains, something from rivers, something from hills, something from backhome. '*A-a-ah, che be-e-e-ella Roma*,' he repeated with a flick of his spread hand. He hugged us and kissed our cheeks and he and the children went on their way across the field. '*Che Iddio vi protegga, soldati*,' he called.

We continued our journey through the night, and next afternoon made camps in several places under olive and oak trees on the banks of the Volturno River. By now we were far away from the steel-bladed winds, in warmth and sunshine.

One night a dozen or more of us lay out under a clear sky, our glowing cigarettes dotting the slopes facing a high bank of stars.

We were contemplating the opposite positions of the constellations, that is, positions opposite to those of skies at home – mirror images presented to us by this other-side-of-the-world's sky. There was the upside-down Pot. There were the Seven Sisters dancing in different formation – Pleiades, known to our people as Matariki, brightest at the time of our new year when crops have been harvested and the earth lies fallow as it prepares for spring. And there was Taurus, who though seen belly-up in the skies of home, is fine and upright tramping these northern skies.

There was a last chip of moon, like a bent icicle, which also took on a mirror image to a backhome moon. It was a moon that at home would be waxing, but on this side of the world was in the position of a moon decreasing. It was as we mused over these matters that Brother Pita came towards us, one of his rare smiles lighting him up. He was flapping an aerogramme, bringing us all to our feet with news of the birth of his son.

Our new camp was dry and comfortable with good hot showers that had been set up by the Americans. Most of our time was spent in intensive training, some of it involving practice on the river with assault boats.

Reinforcements continued to arrive and one day we were happy to welcome Anzac and Matey, two of our backhome cousins who had come to join us on this road to Rome, on our way to win the war.

'That's where we're off to,' I told them. I spread my fingers, lifted my outstretched hand and pushed my shoulder forward, lifted my face, 'Che be-e-ella Roma,' I said. We all practised this.

On leave we went off to see the sights of Pompeii. Therefore, my mountain Taranaki and the other great mountains of home have given their greetings to Vesuvius.

As we moved on there were ever-increasing signs that the battle zone was not far away. The road was congested with traffic – tanks and armoured vehicles; supply trucks bringing petrol and ammunition, tents, clothing, food and utensils; bulldozers and other road-making machinery. Our troop transports moved slowly among it. The road to Rome is ancient and bordered by hills on both sides. It is 'long and filled with many a turning', which is a line of one of the songs we sang on our way. There were ruins everywhere.

And coming towards us out of the war as we moved forward were vehicles so covered in mud as to be barely recognisable as vehicles, the men in them so filthy that they were hardly recognisable as men. Among their traffic was a continual stream of ambulances, some of them Bren gun carriers or armoured cars painted white and bearing the red cross, which had been converted for use to carry the wounded.

The scene worsened as we moved on. By the wayside were rusty remains of burnt-out vehicles and clusters of new graves of soldiers. There were dead men and dead donkeys, and always the pervading stink of death. All along the way were signs – numbers, arrows, warnings of shellfire, and a picture of a decapitated man showing what could happen if you lingered in certain places.

At night we made ourselves as comfortable as possible in roadside camps in some of the more sheltered areas. At other times we found ourselves sleeping in holes and trenches which had the ghosts of our enemies still inhabiting them.

But one day, on this road to Rome, what a scene we came upon. I want to attempt to describe what we saw as we made our way round a feature known to us now as Monte Trocchio.

After miles of winding round hills and through valleys we emerged into a wide plain. On the other side of the plain, ahead of us at a distance of three or four miles, was a mountain range which continued endlessly east and endlessly north, in layer after layer, until it was beyond sight. Through mist and drizzle, as it had been raining most of the way, were high walls of colour; of brown and red, black and grey, all combining with the deep blue and purple shadows cast by rocky sides and rugged mountain summits.

Looking ahead along the line of the road, which had now straightened out across the valley, our eyes came to a particular mountain, which stands at the head of the great mass at a point where the road becomes lost to sight. Though not tall compared to many of the other giants, this is the mountain that takes shape before you. It takes your eye, and it takes your breath away.

Dark and precipitous, this landmark stands at the head of the rest of the mountain range like a great fighting chief leading his people on to a path of war. And there on top of this colossus, we could see, through the mist, a long white shape which could not be snow, which was not cloud. It was unnatural, spooky, unexplainable, until on coming closer we saw that it was a massive building, rectangular in shape, covering the whole of the mountain top. The building was several storeys high judging by the rows of windows that we could see down its outer walls.

The apparent inaccessibility of the mountain face made it seem impossible that men could have done this. It was eerie. Tipu, Choc, Matey and I jumped down from our transport and stood on the roadside to take in the sight.

'That's some ol' fella,' Matey said, 'some real ol' fella.'

We stood to attention and gave our smartest salutes along with the biggest heel clicks ever heard on that road to Rome. Others were jumping down, looking up, shouting, talking, swearing at the sight. And I thought right then that there was no better place to be than on this road to Rome, no greater sight to see than ol' man wearing his wonderful hat, none better to share this sight with than the men of the Maori Battalion.

Here we were, we backhome boys, seeing all of this. We ran, laughing and shouting, to rejoin our truck which was making its slow way along. And how small, how minuscule our army suddenly became on its road to Rome. I thought how tiny we all are and what little reasons there are for what we do.

I know there is more to be known about ol' fella, about his family of mountains, about his white hat, about those who live in his hair. And there is more to learn about this ancient road too, about those who have walked, marched and ridden here.

I've done my best to describe what I saw, tried to write about how

I felt and to give my impressions at coming upon this great mountain range. I look forward to these spare moments when I have opportunities to describe my thoughts, experiences and feelings. But it doesn't really matter if my efforts at expression fall short at times because I am here and I have *seen*.

Ol' man mountain is called Monte Cassino. His hat is a Benedictine abbey first built more than fourteen centuries ago, a time-span which I can't even imagine. It's been destroyed and rebuilt a few times since then. At his feet is the town of Cassino, and at one end of the town there's a castle on a hilltop. I didn't notice the town or castle or anything else on the day we came out into the valley and looked up. Ol' man took my attention completely. It was as though we were directly at his feet instead of yet a plain, a river and a town away. How great he is, this chief at the head of his people, but what a vantage point for our enemy.

On the backhome hills it only needs one pair of eyes on a hilltop, or up in a tree, to discover anyone's whereabouts. A boy, or man, cannot remain still or unseen forever. Eventually a bush will move, a colour will show, a bird will fly, a stick will snap.

High in the hills of Wellington, in among gorse and broom, you can look out and see the city's streets and those who walk and ride there. You can see its buildings and the people who come and go. Whoever is highest is the one who knows, the one who is able to scan every pathway.

There's no doubt Jerry has us in his sights since there are vantage points all round, beginning from ol' man's hat, and from there on down. Everywhere we go we feel Jerry's eyes upon us from on high. Forward battalions, which have been attempting to break through the valleys, have been halted by mountains and rivers, but also by an enemy who sees all and has had time to put up strong defences.

I think of my own home mountain, Taranaki, who is a lonely mountain indeed, a lover ousted from his tribe by a jealous brother whom he fought with red-hot boulders and rivers of boiling spittle. But in the end he had to flee, leaving his homeland and his heart behind, to stand alone, transfixed by the setting sun.

I am my mountain because my mountain is my ancestor, and by my mountain I am identified. My mountain too has his colours, his contours, his imposing presence. He is ever-present in my life. As though painted inside me, he is with me wherever I go.

But for now I live under other men's mountains, which are other men's landmarks and identity, and which will have their own stories of love and war. I think of the people of Cassino town who have left their homes, taking with them their mountains, painted inside them. These are people whose houses and crops have been destroyed, whose roads and bridges and railways have been blown to pieces, whose pigs and chickens are astray in the hills and valleys, and who themselves have taken to the roads and mountains.

Even so I am a soldier and our task is to free the world. I'm happy to be a man of the Twenty-eighth Battalion with such a job to do, Maori Battalion staunch and true.

The New Zealand Corps now reports to the Fifth Army which will take over from the Americans who have been having a rough time. We'll be crossing the river and breaking through to free this way to Rome.

The river we will cross is called the Rapido and is the reason for all the practising with boats that we did back on the Volturno.

15

omnipotentem

I have to try to think of what happened on this day, 15 February 1944, as something that was necessary because we are at war. I have to remember that this is war and that I am a soldier.

Sometime after nine this morning we heard the roar of big bombers coming, hundreds of them, and watched the bombs being dropped on ol' man mountain, on his hat and all around Cassino.

As each bomb hit the earth there were great yellow flashes that spread and coloured the whole sky. From ol' man's head billowed huge clouds of dust as the raid went on and on, as planes came in wave after wave, as bombs followed more bombs. But it was not only the mountain that was hit. The landscape all around, including some of our own positions, was erupting with fire as the onslaught continued throughout the morning.

In the middle of the day there was a period of quiet where we thought it was all over. At first all we could see on the mountaintop were huge clouds of dense orange smoke and dust which blocked out the light of the sun. Then, as these clouds began to clear, we saw to our surprise that ol' man's hat was still there, and that its shape had not altered as greatly as we would have expected.

In the afternoon the bombardment began again.

This time the planes flew lower. They were smaller planes and more accurate, crossing in formations of twelve and dropping their loads. Bright flames shot into the air, followed by funnels of smoke coming out of the ground and standing in columns miles high.

Once the bombing stopped and the smoke finally cleared we could see that the crown of ol' man's hat had been shattered, leaving a ragged outline against a thick backdrop of multi-coloured sky.

This attack from the air was something that had to happen, necessary because the abbey was the greatest stronghold of all, the greatest lookout of all. That's what I thought as I watched. The greatest of all fortresses had to be destroyed.

'But him, the ol' man, he's still there,' Choc said, and I had to think about the truth of that.

'His damn hat too, even if it's busted,' Tipu said, which made us wonder if it was all worth it after all. I mean the fortress, though broken, was still a fortress. Ol' man was still standing in the way, no doubt all covered in enemy eyes as before.

'Not just eyes,' said Rangi, 'but radios, nests of machine guns, barricaded caves, mines all over the place. All waiting for the little Maori boy with his popgun, you bet. Well, can't complain brothers. We been given the very best – the wildest river to cross, a big old mountain in our way – and Heinrich there to try and stop us moving on. To make it sweeter Heinrich been practising all this time on the Yanks and Frogs.'

Brother Rangi went off with his head back, laughing.

After a day of noise and spectacle it's silent. Most of my pals are asleep. As I write I think of the Benedictines and the little I've learned of them through the study of Church history when I was at school. I think of the monks in their abbey in times of peace, and picture them in single file, chanting through columned rooms. I'm reminded of the quiet of early morning chapel; of the swish and whisper of robes as the priest and brothers move about; of light coming through stained glass, and of dust tumbling in these light shafts in the way that mosquito larvae tumble in water.

I think of benediction and white garments and the smell of wax melting; the monstrance, held aloft by covered hands. It glints gold in the light of candles as we kneel for the Adoremus. Pungent smoke pours from the censer as the incense smoulders. There are morning prayers, blessings and genuflections and signs of the cross; the smell of hair-oil; boys yawning on our sleeves.

And I am reminded too, of Sunday Mass among concrete arches, statues and stations of the cross; of red velvet and wood and paint and plaster; the smell of polish and lit candles. There's the toning of plainsong and the singing of psalms. There's the reciting of the confiteor and the profession of faith, 'Credo in unum Deum. Patrem omnipotentem,' all part of the humdrum of school then, but I think of the quiet of it now as I record my thoughts.

At other times, backhome times, there's the quiet of the meeting house when you are the first to wake, and sometimes in the early morning you see the ghost of Maratea passing through. I think of the silence of wood and the silence of the dead. I think of a dead father, or someone dead, lying in a wooden canoe in preparation for a journey.

I think of Ma.

I think about how old this country is.

Everyone's asleep. I write by the scent of a candle.

16

lines

Pita saw Jess look up as she removed goods from the window and knew she'd spotted him, thought he should go on home, but he didn't. A few moments later, when she left the shop, she crossed the road and asked after his hand.

'It's all right,' he said.

'But what did you do?' He didn't want her to ask about his hand, or to have to tell her how he'd injured it.

'At work,' he said. 'I go back to work when the stitches come out.'

Then he remembered that he might not be going back to the job anyway and would probably be working nearby at the railway stores. He didn't want to tell her that.

'How were the sponge cakes?' she asked.

'I didn't have any,' he said, 'but they liked them.'

'Your mother and sisters, your handsome little brother?' She knew a lot about his family, he thought.

'On Mondays we have people in for tea.'

'On Mondays I see you on my way back from my piano teacher's place,' she said.

'On the way to the Club,' he said, though he didn't want to tell her about the Club, or about anything to do with himself or his family.

'I'm just on my way down to catch my tram.'

'Goodbye, then.'

'Goodbye.'

She hesitated, and he thought she might be going to say something more, or that she could've been waiting for him to say something, but she smiled with her disappearing eyes and walked on down the hill to the terminal.

So it seemed she knew Ma and his sisters, and also knew that he had a young brother. But why wouldn't she know when they only lived two blocks away and had now been living there for two years? Ma knew everybody, befriended people, often called on neighbours or had them call in. Ma knew all the shopkeepers around, so why wouldn't she know the people from the cake shop? Jess hadn't mentioned Rangi when she asked about the sponges. That could mean she knew his brother was away at camp. She probably knew all about his jobs and about where he was going on Club nights too. Who knows what they all talked about? Anyway it seemed she knew his family quite well, otherwise she wouldn't have thought it all right to ask Moana his name, or to cross over the road to inquire after his stitched-up hand.

He made his way home through workers on their way to the tram stops or rushing to pubs to drink what they could before the pubs closed at six. A boy on the hotel corner with his bag of papers was calling, 'Ee-ee-vun-ing Pee-ee-yo-ust, Ee-ee-vun-ing Pee-ee-yo-ust.'

Tuboy would like to have a paper-boy job too but Pita didn't want him round the streets yelling like that, putting papers in front of people's faces, jumping on and off trams, going out on the roads to sell to drivers slowed down by traffic or stopped at crossings. In a few months time the boy would be away at boarding school. Boarding school was what he needed, and the Marist Brothers at his primary school thought he'd probably be awarded a native scholarship, which would help even though they already had some money saved.

Although he wasn't pleased about his sisters going to work he had to admit it made things easier. It made his sisters happy too, sorting out money for train tickets, money for stockings, money for Ma, some to put aside for a dress-length that they were going to buy to make a frock. Those were the things he heard them talking about and he could see how it pleased them. Everything was going well for their family. If only they'd been able to keep out of the war. He thought of his sisters taking piano lessons.

It wasn't until after he began the new job that he saw Jess again as she arrived one afternoon at the tram stop just as he was returning from the railway yards. From then on he met her every day after work, except for Mondays when she went to music lessons. He came out of the job at five and was on his way home just as she arrived at the tram stop, so he would wait there with her until the Number Three came along. There were things she knew about him, his family, the Club, that made him feel slow and somehow exposed – as though there was a whole world of talk that went on all about him without him being any part of it. But still, he thought, there were some things she'd never know.

Though he didn't ask, she told him quite a lot about herself. She worked in the cake shop for part of each day, beginning at eleven o'clock in the morning. The older woman was her Aunt Peggy, who owned the shop along with Uncle Malcolm. Uncle Malcolm did most of the baking. Aunt Peggy was teaching her cake decorating just as a hobby, a good thing for a girl to know. Apart from that Jess was studying for her LTCL so that she could be a piano teacher one day if she needed to.

'That is, when I'm married and old,' she said.

Sometimes when she smiled and squeezed her eyes at him he felt like touching her. Music teaching was something to fall back on, her parents had told her.

'If I get left on the shelf, they mean,' she said, 'or if I get married and my husband dies or we come on hard times.' It made her laugh.

He thought of marrying her though he knew he never would.

It felt odd to be standing at a tram stop among strangers, talking to a girl who was also a stranger, while about the streets were paper boys calling, tram conductors switching the trolleys on the overhead wires – sending out sparks – or cranking the lines open with their iron bars so the trams could change lines. The trams came shuttling into the terminus or rattled off in the other direction up Lambton Quay.

Sometimes they walked to the cenotaph and stood there while Number Threes went by. If he was different he wouldn't care that people stared at them, or that friends from the Club saw them and sometimes called out a greeting or came over to speak to them. He often felt uneasy when he was talking to Jess, not knowing what was in people's minds.

But he knew that he was happy spending these moments with her, even though he wondered sometimes if she could be secretly laughing at him.

'I suppose you have a girlfriend at the Club and that's why you don't want to ask me to go out with you,' she said one day. There was light rain falling and the roads and footpaths were dark and steamy. The tram lines glinted hard and silver.

'I thought of marrying you,' he said. She laughed, squinted her eyes at him.

'And what did you think, after you thought of it?' she asked.

'I won't be getting married. Not for years.'

'When the world is free, do you mean?' He couldn't tell whether or not she was laughing at him, but people were talking about that now, about what would happen, what could happen once the world was free.

'And when you do it won't be to me,' she said.

That was true, he thought, but didn't want to say so.

'When you do get married it will be to a Maori girl,' she said, 'a *good Catholic Maori girl*.'

'You think you know a lot,' he said.

She turned away from him and he knew he had offended her, not that he wanted to. It was just that he didn't know how to say what he didn't mean. But then she turned to him again and stared right into his face so that he turned his eyes away.

'Does it mean we can't go out together?' she asked.

'Where do you want to go?' he asked, not looking at her. The question made her laugh. At him? He wasn't sure.

'We could go swimming. We could go to Day's Bay on the ferry one Sunday, on the *Cobar*,' she said, 'or to one of the beaches up the line. We could take the train.'

It was a strange idea to him, to take a girl out to the beach, not something he'd ever thought of doing. Since coming to Wellington the family had found places round different parts of the coast where they could get pipi, paua, mussels and crayfish. There were spots round the harbour where they could fish. When there were relatives coming from backhome, or visitors coming to the Club, a group of them would go fishing and food gathering, wanting to present their visitors with varieties of food from the sea. There was always somewhere to go, even when the weather was not so good.

And while it was true that they often took picnic lunches on warm days and spent some of the time relaxing and taking children swimming, he'd never thought that the beach would be a place to take a girl to. The sea was the place where you went for your food. Yet he had seen people strolling about on beaches in their best clothes, or lying flat on the sand in the hot sun, or just swimming or playing about in the water the way children do. It wasn't something he was used to or that he could see sense in.

'I don't have time,' he said. Or money, he could've added.

It was true that he had little time to spare, most of his weekends being taken up with the Club, entertaining at the army training camps or aboard the ships, or giving concerts in aid of the war effort. As well as that there were the Club socials that they held for the boys from camp when they came into the city on leave. He thought of inviting her to one of them but he didn't.

'Why stop and talk to me then?' she asked.

So many things were new and different since leaving their backhome mountain and since they joined the Club, especially now that there was a war on. Since the war began he'd been in places he would never have dreamed of going into, met people he would never have thought of meeting. It was a new and different world. There was a grand opening of the Centennial Exhibition that they were practising for, and they were going to take part in a welcome ceremony for the soldiers of the Maori Battalion coming to form a guard of honour for the opening of the Maori Court. He couldn't imagine what it was going to be like, only knew that the Centennial would keep them all on the go until after Christmas.

'I don't suppose your family would approve of me anyway,' Jess said. He didn't say anything to that though he knew what she said was true. Ma would never approve.

'What about your family?' he asked.

'What they don't know won't hurt them,' she said.

17

corps

What we understood, as we were being brought back from Orsogna, was that the Yanks were fighting down from the north to crack open this barrier of Cassino. Once that was accomplished, Second New Zealand Division would push through, meeting up with them and holding the way open to the road and the valley.

But we soon found out that the Americans, who had already been in combat for two months anyway, were being hammered to hell and back as they fought their way down. They moved in, hill by hill, fighting for every inch, only to be stopped a few hundred yards from the monastery. For a short time they took a slippery hold. That's how we heard it.

Yes, they nearly made it. But with the enemy holding strong, evil weather setting in and their losses mounting, it was just too tough and they had to pull out. We heard that some of their units had been reduced by three-quarters, and that the remainder, fought out, frozen and weak, had to be scraped off the mountain and stretchered back to recuperate. All of what we were being told was borne out by the sights we had already seen along the way – men and machines barely recognisable.

This failure of the thrust from the north put an end to our hopes of following in through an open door, tanks and all, and running ourselves on to the Via Casilina, Highway Six, the road to Rome. So we were all wondering what was going to happen next. We could just hang round waiting for better weather, we thought, or maybe just push on regardless. Some said there'd be another crackdown from the north that we'd exploit, but we didn't really think they'd try that again. Others reckoned we would be siphoned off to assist elsewhere – on the Anzio coast or somewhere else in Europe. They said staying where we were was a waste of time and that we should just give up on Cassino.

What has actually happened is that our Division has been remade. We've had Indian Divisions added to give a boost, and artillery and tank battalions have been brought in as well. We are now the New Zealand Corps. Other attachments to the Corps are from motor, medical and supply units.

Apparently there has been too much progress made by the Yanks for matters to be left and no advantage taken, so the New Zealand Corps has become an assault force, preparing to go in and press home these gains. Every other force is beggared, I guess. We must be the only fresh meat by now.

So we're heading out, ready or not. If there is to be a doorway we will be creating it ourselves, and we've been told that our Battalion will play a leading part in getting tanks across the Rapido and opening up this new way to Rome.

The place chosen for this breakthrough is the built-up ground that carries the railway line. It is the only position that rises above the water, and it is this embankment which has to be converted into a road strong enough for the passage of tanks and vehicles.

Start times have been delayed because of bad weather and flooding, but the extra time has given opportunities for patrols to go out and gain an understanding of what has to be done. They report that all bridges and culverts along the course have been blown to bits by the enemy, who, for good measure, have heaped up junk and rubble all along the way. Water has caused slips and swamp, and by now there has been so much rain that the whole countryside is waterlogged.

This flooding is all part of our enemy's defence too. It's the result of an unleashed dam which they built during the months while they were preparing for our coming. Any ground not completely under water is spongy and impassable as far as vehicles are concerned. The Rapido itself continues its flow, swift and deep.

So there's a mountain of work for our engineers, who will need every available bulldozer and piece of road-making machinery to help them put their tracks through. All of these roadworks will have to take place in the dark as enemy are constantly patrolling from nearby posts. Monastery Hill, covered in gun-posts, as ever looks down.

When the time comes, we, the foot soldiers of the Maori Battalion, will lead the way in along the railway embankment, clearing the way of enemy as the road-makers behind us make bridges, fill in gaps, remove obstructions. We'll take over the Cassino railway station, holding it open as tanks and trucks head along this new road the sappers have made for them, and by daylight the tanks will be there with us in the station to help secure our position. They'll widen the passageway and continue on to clear the edges of Cassino town, getting a whole army on the road. Round the mountain we'll go, and on through the Liri valley, heading for Roma.

Che be-ella Roma.

But when? All this rain. This spread river. Each day brings another downpour. We look out over flooded land and know that there'll be a further postponement. Never mind. One day, someday soon, final orders will see us off.

Destination, railway station.

18

smoke

The noise. It's in my head. It's only now that I remember the racket that went on. At the time you become immune to the sounds around you because you're so busy concentrating on where you must go, what you must do to stay alive. There's no room in your head for anything else except your survival. But the roar of guns, the screaming, the din catches up with you eventually.

Also the sights that you see affect you more at a later stage than they do at the time. I won't forget men in a row. I won't forget men on fire. I won't forget a tin hat rolling, spinning across the embankment with the head of a man inside.

Sounds and sights wait inside you, along with the stink of smoke, gunpowder, mud and rot and burning flesh. They invade your waking hours as well as your dreams.

Once we reached the start line after tramping through swamplands, wading the waterbound paddocks and getting through the entanglements of ditches and drains, it was a narrow path we found ourselves on. We arrived there drenched, heavy with mud, and finding further difficulties and delays as we came to the congestion of machines and road-making equipment where the sappers had assembled in preparation for their night's work. It was work which could only begin once we'd made our passage through.

What a job the road-makers had in front of them. We knew that there were bridges to be built across the river and waterways, and soon we were able to see for ourselves what else had to be achieved if tanks were to follow. We found ourselves scrambling through craters and hollows and manoeuvring round burnt-out vehicles. Huge mounds of bricks and boulders had been heaped along the way among yards of twisted railway line.

There were more dangerous obstacles to negotiate as we made our way onward, finding ourselves advancing over areas that had been set up with wire traps and stitched down with mines. Only a dozen steps ahead of me, quite early in the night, there was a series of detonations as one of these minefields blew. The whole field was lit for a few seconds and in that moment of light I saw an entire platoon go down. Gone. Men all in a row, as though they'd been scythed.

Throughout all of our progress, mortar and machine-gun fire came down on us from the slopes of Monte Cassino. Every bit of our way forward was being covered by crossfire, and soon stretcher bearers were having a tough time trying to keep up with the growing number of casualties.

Arriving at the station after all the delays, we saw that the rail yards had been barricaded by coils of wire which lay across the entrance. Behind the wire, Jerry had dug in with machine guns and on our approach began giving it to us, full blast.

Men up front flopped on to the wire coils, compacting them downwards while the rest of us ran over, heaving grenades. We followed into the enemy posts with our bayonets and eventually cleared Jerry away from the entrance. All this happened by the light of flares. It was quite a show.

We poured through into the yards and buildings, bombing them and clearing them out, and after a time had Jerry down or surrendering, or on the run. Plenty of them. Some escaped in a truck that was parked behind a building with its engine running. We wasted a few shots on it. But, Maori Battalion march to victory, Maori Battalion staunch and true. By midnight the station was ours.

The next task was to explore beyond the station, attempting to root the enemy out of houses and other guarded positions along the way. The path was heavily mined and fire was coming at us from all directions, so it was care and stealth and a cover of darkness that was needed whenever we were closing in.

We were doing well enough until not long before dawn when the clouds cleared and we were exposed by moonlight, making us an easy target for snipers. Casualties were mounting, so we were forced back to the safety of the station buildings to wait for the tanks to come.

But where were they?

Daylight arrived without our tanks, and there we were once again with nothing bigger to defend ourselves with than what we carried. Naked in daylight, facing a semicircle of fire while the giant stared down from above, we were reminded of Orsogna. Despite this we were hoping that we would not be forced to withdraw. Here we were, the soldiers of the Maori Battalion, chosen to make this important passage and to hold it open. We'd fought hard, cleaned out the station and sent back prisoners. We were now holding our position and, though our own losses were increasing, we believed we had caused havoc among the enemy. Maori Battalion march to glory, take the honour of the people with you. When the instruction came to stay forward we were eager enough to do so.

We found out later that the engineers had been unable to complete their road-making before daylight. No can do. There had been too many hold-ups at the start.

Dealing with the unforeseen hazards of traps and mines had meant further loss of time, and as work went on the sappers were continually harassed by heavy machine-gun and mortar fire from hummocks and hills. Also by snipers from boats on the river. Near morning the same moonlight that had caused us to retreat to safety had exposed them too, bringing their work to a halt.

So daylight came with three hundred yards still unbreached and two hazards still to go. No way for tanks. Tanks would not reach us until after the next dark when the work would be completed, but that next dark was a whole ten hours away.

Popgun soldiers.

Raiding parties began having a go at us as soon as it was light enough, so we had to call on artillery to create a bit of nuisance. Nuisance was all we could manage for the time being.

However a plan was concocted. We were told that the road-makers were going to continue their work behind a wall of smoke put up by the gunners. Their protection, and ours while we held the station, would be a buffer of smoke from a supply of shells which had been intended for use in disguising a departure of tanks and infantry round the edges of town.

Now this screen would have to be put up for a whole day. Lorries were sent off to Naples, seventy miles away, for ton-loads of extra shells.

All right. Enough cheerful.

With our artillery keeping Jerry busy and our gunners making for us a beautiful smoke wall, we could stick it out there in *our* station – ours 'to have and to hold until death us do part'. Enough pleased with ourselves.

'Blue smoke goes drifting by
Into the deep blue sky,' we sang.
'And when I think of home I sadly sigh.'

And this is the song that we've been singing ever since that smoke-shroud day. The song was composed by one of our Battalion boys while on his way over on the *Aquitania*. It's been sung all through the war under all kinds of conditions, they tell me. But I guess it was thoughts of home, not the drifting of gunsmoke or the image presented by thick smoke walls, that our mate Ruru had in mind when he put the song together.

There was nothing 'blue' and 'drifting' and romantic about this dense grey curtain of smoke that it was our gunners' job to keep before us. There was no 'deep blue sky'. In fact there was no sky at all during those hours, as cloud hung low throughout the day and became one with smoke. No time for 'sadly sigh' either, as the empty shells mounted about the gunners and as we skinned our eyes trying to ascertain what was happening on the other side of our wall.

This was a two-way wall. Though intended to hide us from our enemy we found that it shielded his activities from us as well, and every once in a while, through the pall as smoke thinned, our straining eyes caught glimpses of Jerry tanks and gunners. As they made their approaches it was only blasts of our artillery fire that managed to keep them at bay.

For a while.

Night was too long in coming, giving too much time for our enemy to reorganise. After a morning in which we held fire, watched for signs and waited, the machine gun and mortar increased against us. Before long we realised it was only a matter of time. In the early afternoon Jerry came forward.

Like ghosts they were, the Jerry tanks rolling in on us through this smoky armour.

We were caught by point blank fire, with nothing left to do but make a dash for it, fighting for our lives.

Turning and retreating you have no idea what is coming behind you, and I remember thinking that if only I could get rid of my soaked boots I might have a chance of beating a bullet or two. Otherwise I didn't give myself much of a show. We were in disarray. There were men falling all about as we scattered. The stretcher bearers, trying to do their job, were caught up in the mish-mash of it all.

As I ran, a sudden blast and a thump sent me hurtling down a bank where I slammed into a ditch with Matey on top of me, nearly drowning me. I had to shove him off, get my face out of the bog, spitting and gasping for air and wondering how I came to be still alive. But Matey didn't move, didn't speak, and it took me a little while to realise he was a goner. The volley that hit him must have sent him flying into me, toppling us both. It took me a little while to realise the blood pouring all over me wasn't my own. I was lying in a ditch, mud-covered, blood-covered but unhurt, my cousin dead on top.

I didn't want to leave Matey there where I knew he could remain immersed in mud and perhaps never be found. So I waited, hid myself beneath him until after dark when I dragged him up on to a higher part of the embankment where I knew the redcaps would find him.

That's war.

It was very cold. The sodden fields were lit up by chains of fire. Also there was intermittent moonlight as I waited, watching from my hiding places for moments of darkness when I was able to slide myself through mud and water. From bank to ditch, from ditch to broken-down culvert I went, and eventually made my way back – one of the last to come in.

My brothers were out watching for me. They came to assist me, one laughing, one not; one praising me, one praising the Lord.

We were three who had made it back. Of the two hundred who set out there were just sixty-six of us who returned. I didn't find out until the next day about our other cousin, Tipu.

Blame a river, the weather, the moon, a mountain of many eyes.

19

turf

On one Sunday each month, Club members gathered for the afternoon at Uncle Dave and Aunty Pani's place in Seatoun. The Huris' house overlooked the aerodrome and a large area of flat land that Dave Huri told them had been heaved up out of the sea by an earthquake more than a century before. This land was to be the site for the new exhibition buildings being built for the centenary celebrations. At either side of the land were the heights of Melrose and Seatoun, while north and south of it were bays that had been renamed Evan and Lyall after brothers who had never set foot in this country, which was now on its way to celebrating its first one hundred years.

Of what?

First one hundred years of what?

'Of the signing, the signing,' Uncle Dave told them. 'Of becoming a nation. Of becoming one people. You know, the Treaty. We are all one people. He iwi kotahi tatou. One people, one law, one language. Yep. The papers are full of it.'

Aunty Pani and Uncle Dave and the family would cook a meal

for everyone, and when they'd eaten Dave would sit down at the piano where they'd gather for a singsong, resting from their concert repertoire to sing the backhome songs and the World War One songs brought back from France and the prisoner-of-war camps by their fathers and uncles. They would move on to sing the hits of the day, opening up their notebooks where they'd copied down words of new songs they'd heard on the radio.

It was from Dave's house, looking out over the isthmus, that they watched the exhibition buildings grow. Big machines came in to level the land, and while one month they could look out over millions of feet of timber, miles of trenches and drains, acres of piles and floor joists, by the next month there would be a maze of framework and scaffolding to interest them. There were reports on the wireless, pictures in the newspapers, and each month from Dave's they could witness the progress that was being made.

Gradually the buildings took shape, and soon the bare land that surrounded the constructions became expanses of garden, with flowers already blooming. There were plantings of trees and shrubs that were already fully grown. The acres of lawn, Uncle Dave informed them, had been taken strip by strip from the playing field of the local college and lain out like a big patchwork blanket.

'These eyes saw it happen,' he said. 'They rolled it a few times, watered it plenty, now you wouldn't even know it hadn't grown there from the start. Not bad. Not too bad at all.'

On his way home from work each day Pita would buy an *Evening Post* and read about the progress of the buildings, finding information about how many hundreds of workers were being employed and how many thousands of pounds were to be spent on the coming celebrations. There were many letters to the paper that were enthusiastic about the whole idea. But there were also letters complaining about extravagance, especially once war was declared when there was talk of abandoning the celebrations altogether. After six months everything would be taken down again and there'd be nothing to show for it, people said. Money was needed to take a nation to war now.

However most of the preparation had already been done by the time war broke out. Money had already been spent. In the end it was decided that the celebrations should go ahead.

Somewhere in these exhibition buildings there would be the carved meeting house of the Maori Court. It was to be a showpiece, demonstrating the arts and crafts of the Maori to the Pakeha, the papers said. Ani Rose and her cousin Wikitoria were talking about some of their relatives, carvers and weavers, who were coming down from up country to prepare the house as soon as the main building was closed in. Once the Exhibition opened there would be a tapu-lifting ceremony for the new house, and from then on the artists would be there to demonstrate the techniques of weaving and carving throughout the six months of the celebrations.

On opening day the Club was to take part in a big concert in the main soundshell, joined by groups who were coming from all over the country, and while they were on stage the boys of the Maori Battalion would march in, forming a guard of honour behind the audience. They were all looking forward to it, and in preparation were spending many extra hours practising their action songs, haka, poi and stick routines. After opening day, concerts would continue on stage on week nights in the Maori Court until the exhibition ended.

One Sunday they all went with Dave and Pani up the hills at the back of the house, through gorse and broom and snorting horses to the grassy clearings. Here they spaded out squares of turf, returning to lay them and tramp them down to make the Huris a front lawn. The height of buildings, the weight and size of everything, how much concrete and timber was needed, the length of railing for the scenic railway, the wonder of everything, was news every day. Now, once a month, they could stand on this new lawn of Uncle Dave's and look out at it, their view soon to include the exhibition tower that was a hundred and fifty-five feet in height and weighed seven hundred tons. They could wonder at it all.

'As long as they don't sink the land back down into the sea with all their buildings and concrete,' Aunty Pani said.

20

words

We've been moved back. There'll be nothing doing for our Battalion for some time. Just as well, because most of us have been suffering from concussion and all sorts of jumpy ailments as a result of all the blasting during our last business. And we've had too many losses. There are new boys coming in all the time now as our Battalion builds up again. In the meantime we've revived our choir, which helps to keep the crackling and clatter out of your head. But many of the voices have gone.

A few days ago cousin Manahi and friend Johnny came in with new reinforcements. It was a real surprise to see Johnny as we hadn't heard that he'd joined up. Of course we were fooling round with all these new ones, hugging, backslapping, talking about one-way tickets and all that, but couldn't help noticing Johnny was rather quiet, not like the old Johnny that we knew. Now I understand why.

The day after his arrival Johnny said he wanted to talk to Pita, Rangi and me. He was so serious that we thought there was something wrong at home. We all sat down together and waited for him to speak, wondering what the matter was.

After some minutes of Johnny lacing and unlacing his fingers and looking into the threaded or unthreaded cup of his hands he said, 'I want to marry your sister.'

I wanted to laugh at the look on his face, but at the same time I was relieved to know that Wellington hadn't sunk back into the sea, our family still had a roof over its head, Ma hadn't been hit by a train, our sisters hadn't been taken into TB wards or gone running off with Americans. The Uncle hadn't been thrown out of parliament.

Anyway, here was Johnny.

It wasn't my business to laugh, or even to speak at that moment. It wasn't up to Rangi either, who folded his arms and leaned back, taking himself out of the picture. He waited with his eyes grinning but his mouth not. Almost not.

We both waited.

Johnny lived out of Wellington so wasn't a member of the Club. Pita and Rangi had met him on one of the Club excursions when a new meeting house was opened in Waitara. I'd met him at different times when he came down to visit his sister, who was one of our Club girls boarding with her aunty and uncle in Seatoun. So now and again Johnny would be at the Sunday dinners that Aunty Pani and Uncle Dave put on for all of us. They were good days, and I was sorry, once I went away to school, to miss those Sunday get-togethers. If it was holiday time I was always reluctant when I had to leave there early on Sunday afternoons in order to catch the bus to return to school. At some time during the Sunday afternoon Johnny would be asked to sing, because among all the good voices his was the finest of all. He was a good pal too.

'What've you been up to with our sister,' Pita asked, as grim as knives.

'Nothing. No, nothing,' Johnny said. 'Your sister . . . she's . . . not a girl like that.'

It was the right answer.

We waited.

'Our mother,' Pita said, 'would want our sister to marry in the church.'

'I agree with it,' Johnny said.

'Our mother would want our sister to marry a Catholic,' Pita said.

'On the way across . . . ah . . . spoke to a priest on board. I want to convert to the faith and . . . marry your sister.' He stayed silent for a moment, then he said, 'There's the farm. I can make a go of it . . . when we get rid of this war.' It was the right thing to say.

'What does our sister say?' Pita asked.

'Haven't spoken to your sister.'

'What does our mother say?'

'Haven't spoken to your mother.'

I was busting. I knew Rangi was too.

'Not yet,' said Johnny, 'but give me the word. You give me the word then I write to your sister.'

There we were, waiting, Rangi and I leaning back, keeping ourselves out of the way, ready to burst, Johnny hunched over his folded arms and looking at the ground, Pita with his hands on his knees, his elbows jutting, his cheeks puffed out, looking out to the mountains.

Finally Brother Pita stood.

'Write to her,' he said, and held out his hand. At that point we were able to explode, laugh out loud, jump up out of our seats. Johnny became the old Johnny again. We hugged this new brother-in-law, thumping him, telling everyone about him coming all the way across the world to ask for our sister's hand in marriage. In the middle of all this, Pita said, 'Which sister?'

Ha, ha. What a time we had.

It was our sister Sophie who Johnny would write to. We stood him up there in the choir, made him sing. What a time. Plenty laugh. Plenty song.

The next attack on Cassino will come down from beyond the flooding where the river is fordable. Tanks will be brought along roads already formed and taken through the town – a head-on

136

clash – then round the mountain. There'll be help from the air this time and rumour has it that the bombers will come over one fine day soon and that Jerry is going to be blasted out of Cassino. When will that be? There's nothing but rain.

Our Battalion won't take part in the attack as we have had too many losses and have to regain strength. But once the bombing stops, the guns and tanks will head through the town and the Twenty-eighth's job will be to go back in and hold the railway station once it has been recaptured. That's good. We've earned the railway station. Men of our Battalion have already died for it. This time the ground will be dry.

We've pitched a couple of tents beside our canteen truck and that's where we get together at night to listen to the radio, make cocoa, drink wine, yarn and sing. We've even managed to rig up a couple of electric lights using a patched-up generator to power them. These are the times when Brother Pita gets hold of me and starts bending my ear, as he did again last night, no help at all from vino. To begin with I was happy to sit and listen, or I should say just resigned to it. After a while I was longing to escape. I didn't want to hear what he had to say to me. I wanted to halt him, but didn't know how to do that without seeming disrespectful or unbrotherly. None of it was any business of mine.

Anyway, in the middle of it, and fortunately for me, Bootleg walked in on his hands and began singing his song without words. While he was opening and shutting his big mouth, stretching and twisting his fat lips, a big fluffy moth which had been cracking its head against the lights we'd hitched up, fell spiralling down and swooped in. Into Bootleg's mouth, that is. He swallowed it, an upside-down swallow, reverse Adam's apple, and kept on singing. The place was in an uproar. That's when I took my chance, grabbed a uke off Manahi, and when everyone had stopped laughing and Bootleg had finished his wordless song, I plinked away, re-tuning the instrument. I opened my own mouth, which had been shut for the past hour, and started us all on a new song.

21

light

When the lights came on Pita saw Jess coming out of the audience towards the stage. Light on her face. Disappearing eyes. White collar on a dark dress like an altar boy, stepping forward to talk to his sisters. Timi, beside him, dropped his chin on to his chest and lowered his voice.

'Aa, your sisters. She talks to your sisters, but *you* she's after I bet.'

Pita felt caught out, spied on.

'Come on,' he said to Timi, 'get this off and we go for a beer.'

He turned to the far stage door and went out to the washroom, changing out of costume and cleaning the lines of moko from his face, taking his time. He didn't really want to go for a drink tonight. It was pay day and they'd brought Tuboy with them. Pita wanted to give Little Brother money for the roller coaster or a Jack and Jill ride, wanted to see him have a good time. Now if he went off looking for Tuboy he'd probably bump into Jess.

Ever since the Exhibition opened he'd been too rushed to see Jess after work, running straight from the railway station to catch a tram that would get him there on time for the nightly concerts. Sometimes on the way into the building, he'd meet up with Club friends and they'd have time to put their threepences on the end of the bar for Centennial lagers. The barman would slide these along to them and they'd have to drink them hastily before going to change for the performance. At other times, especially on a Friday when the trams were crowded and slow, there wasn't time for a drink or even to exercise their voices before going on stage.

He'd already decided he wasn't going to see Jess any more. Their family had found their 'better life'. The Uncle had provided Little Brother with shoes and a uniform for boarding school, and with Ma's widow's pension and the work they'd been able find they could pay their bills, get their meat and groceries, buy wood to start the copper and have enough coal for a fire on the coldest days of winter. When Fred brought them someone in need of a bed or a meal they were always able to provide, and there were always pence for the collections at Sunday Mass. Ma had a coat and hat to wear to church and to the hospital visiting that she did for the Club's welfare committee.

God had been good to them. With God's help they'd been able to realise dreams, and he knew in his true heart that Jess wasn't part of those dreams.

Of all of them it was Ma who had most easily found her way in this new place, Pita thought. Somehow she made everything fit around her, never tried reshaping herself, never sought the city's love or acceptance. She treated it all like backhome and she treated the neighbours like backhome people, walking into their yards, calling through their doors, looking after them with their new babies and taking their children home with her sometimes. She shared out their wood and coal, their flour and potatoes, sent Tuboy next door with Maori bread or fish.

But ever since they'd arrived in the city that morning over two years before, buttoned to the throat in other people's clothing, it was from 'backhome' that Pita had been trying to free himself – from rage, hunger, hiding in trees, waiting, lying awake and listening in the dark; from dreams of finding his mother dead, strangled, chopped in half with an axe.

He believed it was backhome that pinned him, gave him his slow walk on the footpaths. It was backhome that kept his eyes switching from side to side on city streets because he didn't want not to give recognition to those coming towards him. It was backhome that made him fearful of putting himself somewhere where he could be watched by a thousand eyes.

And it was the thousand eyes that made the colour of his skin a shame, that made him catch his breath before going into the greengrocers or getting on a bus, that made him unable to go into a shop without buying something. It was the thousand eyes and the thoughts that went on behind them that halted him. Because he didn't know those thoughts, had no way of discovering them even through the talk that went on around him at work and about the city. What did words mean if they didn't mean what they said? Maybe his brothers and sisters followed Ma's example, allowing the city to make its own shape around them. Perhaps he was a man alone in a family, not having learned to talk about the weather or the government or the price of things, and who felt embarrassed when the men at work spoke the way they did about their wives. He hadn't learned to be offhand either, and didn't know whether or not people were having him on when they smiled and talked to him.

How did you learn to say what you didn't mean? How did you know when not to take what people said, literally? He decided he was too backhome and ignorant to understand all that, too in-a-tree waiting and not enough school. So he kept himself quiet and worked hard, hardly opening his mouth because he always felt conspicuous. It was as though he had two heads sometimes, as though each of the heads wore a bell. He wished he could be more like Ma or Little Brother who seemed to fit anywhere, under any mountain.

But this was home now. He never wanted to return to the old place, so he had to shape himself into this new life, discover what it was that he had to do, find out who he had to be in this city of a thousand eyes. It was easier now that they'd found new friends and the Club to belong to. The city was a place with a family future, and though it wasn't his known world, he knew he just had to work hard, keep himself quiet and be good enough to live in it.

However, it was on the opening day of the Maori Court at the Centennial Exhibition that their known world came to them. That's how Pita saw it. On that day it was as though you didn't have to try to change who you were, because suddenly a place had been moulded to fit you. You didn't have to be aware of a thousand eyes, because the eyes were your own. On all of this concrete, on all of this land, which had once been thrown up out of the ocean by the dance of Ruaumoko, there was a space that was right for you and so you became fortified.

By the time he and the others of the Club arrived on opening day, the soundshell area was already filling with Maori coming from all regions to take part in the ceremonies. There were people they knew and people to meet, bringing with them their language, their stories and their gossip, their special prolonged greetings and manner of leave-taking, their songs and their humour. The arena was full of life and activity as people began to prepare, the younger ones putting on performance costumes and drawing the curled lines of moko on each other's faces, the elders donning their feathered and patterned cloaks, their woven head-dresses and their greenery, their earrings and ornaments made of bone or greenstone.

Children played among them, and everywhere there were last-minute rehearsals taking place. Ceremonial weapons were being unwrapped from blankets, girls were practising their poi movements, while voices and instruments were being tuned.

It was as they all assembled on stage that the Maori Battalion marched in to the back of the arena to form a guard of honour. The soldiers were three weeks into their training and three and a half months away from going overseas, and it was the sight of them that made the performers' feet tramp the boards more loudly as they did the haka of welcome, and that caused their chests to fill out and their voices to intensify. This was their own Battalion, rifles on their shoulders, bayonets glinting in the sunlight as they stood to attention while the inspection of the guard took place.

Afterwards, they all made their way inside the buildings for the tapu-lifting ceremony of the new carved meeting house. It was the turn of the soldiers to lead the haka that began proceedings, and as the dance concluded, two elders began the incantations, moving across the open space in front of the house accompanied by the woman they all recognised as Te Puea Herangi. They had seen Te Puea on newsreels at the pictures wearing her white headscarf and talking to important men dressed in suits. They had all expected her to be taller. It was she who had stood firm in refusing to allow her people to go away to fight for God, King and Country. They had their own god, she said. They had their own king. They had their own country too, but much of their country had been stolen. Why would they want to fight for the people who had stolen their country? She was small and not very different to look at from some of their backhome aunties.

Te Puea led the way into the new house, freeing it from all ill-fortune and wrong influence, so that all people could now enter it safely.

They followed the crowd into the house, taking in its carved figures, its woven wall panels and scrolled paint decorations. It enfolded them. In it they thought, heard, spoke and understood in their own way. Their space and their place had dropped there for them and there was nothing that could intrude, even when they went out together to explore the many other courts and amusements of the Exhibition. Over the next days and weeks they were able to make the house more and more their own.

Now Jess had turned up, and though the sight of her had made his heart flap about like a marooned fish, he suddenly felt cornered.

'Dodging her, or something?' Timi asked into his beer, looking at him sideways. 'We seen you talking at the tram stop. You like her, don'cha?'

Pita didn't reply. He drank his beer and ordered another. When they'd finished he stood. 'Let's go and find the others,' he said.

Over in Playland he saw Tuboy high up near the ceiling about to go down the slide with Jess. His two sisters were there in the crowd, looking up.

'We got him a ticket,' Sophie said, 'but too scared to have a go ourselves.' He knew Sophie was letting him know that it was she and Moana who had bought the ticket, not Jess. He was grateful to his sisters.

People were coming down in twos on the mats, screaming and shouting, swooping from side to side in the chute as they plunged. The beer inside him was making him smile, anchoring him to the spot as their brother came into view with his head back laughing. Jess seated beside him, clinging to him, screaming. They stepped off drunken, stumbling, clutching each other.

Outside they joined Timi and some of the girls at the entrance to the Crazy House. Their friends were looking up, holding on to each other and laughing with tears running down their faces, as the giant sailor, high above, rolled forward and back, from side to side, spreading his giggles and his ha ha ha, ho ho ho out across the crowd, which was now beginning to disperse.

At the tram stop one of the girls asked Jess where she lived, and Jess lifted a hand towards the hilltops.

'Up there,' she said. 'I take a tram into town and then catch a bus up the hill . . . that is, unless someone wants to walk me home.'

It was such a wrong thing for her to want, or say, in front of everyone, Pita thought. It was as though what his friends and family thought about her didn't matter.

'Don't look at *me*,' he said to her, which came out rough because he meant it to.

'Yes why *don't* we?' his sister said, as though she really believed that what Jess had said had been directed towards all of them.

'Which way?' someone asked.

'Straight up.'

'What you need is . . .'

'Goat's feet or . . .'

'Wings.'

Everyone was having something to say to cover the awkwardness of the moment as they set out – ten of them altogether – on the steep footpaths that were lit here and there by the orange light of street lamps. They went up, passing by white fences, white gates and coloured letter boxes, behind which houses clutched against the dark hillsides like waiting spiders.

'It was the loveliest singing I've ever heard,' Jess said from beside him. 'I loved the dancing too.' He could see the tips of her shoes stepping, one then the other on the black pavement. He could feel the touch of her coat sleeve against his arm.

'And all that jumping up and down, all of those faces you pulled at us. I could've died.' She laughed, and though he felt there was something that needed justifying he didn't know what it was, didn't know what to say. The night was all mixed up, a confusion of talk and laughter, a smell of road and soap and flowers. There was nothing he could say, no way of explaining anything.

Near the top of the road they climbed a hundred dark steps under an overhang of taupata, wattle and five-finger trees. Coming out from that dark space made everyone laugh, while being up high, being on top of the world, made them gasp.

Looking out, there was the whole lit-up city, the two dark chunks of water on either side of the strip of land, and lights swooping down the hillside before them, row upon row. And there, way down there, was the great expanse of the Exhibition – lights like nothing they'd ever imagined, something which none of them had ever dreamed being part of.

But were they a real part, or had they just been placed there as if by accident, Pita wondered now. In among all these grand lights and buildings, how did a little house made of reeds compare? A house inside a building. A fragment of something else that was quite overwhelming.

Below them, the main avenue shone in a pathway of gold light which continued all the way along until it deepened, thickened and became a fiery orange-red, sweeping upwards and over the tower. The tower was the centrepiece, seen for miles around, from where for sixpence and a spiral climb, they knew they could look out over the far reaches of the isthmus and beyond.

Crossing this main avenue were more pathways in many colours of standing light. But over and through all of it were other changing and turning beams, so brilliant that it was as though the crown jewels – at present on display in the British Court – had been taken and formed into emerald, ruby and sapphire shafts, ascending and descending through all the hues of orange and yellow; scarlet, cerise and purple; mauve and turquoise; tints and taints of blue and pink and gold. These rotated and spiralled, continually changing across the whole vista. They played over the lit-up fairground, over the lagoons, and through the jets of water which spouted high in the air from the central fountain and fell in coloured showers into a wide pool.

Jess, her face, the collar, her hands – which were palm outwards and lifted away from her sides – all tinted by street light, and with all this at her feet, was showing them the great wonder of buildings, water, light and colour.

'Isn't it lovely?' she said.

He felt so barefoot.

She pointed out her house just below the road, where faint light showed round the edges of the windows.

'The inseparables,' Jess said, scrunching her eyes. 'Escorted home by the inseparables,' and they stood, watching her make her way down the zigzag path by white wooden handrails, gliding, like a candle being carried in an Easter procession.

22

deluge

The town has been completely annihilated. Even the bombing of the abbey was nothing like this bombing of Cassino. I've never heard or seen anything like it and don't believe I ever will again.

Cassino is a small town, I'd say no more than half a mile square though it's difficult to judge from a distance. During enemy occupation over several months it has been strongly fortified and set up with gun-posts concealed in and around all of its buildings. This is what we've heard and it's sure to be true since the town is a key point in the defence of the mountain, as well as the defence of the roads that give access beyond it.

Anzac and Choc and I were out in the open when the first planes came across, but the noise was so deafening and dreadful that we ran off to watch from the shelter of a nearby *casa*, hoping this would help drown out some of the sound. When we arrived we were surprised to find people there – two women and three children – as most civilians have left the battle zones by now. I don't think they live in the house as they had their bundles with them. They were probably sheltering there while escaping from the north.

One of the women was very old; the other, who was much younger, we presumed to be the mother of the children. As we entered the house one of the kids ran and leapt into Choc's arms and stayed there with her head buried in his shoulder. She wouldn't leave him so he walked back and forth trying to comfort her. The mother, clutching the other two against her in a corner of the room, was crying and covering their heads, while the old woman was going nuts, flinging herself round the room or sometimes crouching on the floor with her hands over her ears moaning and talking to herself. Poor things. We felt very sorry for them because even though the planes were not coming our way they were terrified. We tried to explain but couldn't make them understand.

Formations of bombers passed over the town, twenty to thirty at a time, dropping their loads. On first looking up the bombs appeared to be hanging, wavering in the air. Suddenly they were hurtling earthwards.

Days of rain, weeks of rain had called a halt to any attack for some time, but now, after so much ordinary rain this was a deluge of a different kind. It hammered down on the town from where chimneys of thick dark smoke vented. It was as though hell had been unleashed from there in the earth.

The columns corkscrewed upward before spreading over what had been the town of Cassino, forming a black canopy. This went on all morning until, as a kind of finale, groups of fighter bombers came in, strafing and dive-bombing. The town was blasted to smithereens and it was burning, taking Jerry along with it. We concluded that there wouldn't even be a rat left alive in there.

As soon as the bombing stopped our artillery opened up and we knew that the Twenty-fifth Battalion, led by tanks, would be starting out for the direct push through the town. Our Battalion was moved closer as we prepared to go in and hold the railway station once it had been occupied, but rain began again, coming down full pelt. Days of dense cloud and rain followed. The nights were intensely dark as the rain continued.

But it was not as we thought and it was difficult to believe after what we had witnessed. Jerry was still alive, fighting and holding strongly throughout the ruins of Cassino. Our tanks made little headway into the town, being hampered and stalled by mud and all sorts of debris, and by holes which quickly filled with water. Twenty-sixth Battalion, which was meant to get through and take the railway station, came nowhere near it, having to draw back again and again from the rising end of town where there was strong resistance. It was no-can-do. The rain thickened and carried on.

We knew our army would be doing its utmost out there in the ruins and the rain, and even though progress was slow and we heard of the many setbacks, there were some encouraging reports as well. Castle Hill was captured after a real ding-dong. The Indians were holding there and, though they'd been thrown back from attempts at ol' man's hat, they kept on trying. Good on them. What a job they'd been given, we thought. But what a prize.

Twenty-sixth finally made it into the station, so it was a matter of time for Twenty-eighth as we awaited the call to go in and take over from them. After we'd done our job we'd be on our way round ol' man mountain with the rest of the troops. As we waited Royal Sussex made a final attempt on the mountain top, but though they were unsuccessful we received the news that the Gurkhas had occupied Hangman's Hill.

Though the Gurkhas are the most skilled soldiers of all when it comes to mountain fighting, we couldn't help feeling sorry for them. They're small men, brave soldiers, full of fun, and they sure like their vino. But this place they were hanging on to, a couple of hundred yards from the Monastery, was a cliff-face. Poor beggars had to leave greatcoats and blankets behind because they were carrying all their own ammunition and had to lighten their loads. But it was freezing. There was no way to get extra supplies of ammo up to them, and too bad if they ran out. No way to get hot food to them either, and God knows what they were doing for water. It was wet and miserable the whole time and the winds were full of ice. What could anyone hope to do under such conditions, we kept asking ourselves.

Anyway all we could do was keep hoping it would all work out in the end. There was all hell going on for the New Zealand Army in the upper end of town. Our *compaesani* were having a devil of a time.

Orders have changed. We've now been told that we're not going in to hold the station but getting back into battle instead – going on the attack. Yes, ready or not, it'll be march, march, march to the enemy, fight right to the end, for the Maori Battalion.

Our job is to clear the way towards a couple of hotels – the Hotel Continental and Hotel des Roses – in the troubled part of the town. We'll take over the two buildings, holding the way open to Route Six while the Indians storm upwards from their possie on Hangman's Hill to take the Monastery.

It's close stuff, bayonet and grenade, that they want from us. 'Dig them out of every nook and cranny,' is what we've been ordered to do, which is the kind of action the Maori Battalion is known for. Yes. Sooner or later we'll be setting out for a night in the Continental and a day in Hotel des Roses. Maori Battalion march to glory, take the honour of the people with you.

Start line, botanical gardens.

Leaving time, midnight.

Start time, 3 a.m.

But in the meantime we wait. Much of war is to do with waiting, for weather, a right time, darkness, daylight, a word. I'm glad of my notebook and the way writing in it helps fill in waiting times, pleased to have the pen in my hand.

I look about me. My companions 'wait' in different ways. Most sit and yarn. Some are going through their packs again, or spitting good luck, *buona fortuna*, on to their bayonets for the hundredth time. Several are asleep with their heads on their packs, and Choc is really out-the-monk, snoring. Others sing, voices low. The songs they sing are waiting songs that are often sung at home – but now we have a repertoire of Italian songs as well.

River and Tahi are writing letters while Jacob reads one. He sits back to back with his cousin Tipene who is perusing his bible. Perhaps, like Deerfoot of the Forest, Tipene will go out to fight with the good book in his breast pocket. A bullet aimed at him will lodge in the book and he will be saved by faith, by goodness, by a miracle, by God. Or was it a crucifix, hanging on a chain about his neck, which saved Deerfoot from a bullet in the heart? I can't remember.

There are two men, Hemi and Gary, who joined us in Maadi. They're cousins. Hemi and Gary spend their waiting moments tapping rows of nail holes to form intricate scrollwork into the butts of their rifles. In transit camps, out on ridges, in snowbound shelters, we have watched the motifs grow – central knots opening in outward spirals which become tendrils, coiling and uncoiling, but always finding a place to return to, a place of rejoining. The two men are so much alike in height and build and looks that they could be twins. You never see one cousin without the other.

My brothers?

Rangi is one of the sleepers. Pita, though he sits with the singers, is not singing. I catch him looking my way and believe he's praying for me. Okay, that's good. As long as he doesn't come sprinkling me with his holy water. I understand my brother better than I used to now that we've spent this time together. We've grown up in the same household, yet our lives have been so different. When he talks about the past, the backhome days, our father, what he has to say hardly ever matches up with my own feelings, memories and understandings of our early lives. I think I've been fortunate, unaffected by some of the hardships that my family has suffered.

When I write down Pita's stories I like to fill them out by putting in my own descriptions and observations, my own slant here and there. Sometimes I think that I find the right words and create just the right feeling. I get satisfaction from that.

In a moment I'll pack my book and pen away. Even on the warpath there are times of waiting, time to pick up a pen. Perhaps, as with Deerfoot of the Forest, a bullet aimed at me will lodge in my notebook, etc.

Time to go.

23

monkey

With a month of the Exhibition still to run Pita found he couldn't do the performances any more. After Jess's comments about their faces, their jumping about, he began to feel more and more like a showpiece or a clown act. A drawcard. He couldn't stop wondering about this, and once on stage he couldn't help thinking about the thousand eyes and about what might exist behind them. What did the eyes see?

Who were they now that all their people had gone, and now that their performances were no longer among themselves or for themselves? What were language, dance, movement, song – which was part of the sap of them all – to those who didn't know, deep inside themselves, what they were about? Who were they to these different eyes, the eyes of people who crowded their hall every night and applauded so generously, or who exclaimed over the reed-lined meeting house with all its decoration and sculptures? Who were they to the people who gathered round the carvers and weavers throughout the day as they demonstrated 'the arts of the natives of New Zealand'? This audience touched wood, listened to the carvers' stories, talked to the girls plying their strands from front to back as they moved along the panels, creating their patterns. Were these not the same eyes as those belonging to the men who didn't move over for him on the canteen bench, or who treated him like a boy, a sweeper, when he'd been a man all his life? Were they not the same eyes as those belonging to the woman behind the shop counter who couldn't see him standing there?

In this enormous construction, and with all that went on around and inside it, were their arts, their dances and their music just another 'attraction'? Were they exhibits too?

Near the end of their nightly performance, a highlight of the programme was when the girls sat on stage in formations of eight to perform their stick routines. This began with a simple tapping and passing of the pairs of sticks in time to singing. But as the item went on, the various movements – sticks passing from one pair of hands to another, spinning, rotating, criss-crossing – became more complex. The rhythm became faster until the actions on stage were as a flow of hands weaving magic over an ever-changing pattern of airborne batons, luminous and flickering in stage-light. The performance always excited the audience who would remain silent and attentive right up to the moment when the sticks began flying from left to right across the stage, decreasing in number, the clicking and tapping becoming fainter as the batons disappeared behind the curtain. There would be an outbreak of applause and people would stand and call for an encore.

Could the girls with their magic hands and their flying sticks be viewed in the same light as 'living wonders', such as the magicians of the Chinese Theatre; or the acrobatic sensations in their brightly coloured costumes, flipping and tumbling, and throwing high into the air nature's mistakes – Chang the pin-headed midget and King Chong the amiable dwarf? Could they, with their intricate poi actions, practised and synchronised to perfection, be described as 'marvels', like the girl motorcyclists riding the Wall of Death at a mile a minute – round and round and up and down the vertical sides of a cylinder, riders releasing the handlebars and standing with arms outstretched as the bikes rose higher and higher in the tube?

152

Were they all part of a sideshow now, something to stare at, exclaim over?

Giantess, Mexican Rose, the fattest girl in the world, was twenty-three years old and weighed fifty-four stone. He'd seen a picture of her in the *Evening Post*, sitting at a table with a rolled roast of beef and a hock of ham on a large platter before her. She was slicing meat and smiling, reaching across the table with arms that looked like fully puffed windsocks. On one side of the platter was a dish of vegetables, on the other a long loaf of bread. The table at which she sat looked tiny. It was set with a china cup and saucer, china plates and bowls, which all looked tiny.

Moana and Sophie, who had been to see Mexican Rose, said she was a pretty girl with a kind face who had a nice way with her. She had told her audience that she'd been on exhibition since she was ten, that she did all her own housework, drove a specially built car, had never had a day's illness in her life and had taken part in several movies.

'She's got square feet,' Sophie said.

'And she has to have twelve yards of material to make herself a dress,' Moana added. 'That's about from here to next door.'

Pita came to realise that their carved house, which was like part of backhome to them, was being viewed in a similar way to the diorama which took up 64,000 feet of the Dominion Court and was a model of the whole country. The diorama showed in miniature the country's mountains, rivers, valleys, lakes and harbours; its towns and cities; its wharves and railways; its attractions, its agriculture, its industries. There was a railway running the length of it and model trains tooting along. There were cars on the roads, ships in the harbours and tugboats moving across waters of miniature ports. Reports in the newspapers about their meeting house and their arts and performances used some of the same words that they used to describe Mexican Rose and the diorama.

More and more over the weeks he wanted to drop out of the concerts. He still wanted to belong to the Club, go to the practices, assist with fundraising and the welfare work, help run socials for the soldiers and their visitors when they were in town – but he didn't want to be a performing monkey any more. The reason he stayed on was because he didn't want to let the Club down. They were short of men now that more than half of them were away.

At first he tried to explain to the others how he felt, which was difficult because he didn't fully understand his own feelings. But he knew that something was wrong.

'Who do they think we are?' he asked one day when Timi opened the newspaper at the review page where they read about the '. . . glistening torsos, as of the noble warriors of old, posturing and stamping forward with horrific facial expressions that had the crowd quite carried away.'

'What's that all supposed to mean?'

'Sweaty bodies. All them, they like sweaty bodies.'

'And ugly faces. They love it.'

'They keep coming back. Some of them been back a few times. Can't keep away.'

'A chance for us to show something . . . something of *us*, to *them*.'

'They love it, see.'

'Just like they love "Hitler's Horrors of Mechanised Murder"?' he asked. '"Giant Torpedo and Nazi Mine Captured in the North Sea"?'

Sometimes, when he complained and told them he was fed up, they thought he was talking about being tired, short of time, short of the tram fare and sick of living life on the run.

'Yeh, bloody worn out,' his mates said.

'Leave work, no time for a feed, run for a tram, wet the whistle with a lager if you're lucky, then you're on.'

'Go home, fall into bed, get up . . .'

'Same over again.'

'Another month to go.'

Increasingly there was a feeling that he had of not being real or of not knowing what was real. Or there was a sense that he, all of them, were being owned. These ideas were difficult to pinpoint and difficult to explain when he tried to discuss them.

The worst of it was that he didn't know why, despite everything, he still had a desire to please these audiences, why there was the need to seek the acceptance and approval of those of the thousand eyes. What was it in him that made him want the applause, look for the reports in the paper, count up the encores, just as they all did?

During the last weeks he made work the excuse for not being able to take the stage. He couldn't do it anymore. And if there were meant to be concerts during the final nights of the Exhibition they were cancelled anyway.

The Maori Battalion was preparing to leave the Palmerston North camp for the journey to Wellington where they would board the ship that would take them off to war. Everyone from the Club was talking about the farewell concert and ball that were to be held in the camp town of Palmerston North. His sisters and Ani Rose had taken time off work so that they could attend.

On the night before they left for Palmerston North, Pita came home from work to find he could hardly move in the house for spread material and pattern pieces. The girls were making ball gowns, tucking and pinning and smoothing the paper patterns in an effort to make them fit the material. They were having trouble with bias and trouble with stripes, he heard. And when he tried to edge past, a piece of pattern tissue caught in the air movement, wafted up and came down in wrong angles. The girls all had pins sticking out from between their lips as though their faces had become pin-cushions, but Ani Rose still had enough mouth remaining to be able to speak. She was having a go at him out of the side of it. Pita felt pleased about the dresses, thought his sisters were pretty. And Ani Rose.

When he came out into the sitting-room the next morning the girls were still up, whipping their way round hems with needles and trails of cotton.

Pita didn't attend the concert or the ball but travelled up to camp on the last day, with The Uncle and Tuboy, in The Uncle's car.

'Maybe fighting in their war will make the brown man equal to the white man,' The Uncle said on the way up. They all spent the morning in the army canteens with Rangi and friends.

When it was time for the soldiers to assemble for the march out of camp, the families went along to the railway station for what were to be the final goodbyes. Pita was sorry now to see his brother go. Rangi was the one who knew him better than anyone, the only one, apart from Ma, who understood his moody heart. He wondered if he'd ever see his brother again, thinking that Rangi was far too brave, too unafraid to keep on living through a war.

'I'll be back,' Rangi said as they hugged each other. 'Don't worry, Brother,' he said, raising his eyebrows to heaven, 'that fella up there only wants the good ones.' His brother was unable to hide his excitement, couldn't wait to be gone. Tuboy, chatting to the soldiers, was excited too, wanting war to go on long enough so he could be part of it, but that would never be.

The train pulled out and they followed in the cavalcade of cars going to Wellington, expecting to see the soldiers again before they boarded the ship. However when they arrived at the wharf where the *Aquitania* was berthed, it was to see the troop train taken immediately on to the wharf and have the iron gates closed off behind it. People were shut out and angry. It was only because the Ngati Poneke Club was the official farewell party that they were allowed through, being driven by bus on to the wharf early next morning.

From the wharf they went on board a destroyer which was to act as escort to the troop carriers, and once the *Aquitania* moved out into the stream the destroyer followed and they began singing their farewell songs. As daylight came, with the gates now open to them, the crowds came through to find the ship far out in the stream.

Mists, like webs, were down about the city. Buildings, the harbour, ships out in the water, the seagulls that cried and circled over sea and shore, were all caught up in the tangles of it.

Life was just as busy after the close of the Exhibition. The Club was invited to perform in concerts for patriotic funds or to entertain on board supply ships that came into Wellington. There were camps and hospitals to visit, and radio broadcasts over 2YA on Saturday evenings where Pita was persuaded that they needed his male voice.

Although he avoided taking part in the concerts he continued to go to the training camps where they would put on a few items, have singsongs with the boys and hang about in the canteens with them. In the weekends he'd help with the Club socials and meals that they put on at the clubrooms for soldiers on leave.

On Monday nights on the way to the Club they'd meet Jess returning from her piano teacher's place and he looked forward to that. He'd stop while the others went on their way, and even though Jess wasn't for him, he'd walk to the tram stop with her before returning to catch up with his friends again. Sometimes he saw Jess at the tram stop after work. He'd speak with her briefly then hurry home for tea before the pick-up trucks arrived.

Eventually came letters from Rangi describing the journey, telling about life aboard the *Aquitania*: '. . . fit for kings and queens or some of those flash film stars in their monkey suits, ball dresses, diamonds. Corker. Well we went creeping around, too scared to call out, sing, fart, anything, for a few days. Some seasick anyway, and homesick too. Anyway used to it now. Reveille at six. Then we got three training sessions a day, mess at five and we have a good singsong and a laugh, a few high-jinks on board, or we go off somewhere for a game of two-up. A great ship, a beauty. And miles of water like I never thought of . . .

'. . . Not what we're used to all this flash food we been having. But anyhow had a feed of titi the other night. A couple of our mates sniffed them out somewhere in the hold, a whole drum full. Ask no questions and they tell you no lies. Don't worry Ma, us boys won't go hungry. Mutton-birds. Beauty feed. Nothing like it . . .

'. . . Stopped off in Fremantle and went ashore on an oil tanker. On leave till midnight then we came back on board and sailed off next morning, to where? Who knows? England, Italy, Africa? Anyway the boys reckon anywhere will do, now sick of all this water day after day, but saw flying fish the other day.

157

Up and over the waves. Beauty. That was a sight . . .

'. . . They reckoned us Maori boys wouldn't be allowed off the boat when we got to Cape Town because of the colour bar there. Not too happy about that. Looking forward to getting our feet on any old sod. And true it was. We got stuck here on board for three days while other units were off enjoying themselves. Three days looking at Table Mountain covered to halfway with mist, thinking of home and feeling pretty wild. Anyway on the fourth day we were allowed off at last and got taken into Cape Town by bus, escorted everywhere like we were just kids not allowed out of sight. They reckon it was for our own protection. Well I don't know about that. The scenery is just like home with hills and paddocks and trees, but white houses all made of stone. Off we went to have tea with the mayoress. We sang a couple of our songs. On show as usual. After that we only had about half an hour to ourselves going round town. Pretty fed up about it.

'. . . No leave in Freetown, but swapped a shirt for fruit and coconuts when these black fellas come round the ship in their canoes. Nice oranges and coconuts too, but after a while the ship's officers turned the hoses on them and someone shot a hole in one of their boats. Off they went paddling for their lives, and that's the last we saw of them. Off in their new clothes, a few blankets too. Where to after this? God knows . . .

'. . . One of the stokers jumped overboard and drowned himself. They reckon it was the heat, then we heard another stoker died, don't know how. They say he did away with himself too. Poor jokers . . .

'. . . Keep on changing course so hope someone knows where we're going. Anyhow, looks like we might be getting close. Everyone's on the lookout. There are subs around and we came across the wreck of a ship, oil and rubbish in the water, empty lifeboats floating all about, spars and wreckage everywhere. Later, dead ahead, sighted a burning tanker, flames shooting up a hundred feet. Not too good at night, down below in your cabin and thinking you might get a torpedo up the jacksy . . .

'. . . This morning, 16 June, arrived off the port of Gourock and will go ashore tomorrow morning. If we thought we'd be in a fight, swarming onto land with rifles at the ready, well no. It's somewhere in Scotland. Nearly midnight and it's not dark yet. From here we go by train to England.

'... Today all polished up and on parade for the King's inspection. Thought he would be a big joker, this King we're meant to be fighting for, but not big at all, a bit of a shorty. Won so many cigarettes at cards the other night I had to dish them all out again so I could win some more. Anyway, lost after that. Getting bored waiting around ...

'... Pleased to get away from England after all this time. What a cold miserable place. Now going back the way we came. And from one extreme to the other. Hot, but the *Althone Castle* is a beauty ship. Good food, too. Found ourselves berthing in Cape Town again and thought it might be the same old story. Anyway we were allowed off this time. Had the same leave as everyone else and all our money changed to South African. Had quite a good time and people treated us all right, but it was like we were on show all the time. You walk around all stiff as though you got a broomstick up your bum. The coloured people put on a dance for us. On the last day bought a whole lot of crayfish and when we got back on board filled a bath up with them. Threw a couple of buckets of seawater in and they kept for long enough. Only trouble was they got out a few times and came crackling across the floor.'

Usually the letters were to the whole family, but one night when Pita arrived home there was one addressed to him. It told of places Rangi had been, people he'd met and of impatience at inaction. '... And your girl Jess,' he wrote in conclusion, '... Don't hold back. Get her in the sack and give her a good rattle. Give her a go. Why not? You want to. She's singing out for it. Why not, if she wants and you want? True, no bullshit, man. You won't go to hell ...'

Pita was angry. A dream. A dream girl, that's all he wanted her to be. Now he felt the dream had been taken from him. How could he ever face Jess now, even for a few moments at the tram stop?

And yet he knew, he knew.

Underneath it all he knew it wasn't true. It made him angry with his brother. Now he had to admit it wasn't true that all he wanted Jess to be was a dream. Rangi made him wild, because even if it wasn't true that a dream was all he wanted her to be, it was still true that a dream was all she *could* be. It was still true that she wasn't for him, not even when the world was free.

It was Club practice night, the night that they would meet Jess on her way down to catch her tram. Earlier that day he'd thought of some of the things he might say to her as they walked to the stop together. He'd decided he would invite her to one of their Club socials. She'd often spoken of a sister and brother-in-law who lived in Courtenay Place, and he thought that if he asked her to bring them along too, it wouldn't be quite the same as asking her to go out with him. He could just mention it to her and hope she would come, or maybe hope she wouldn't. Now, since reading Rangi's letter he thought he probably wouldn't mention the socials, wondered if he should see Jess at all. It was all wrong somehow.

He left the Railways job. The pay was poor, and the work – sweeping the warehouses and emptying the bins, fetching and carrying for so many bosses – made him feel like a boy around the place. It wasn't comfortable being a twenty-six-year-old man with no ambition to go to war and no excuse not to go. The men he worked with were mainly much older than he was, though there were some younger ones who the army had turned down for medical reasons. The men hardly spoke to him as he ghosted by with his broom, except to ask when he was leaving his soft job and joining up.

Several of the women and some of the men from the Club had been manpowered into the Ford factory as part of the war effort. The pay was good and they were able to work fifty hours a week. So he left the 'for-life' job and took one in essential industry at Fords.

It was hot work in all the protective clothing he had to wear, and the hours were long, but he felt happier there where he was not so much under the critical gaze of men who thought he should be away fighting for his king and country. He went into munitions where he could earn danger money in the powder room assembling mortar bombs, arming hand grenades or weighing out gunpowder to press into pellets for detonators. Most of the workers were women and that made it better somehow, though he wouldn't want his sisters to be doing that kind of work. Being war work, he felt more useful there, and less visible.

Since he worked late and took on as much overtime as he could, it meant that he was unable to attend Club practices on Mondays, and also that there were no more meetings with Jess on his way home from work. In some ways he was relieved about that. Sometimes friends, who called in with Sophie and Moana after Club, said that Jess had asked after him, though his sisters never mentioned it.

A dream, but Jess made him uneasy. His brother had made him uneasy, and now he wanted more than ever to put Jess out of his mind. After all there was Ma, the family, the future, and they were doing all right. There was a war, but what a time they were in really. He had a job where he could earn good money so that the family could have what they needed and, above all, with the help of the scholarship and The Uncle they were able to keep their young brother at school.

Tu had been away at school for two and a half years by then and all his school reports had been excellent. The family looked forward to Tu coming home for part of the holidays with his books and certificates, and Pita was always pleased when Ma insisted on him wearing his school uniform to Mass on Sundays, or to the Club bazaars and socials. It showed people. There was a war but they were doing all right. He liked seeing his brother reading his schoolbooks and there were always things he felt like saying to Tu but he didn't know how to say them. There were things he felt like pointing out because life was different now and there were great opportunities for kids like him. A kid like him could make his way right up there and be as good as anybody.

24

roses

Botanical gardens. Now that I think back, how soft-sounding, sweet-smelling and peaceful it is as a description of our starting-out place. And as I write, the two words remind me of a day in Perth, being drunk and singing with pals who eventually slung me under bushes in a public garden where I slept. I woke in the late afternoon to the smell of roses and the sound of the friends out on the grass playing with souvenirs. We were all boys then, long ago. I remember that all the way to the ship in the returning slow train to Fremantle, we sang songs of home.

After days of being ready, but not knowing what we were really preparing for or when we would start out, it was a relief to be on our way – more than just a relief. There's a certain exhilaration which accompanies you when you all set out together, a feeling which is maybe spurred on by a hint of fear. What I recall is a kind of spirited joy as we went off along Route Six in the dark, a kind of pride, which seemed to be something to do with love, because of who you are. It's all of you, a bunch of you wanting to give each other your best. As I write I wonder if exhilaration and elation are somehow related to that bodily kind of fear told about in books, where flesh creeps, hair stands on end, the spine chills, knees knock together, hearts beat double or maybe stop beating altogether. Or is there something higher sometimes, which overtakes fear? I try to recall fear. Is fear like pain, which once over is difficult to remember? I struggle with these thoughts, struggle to find words, struggle to remember, struggle to know myself.

It was just before midnight when, under light shellfire, we set off in single file on the road to Cassino town. Though there was mud flying everywhere, the shells, intermittent and driving into the soggy ground, were not doing the amount of damage that they can do when exploding and shattering against rocks and walls and the hard surfaces of roads. We made it all in one piece to our 'Gardens', which turned out to be an area of stinking bog, flowering with huge bomb craters the size of trucks and all filled with mud and water.

'Home sweet home in the cowyard,' someone said when we arrived there.

'Some bigfoot cows, you reckon?'

'Big bastards.'

All about us were the smashed-up municipal buildings and the sodden rubble and ruin of public parks. And ahead of us, beyond the 'Gardens', was what was left of the pulverised town, stretching away into darkness towards the mountain. It was in the far corner of town that Jerry was putting up strong resistance, determined to hold there, safeguarding the road and the mountain – but how he had survived the bombing in the first place we still couldn't understand.

All right. That far, dark place was where we were heading.

Off we went through the muck with our gear and clothes becoming soaked and heavy, scrambling and sliding by the water-filled holes and over the bisecting road to get us into the central area of town. But even as we scrummed across those incredible gardens I remember feeling a light-heartedness and a willingness, and I can truly say that there was nowhere else in the world that I wanted to be than with my Battalion. There was nothing else in the world that I wanted to be doing, but going in to help clear a south-west corner of a maimed town on the way to win the war. I remember thinking about tanks – that maybe there was another way in for tanks, because it was obvious from the start that they would never make it through there.

On the other side of the bog we found ourselves crawling over fallen masonry and debris, manoeuvring over heaped and slippery wreckage with the aim of searching Jerry out of 'every nook and cranny'. But we were only minutes into the town when a machine-gun blast sent a bunch of us rolling into broken culverts, against pieces of wall and in among debris and shadow, unable to tell where the fire was coming from. Our mates to the rear managed to take themselves back out of the way after the first bursts, and we hoped, as we lay pinned and listening in the dark, unable to twitch for fear of another sweep coming our way, that these mates would be out hunting for the gunpost.

After keeping low for several minutes we heard a double explosion, and then another. There was a shout, giving us the all clear before all became quiet again. There were six of us hiding there, but as we crawled out of our holes into a nearby cellar to organise ourselves, I could see that River and Tipene were in trouble. 'I think I been shot in the bum,' River said.

So he had. The seat of his pants was in shreds and we could see by matchlight that his backside was shot up and leaking like an old sieve. Tipene, also caught by the fire, had a shattered arm. They both needed to be taken out of there.

'I'll go out for a shufti,' I said.

I left them lighting their cigarettes and went back out over the junk, keeping my eyes peeled in the dark, my ears flapping, but the way seemed to be clear. It wasn't far to the junction as we had only gone fifty yards in when the gunner pinned us. I was soon able to locate the route the stretcher bearers and escorts were taking and reckoned we could bring the two men out safely to that point.

'Now we got to get your fellas' arm and arse out of here,' Choc said as we slung River between us. Tipene followed behind and Hemi and Gary led the way out to the medics, our only trouble being the rough ground we had to cross and the general fire of mortars landing in the direction of the road. After we'd delivered the men, the four of us went back into the tangle, heading in the direction of the first hotel, aiming to catch up with the rest of our platoon.

On our way we came across half a platoon from another company, but radio contact had been lost because signallers hadn't been able to keep their equipment dry. The formations that we started out with had disintegrated. There were no orders for us to follow as we were now without our commander, so we pushed on together.

Getting through the town was like being in one of those bad dreams where you set out on an important journey to find that there are obstacles blocking every pathway. At one turn giant parrots bar your way, and as you approach they rattle and scream and come down on you out of the trees, their beaks curved and white like descending moons. You run in another direction where pigs growing to the size of horses will not let you by. Setting out again, roads fall away and you find yourself standing at the edge of a cliff or a chasm. This goes on until you wake at last, never having reached your destination.

But there was no waking from this nightmare of Cassino as we attempted to clear a way in a town that bore no resemblance to any maps we had been shown as part of our preparation. 'Via this, via that,' we'd been told. 'Turn this way, turn that way.' But there was no this way, that way, no via anything. How could there be after such a pounding?

And what we came across, entangled in all the jumble and waste as we made our way, were reeking, water-swollen corpses of Germans which had been there since the bombing and the first forays into Cassino. We didn't realise at first, after slipping and scratching along, and sliding over mud-caked rubble and stone in the dark, that on striking a soft surface it was rotting flesh that our hobnails, our hands, our knees were sinking into.

Coming across the blue and stinking bodies brought you down to earth after all those first fine feelings you had when setting out

– though the feelings of horror and revulsion were not so much then, as now. Feelings and sensations become delayed when you are in battle, there being no time to dwell as you focus on what you have to do for yourself and your mates and survival. Never mind about God, King and Country at times like those.

Scattered on top of that under-layer of bodies were the newly dead, Jerries and Kiwis alike.

We groped our way forward through the ruins and over the disintegrating pieces of men – through the rotten stink of it all – soon finding that this place where we thought there wouldn't be a flea still jumping, was infested with Jerry. Live ones, that is. Because though we believed that this part of town had been cleared of the enemy by other battalions, there he was, hidden behind every piece of wall, in every broken-down *casa*, in among every jumble of rubbish.

But still, in a roundabout way we managed to move in the right direction, and as we came somewhere near to the first of the hotels a scout found us and took us into the cellar of a *casa* where our sergeant and our two platoons had assembled – or the remnants of our two platoons, I should say.

There was not much of the night left as we formed up to rejoin the attack, moving out once again across the slabs and hills of wet and jagged rubble, the nests of twisted iron, an overturned tank, more bodies – doing the best we could with grenade and bayonet while every 'nook and cranny' discharged enemy fire. Coming from the hill-slopes, shells burst and shattered all around us, machine-gun fire scattered in pathways through the dark, and as we ploughed on, attempting to keep our formation and our forward movement, the area was lit by tracer fire and the occasional glow of flares.

Over the rough and gory ground we crept and crawled, cleaning out one post only to be fired on by another. Keeping pace with me was Choc. Underneath all the clamour of war I could hear him whistling through his teeth.

The very earliest squint of daylight put up against the skyline the eerie shape of the Hotel Continental, brokenly standing against the base of Monte Cassino where the road wrapped round. It was higher than the other buildings, this main centre of resistance, which, as we sought entry to it, we found to be manned on every front. Guns were set on every platform, behind every mound; and at the hotel's very centre, concealed inside the building itself, was a tank – maybe there were two – bringing down a rain of fire on all surroundings. We came to understand, as the day progressed, why other units, struggling for nights and days, had found the way impassable.

Our attack disintegrated into a kind of foraging as we moved forward and back, sometimes dragging the wounded with us to any shelter we could find. There we would do our best with bandaging. We'd supply the men with cigarettes and rations then we would have to leave them, with the more able attempting to keep the rats away from the dying and the dead, knowing there was no hope of being evacuated before nightfall.

It was cat-and-mouse out in the town, life or death without let-up. Sometimes you were the cat, sometimes you were the mouse, there being no line between you and your enemy. In this great mix-up any shelter that we went into was likely to have our enemy harboured on a floor above, or in an adjacent *casa*. All we could do was clean out where we could – otherwise we were the ones to be cleaned out.

But maybe a cat-and-mouse chase is not a good comparison with what took place in Cassino. The image presented by a cat bounding after a mouse, and the zigzagging efforts of the mouse to escape, is too clean, too clear and too sharp-angled, the pursuit too quiet and clever. Also that kind of hunt is something that is right, I think. It's something ordained. Our stalking round town, our being stalked, was rowdy, filthy, stinking. It was brainless, all plans having gone haywire, and it was wrong too. I think about that now. I think that maybe there was no honest plan for us at all. Maybe we were just a distraction in some larger and more favoured objective. Because of what other use were we? Maybe we were just a little glass marble rolled in against a gigantic and immovable steel ball in some grotesque game.

As we struggled through the morning, our tanks attempted to come from behind the hotel on a track made in secret by the road-makers. This is something we found out later. But when the leading tank blew up on a minefield, the way became blocked and other tanks following became targets for bazookas. So there was no help from that direction, and even with other battalions brought in left and right of us, still the defence was impenetrable.

Near nightfall, Choc and I, to escape a stream of fire, found ourselves crawling along inside a broken-down sewer. As we waited, hunched and covered in shit, expecting the next blast, Choc whispered up the drain, 'Don't nobody pull the chain.'

Dead in a sewer. Drowned in shit. Think of that.

25

yellow

But one afternoon, after he'd been working in Ford Munitions for seven months, Pita found Jess waiting for him at the end of the platform as he came off the workers' train. They went to the station cafeteria together, going to the counter to order coffee. Although all the munitions workers had to shower after removing their protective clothing at work, he was conscious that the gunpowder could still be streaking him. He felt yellow, knew his eyes would be red and swollen from the effects of it.

Her eyes held on to him as she sipped the steaming milk with the thick essence of chicory and coffee stirred into it. She spoke about her job for a while then she said, 'I suppose there's someone, a girl at the Club.'

Pita didn't know what she meant at first. The girls at the Club, if they knew she'd come to meet him off the train, would've said she was throwing herself at him, would've described her as 'fast' with her painted nails, bright red lips and tinted cheeks. They would've said that all that stuff on her face made her look cheap. 'Raddle' was what the men at the meatworks called it. He could feel her eyes on him, staring into him, and he looked away remembering Rangi's letter.

'Victory Red,' she said. 'Patriotic lipstick. It's new. Do you like it?'

'It's ugly,' he said.

She lowered her eyes, then shrugged and looked up at him.

'Of course. You don't approve. I put it on when I'm going out at night. Not that I go out much these days. But I thought I'd come and see you because I have tickets for the pictures. There's a double feature – *Second Chorus* with Fred Astaire and Paulette Goddard and *Safari* with Madaleine Carroll and Douglas Fairbanks Junior. At the Paramount. My sister, who's a volunteer down at one of the clubs, had them given to her. She and her husband were going to go and see it but now she has to work. I wondered if you'd like to come with me.' She was looking into him, and then she smiled and pushed her lips forward. 'I could always go back to Tangee Natural.' She held up her hands to show him red fingernails. 'And Cutex Clear that I wear to work.' She scrunched her eyes at him, laughing, looking hard at his face and waiting.

'I can't,' he said.

'There's someone else, a girl at the Club?' she said, not moving her eyes from his face. 'An unpainted one?'

'Busy,' he said.

'Do you go out dancing?'

'With work, and doing the rounds of the camps.'

It was true. Right at that moment he knew that the others would be waiting over at government buildings for the truck to take them to the camp at Trentham.

Yet it wasn't quite true.

He didn't have to go, didn't always go when he felt too tired or didn't have money to spend at the canteens. He was aware of Jess watching him, as though she was watching him tell lies. It always made him uncomfortable the way she let herself stare straight at him. The bosses did it too, the old guys at work, especially the ones at the Railways. It was as though they thought he was lying to them even when he hadn't said anything, or as if they were about to catch him doing something wrong. It was as though they thought he might thump them, as though they thought that if they didn't keep an eye on him, he might steal something.

'Or you don't want to be seen with me,' she said.

That could be true too. The thousand eyes, the painted face. He didn't know what she wanted with him.

He didn't know what he wanted.

'And perhaps you don't like me at all,' she added, which could also be true. It was the way she stared into him. She choked him, puzzled him, angered him, made his insides twist and shudder like a gaffed fish.

'You'd rather I hadn't come.' Now her eyes left his face again. 'You'd rather not see me again?'

Never again?

But there was the way her eyes disappeared so that all you could see was the light that shone from in them. There were her bare, speckled, untouchable arms that he could see as the sleeve of her jacket slipped back – arms that were pale underneath with veiny wrists as blue as stamps on meat. Just at this moment there was the railway cup hanging heavy on a curved finger of one white, bony hand, and there was the other hand that lifted, drawing a strand of hair back behind a milky ear.

'You glisten,' she said.

A papery skin had formed on the top of the coffee, and when he dipped a spoon into the cup and drew it upwards, the skin lifted like a little tent round the spoon handle.

'Your skin,' she said.

He thought he must be yellow. He wanted to leave.

'My brother,' he said.

But how could he tell her what Rangi had written, how explain the amputation of a dream? Or how explain that there were some dreams that you could make come true because you wanted to, needed to, had to. There were others that you wanted to stay just as dreams.

'Your brother?' Jess prompted.

'Wrote me a letter.'

'And what has he to say, this brother of yours?'

'That you're my girl,' he said, though that wasn't the way Rangi had put it at all.

'And it's not true is it, that I'm your girl? Is that what you're telling me?'

'That I could do you wrong,' he said. It wasn't the way to explain what Rangi had said, and not what Rangi had meant either. He could only look about as he said it, at damp walls, steam, flies criss-crossing. But when he let his eyes flick by her face he saw that she was still looking hard at him as if trying to understand something.

She smiled without disappearing her eyes.

'Ah, but you wouldn't do that now would you? Oh no.' Laughing at him it seemed, but then becoming serious, a bit wild he thought.

'So what about me then?' she said, 'Did your brother ever think of that? Did he ever think that I might do wrong to the good Catholic boy, that I might get my piano hands on the Maori boy, the painted claws, into the glossy skin?'

Pita had to go.

He stood and walked out of the cafeteria, past the platforms, through the high doors, crossing the brass and mosaic floors of the station and hurrying out towards the government buildings where, across the road, the others would be turning up to wait for the transport that would take them to the army camp.

But as he was about to cross he changed his mind about going to Trentham. He was in no mood for company.

He started up Molesworth Street on his way home but when he came near to the Sacred Heart Cathedral, he saw that the lights were on in preparation for evening devotions.

Going in, he crossed himself with holy water, genuflected and went to sit in a side pew, away from light but under the eyes of the Mother of God. Her face, her folded hands, her feet that crushed the head of the serpent, were pale reflections in the darkened alcove, paler than the garments that she wore and more glowing than the garments' gilded edges. Pray for us sinners, now and at the hour of our death. The words kept turning in his head as he sat. After a time he kneeled to pray.

26

chatanooga

I'm surprised to find myself alive. Or am I alive? Dropping down, I had to believe I was dead so that others would know it too. Is belief all that exists? Is there really an edge that separates what is real from what is not, or is there no such separation? Sucking into shadow, do you become shadow? If, like a lizard or a fish, you are so indistinguishable against rock that you are undetected by the globular eye of a fly, or any eye, have you become rock?

Rangi said to me, 'You don't risk your life.'

'Look who's talking,' I answered.

At the time I thought he was ordering me, letting me know that I wasn't to do as he did. But round and about in the mayhem of Cassino I discovered what he really meant, thought about what his words were truly saying to me. I thought about Uncle Ju too, and how he used to instruct me.

'It's to do with timing,' Uncle Ju told me many times by the creek-sides of home. 'It's to do with timing, it's to do with speed,' he said. And it was once I became skilled in handling the taiaha, once I had learned the dance of feet, the importance of gesture and eye movement and facial expression, that Uncle Ju began to teach me combat movements as we faced each other with our weaponry.

My uncle had fashioned two taiaha from strong wood, one for each of us. They were about five feet long and Uncle Ju had planed them and shaped them to a suitable weight and a fine balance. At the top of each he'd carved a chiefly face, their elongated tongues forming the tips of the taiaha, while at the narrowest part of the shafts he'd tied circlets of white feathers. Our new weapons resembled an old carved taiaha that Uncle Ju had on a wall above his doorway.

'There's more than that too,' he said. 'Speed and timing, but there's more.' And as time went by I began to understand what he was saying. The 'more' was to do with understanding yourself, knowing the other man, knowing the world immediately around, above and below you; and it was once I began engaging with my uncle, my teacher, that I had to step up the agilities of the mind to match the physical agilities. I found that wielding a taiaha against an opponent was not only to do with being quick enough and being able to judge the moment, but was to do with blow and parry and angles, feint and balk and causing a diversion as well. It was also to do with the illusion brought about by the glint of light on shell, the shortening or extending of a shaft, the use of shadow or light or the contours of the ground. It was to do with the colours and markings of earth and sky.

'But it's more, it's more,' he would say, urging me, and I learned about distraction – sibilant and guttural noises and the timing of these, about a flurry of feathers, which if close enough to your face your eyes cannot ignore, but which if far enough away could be a bird turning itself among the foliage. Also there is distraction which is caused by the widening or narrowing of eyes, and by whatever else your eyes or your opponent's eyes can tell or refuse to tell.

Now, on this upside-down side of the world, in saying, 'You don't risk your life,' Rangi was telling me that when he ran out alone, climbing on to a moving tank to drop a grenade into the hatch before disappearing, with the whole ground exploding and the surrounds lighting and flaming, that he was not putting himself in danger.

I think it's true. There are all the normal dangers that none of us can avoid, but Rangi was telling me that he knew himself, understood what he was capable of doing by taking into account everything around. He became shadow because there was a moment when cloud passed across the moon or against a hillside, and he knew how long that moment would last. He became silence because all around there was bedlam. He became ground or wall because there was a hollow, a bend, an angle that fitted him into it. He became darkness because in light and fire he could see a spot that would absorb him. When he went out alone there was no circumstance that he had not accounted for, no shadow unseen, no distance uncalculated and no obstacle unconsidered. When he said, 'You don't risk your life,' Rangi meant, 'I don't risk my life. I do only what I know I can do.'

One morning – I don't know when, or if it really was morning – after another night on the town, pitching ourselves uselessly at the approaches to the Continental, we were drawn back into shelters bound by a wedge of ground we had cleared, this triangle being the total of our gains.

Our *casa* had once been a two-storey house. Roof and walls of the upper storey had collapsed in on to the floor, a section of which had fallen through to ground level, of which three outer walls and part of a fourth were still standing. Some of the inner walls were down too, and the rooms were piled with slabs of concrete, chunks of ceiling and rafters, broken furniture and two dead men. But not minding any of this, nor minding hunger or the filth of our clothes, and with our boots still on, we rolled ourselves in among the debris while a section from reserve set up gun-posts at the doors and windows. And with all the musical instruments, large and small, rattling, drumming, crashing, booming, thumping and bellowing as from a paddock next door, or a room next door in a house fragile and made of wood, we faded into death-sleep.

I'm not convinced that I'm alive, and have come to a sense that living and dead may inhabit the earth together. Do past and present exist, I wonder? Do *we* exist, or is the whole of life an illusion? Perhaps our true and only state of being is a non-physical one.

When I woke it was to the dull light as of early evening. Some of the rubbish had been cleared or formed into protecting screens so that light would not show. Ben was trying to get a signal on his set. The dead men had been removed to the cellar where six more had been found floating in waist-deep mud and water. The reserve boys had shifted them all up on to shelves, afterwards making a drain to take the water away. They'd cleared a passage in case another escape route was needed, and had heaped brick and stones into a corner of the cellar to be our lavatory.

Our sergeant was brewing tea in a fireplace he'd made, using the last supplies of water. He'd been through our haversacks and pooled any rations he could find. There wasn't much at all.

'We need a scout,' he said, handing me a cup. 'Our carriers haven't turned up. I can't go myself . . .'

'I'll go out for a look-see,' I said.

The tea, with a good dose of sugar in it, inched down and settled in my stomach as though it could have been a full boil-up of pork, vegetables and seasoned dumplings.

'Ben here can't get through, or not good enough. We know the carriers started out, but they haven't come.' He gave me a tin of meat from which I ate two spoonfuls before handing it back.

'I'll eat when we get back with supplies,' I said.

'If you bloody make it,' Choc said as he woke, not happy that I'd volunteered, knowing that my brothers, away in other shelters, wouldn't approve.

'And if I don't, what a waste of two mouthfuls of bully beef that would be,' I said.

Just then there was a juddering burst from one of our Brens at the far window, followed by the dull thudding sound that bullets make when they enter a man, or an animal.

When I went out, as night came, there were three dead men up against the wall of the next building, caught because of the sound of their boots on stone. The hobnails, I thought, are a curse. They rattle, they send out sparks, they suck you into the mire. I decided to leave mine behind, so pleased to remove them because they hadn't been off my feet for nights and days.

And quite suddenly, sneaking along, stooped, watching, my eyes becoming accustomed to the dark, with no pack on my back, with socks on my feet that could have been knitted with needles made from number eight fencing wire, and just my rifle and me, I felt a sense of joy and freedom.

I kept my eyes out, knowing that every *casa*, every mound, every hole, every shadow, every dark wall or doorway could be inhabited by the old bucket-head enemy. I moved only when I knew I could, waiting for shadows to push by, finding my silent way to a dark wall or doorway to ensure a house was empty before looking out for my next passage. And there *were* shadows passing. There were enemy beginning to re-enter these houses that we had earlier cleared. I was curious as to how, with all our shelters guarded and our patrols out and about, the enemy could be reoccupying.

About fifty yards from where I judged the road to be I came across two of the carriers. They had been cut down by mortar, themselves and their loads all in pieces strewn over ten yards of ground. I searched the area as thoroughly as I could, but since I found no sign of the others I guessed they'd been evacuated with wounds or taken away as prisoners. I thought I had better return to the shelter to dredge up a new collection party. Our rations and ammunition supplies were running low.

I headed back and was only twenty yards from our post when, waiting in the darkness of an arched doorway to make sure the way was clear, I heard the sound of boots on stone. The archway, which was nothing but a doorway with a short piece of wall either side of it, was in deep shadow because of a high pile of rubble behind it.

Outside the doorway was a comparatively clear piece of ground which I had to cross, but which I imagined could be open along the sights of Spandau sitting at any nearby window. I flattened myself over the darkest side of the rubbish pile just as two men stepped through. They waited there for some minutes, close enough for me to touch. I thought it would be easy enough to take them as my prisoners if only I was sure there were no more of them on the way. While I was considering this they left, going round and out behind the rubble. It was the route I had intended taking too.

I stood and worked back towards the doorway just as a third Jerry soldier sidled in with his rifle pointed. I came upwards with a two-handed clout of my weapon, knocking his rifle from him, lifting him off his feet, and as he went down, criss-crossing him with my bayonet. As I did this a bullet pinged the tin hat off my head. There were men and more bullets coming my way so I dropped down, scooping up handfuls of blood which was pooling out of the man on the ground, and smeared it over my head and face. I lay there, dead. I felt a bit scared too.

The snipers ran forward, one of them stopping for a moment to boot me in the side, boot me in the arm, boot me in the head, while the others began dragging their gurgling comrade back into the doorway. Now shots were coming from the other direction and the kicking one fell. The other two left their companion in the doorway and licked out of there.

The bullets that scared the Jerries off came from the guns of Choc and Anzac who were out watching for me. Did they get a surprise when my gruesome head popped up?

Back in our *casa* they showed me around as though I was some great bloody prize.

'Tu Bear,' they said.

'Dead man walking,' they said.

And I thought the latter could be true, since during my recent convincing of myself that I was a dead man, in order to convince others, I had not breathed, blinked, swallowed or allowed my heart to beat – though I do remember that my heart had some fear inside it.

Of what? Ending up dead? Or of batting an eyelid?

We could all be dead men, I kept thinking afterwards. We should be dead after all that had happened. Yes, we could be an assembly of the dead who, if touched by the light of the sun which we had not seen for days, would meld back into earth's formations. After all, we were not now who we were before. We were not now the blackened, fit men who had crossed from desert regions in a crowded boat. How long ago? Now we were pale ghosts of men whose bones were coming through to live on the outsides of our skins. We were men living in dens and rubbish piles, who crawled on hands and knees in a succession of nights and days in a world without colour. For this was a black, white, grey, flickering world we were inhabiting, as of some macabre newsreel which we could have been at once watching as well as taking part in, in a world where even blood flowed grey and dark, and where orange-red fire infused in shell blasts seemed to be an aberration. It wasn't the known world, so why shouldn't it have been inhabited by ghosts? Why should we not have been those ghosts?

'Meat head,' my mates said, shoving and slapping and hugging.

'Not on the menu,' I told them.

Though there was no clean water for washing and though we were all wearing the same stinking clothes that we'd had on for days, the boys had shaved and cleaned their faces using the dregs of tea.

'Ready for dinner,' they said.

Hemi, by the light of a candle, was drawing whorls of moko on the cleaned face of Gary with a piece of charcoal, making him into a chief from olden times.

I told our sergeant what I had found, and since he wouldn't allow me out on porter duty, I peeled off my shredded socks, smoked a cigarette, drank another cup of tea and went to sleep bloody-headed. And I died again, or remained dead. Another man's blood was painting me. Both the other man and I were dead, and both alive.

I awoke, still not sure that it was life I woke to. I was feeling cold and hungry – sensations usually associated with the living. But still I was unconvinced because flies were in love with us in the same way that they love dead men. They were in love with our eyes, our lips, our skins, our backsides. If we were not dead we'd have waved at them, slapped them down. Instead we left them to circle, creep, spit, lick. In love they were, giving to us completely their emerald and sapphire selves.

On the other hand there were feeders and egg-layers in love

with us too, who as a rule love only the living. They crept and hopped all over us, attaching their drinking mouths to flesh and tunnelling under our skins. How could we know whether we lived or not?

Perhaps there's an in-between state where ghosts walk in and out of you, or where you could be your own ghost coming and going?

I don't want anyone to read what I have written, wouldn't want anyone at home to get hold of my notebooks. I'll burn them once all this is over. One day it will be over. I've told my mates that if I die for once and for all, they're to chuck the books down the hole with me.

The porters arrived with supplies and the rations were divvied along with tins of hot cocoa delivered in bags packed with straw to keep them hot. The ghosts warmed up after that. After that there was a little bit of colour in Cassino as we began unloading the grenades, putting them in carrying bags and refitting the belts with ammo, preparing to go out on patrol.

'Won't be around to chuck nothing down no hole,' my mates said.

'Be in a hole ourselves, likely.'

'And lucky if you get put in a hole anyway. Out there growing maggots and that's all, that's the end of the story.'

'Stiff out of luck,' I said.

We soon found ourselves out once more in the wreckage of the town, finding that places we had cleared the day before had now been reinfiltrated.

But how?

The answers to that question were in what we came across as we moved about, doing the best we could in the shambles.

I know that others feel differently from me. I know there are many who have loathing in their hearts for our enemy and who want retribution. One day or night these ones will go out fully armed, without orders and alone. They'll find their way to an enemy hideout to seek personal revenge for a brother or cousin who has died – maybe in a much earlier battle. Or perhaps the vengeance they want is for a father killed in the earlier war. Once the task has been completed they return and sleep peacefully, but sometimes they do not return at all. I look for feelings of hatred in myself but don't find them. I've never yet felt hatred for anyone. Also I don't find any strong understanding that Jerry is my enemy anyway. Perhaps he is mankind's enemy, which could make him my enemy. Perhaps he is freedom's enemy, which could make him my enemy. But even though my job is to beat him, get rid of him, he has no particular enemy face for me.

In the absence of hate is it possible to feel some kindness, some warmth, some admiration for one's adversary? What I know deep in my heart is that this enemy cannot be scorned.

What we found in this town that we believed had been blasted from out of the earth, what we came across, as we stumbled, crept, ran, crawled in the shreds and fester of the town, were a series of strongly reinforced cellars; also ground-floor bunkers that were finely constructed and solidly made and all undamaged by bombing. In the most surprising of places there were carefully disguised gun-posts and blockades, while from out of every slit or peephole, from every fragment of masonry a gun was spitting. Mines had been threaded along every pathway and we discovered covered ways, leading from the slopes, by which men could be brought into the town at any time of night or day, or which could be used as escape routes when needed. In this way, crews could be relieved regularly and safely, and could move easily from one shelter to another, disappearing and suddenly appearing again. There were fortified shelters, camouflaged and strengthened lookout posts, and back routes through concealed passages that led under courtyards and returned to the mountains.

So, as our legs sagged, as our eyeballs leaned out of our faces and our arms became sandbagged, we found ourselves up against fresh fighters. We came across fresh patchworks of mines. Areas taking all day to clear could by morning have new machine-gun nests built in them, or could be hatching out whole new broods of snipers.

Considering all of this, though all that we set out to do was not accomplished, I think we did more than hold our own. We cleared large areas, sent back dozens of prisoners and gave as good as we got under the circumstances. I want to believe that our enemy would think that we too are a force that cannot be scorned.

Tonight we had a drink for Choc. It was a swig from a flask of brandy sent along with supplies. He's gone. Stepped into a booby-trapped doorway. Up he went. No more whistle. No more Chatanooga Choo Choo.

27

shadows

As more and more overtime became available, Pita stopped visiting the training camps after work. On nights when there were extra hours he'd hurry home when the shift was over to say the rosary with Ma, his prayers being not so much for his brother's safety but for the family. He would thank God that Ma had not received bad news that day, prayed that the war would quickly end and that they would soon see the whole family back together again. After the rosary he would listen to late news from the BBC, tuning in just as Big Ben chimed and the bulletins began.

Ma went about her days looking in on neighbours or having them call in, just as she had always done. She worked for the Club's social committee and visited the hospital with the Maori Women's Welfare, as she had before the war began. When food rationing came into force she saved family butter and sugar coupons so that she could continue to make biscuits for patients in the tuberculosis wards.

'Bread and dripping for us this week,' she'd say, 'I'm making brownies,' or 'I'm saving for a ginger cake, Anzac biscuits, boiled pudding.'

But unlike his sisters and Ani Rose, who were so involved with patriotic work that they were seldom home, Ma refused to do anything that she considered was for the war effort. She never visited the boys in camp, not even when Rangi was in training; and she hadn't been persuaded, even by The Uncle, to go with them to Palmerston North to the final farewells.

Eventually, visiting the wounded who had returned in hospital ships did become part of her work in the wards, and she didn't refuse to help at Club socials when she knew funds were for meals and suppers for soldiers on leave about town. Once the Americans became a presence in the city she thought it right that they all did their bit to make them welcome. 'Maybe there's some family on the other side of the world looking after our boys,' she'd say.

One Sunday night, when Pita was helping Ani Rose to put up the blackout curtains, she told him Jess wasn't at the cake shop any more and that she'd been manpowered into essential industry.

'Just grabbed by the Manpower on one of their raids round town,' Ani Rose said, 'and her aunty has to manage the cake shop on her own. They do mostly bread now.'

'Manpowered where?' he asked.

'Her aunty just said to essential work.' Ani Rose was watching him, flicking her eyelids up down, up down.

'What is it,' he said, as he hooked the curtain to the top of the frame, 'why is it I need so much watching?'

At that Ani Rose let her eyelids drop for a moment, then shrugged her shoulders. He knew she was wild with him. He knew he should marry Ani Rose.

'Telephone exchange, making soldier uniforms, boots and helmets, the foundry. They're all wanting girls,' Ani Rose said. 'They haven't got enough girls. The cannery, freezing works, ammunition, tin factory too.' Then she said, 'But they wouldn't, would they, a girl like that?'

But a girl like what? A dream girl? A girl with the whole lit-up world at her feet? A girl who squeezed her eyes, lifted a white hand to put back a wisp of hair? Or a girl who threw herself at him, who was 'cheap'. A girl getting her red claws in, a girl 'singing out for it', a girl who was not for him even when the world was free.

'Like what?'

It came out rougher than he meant, and now Ani Rose turned her back, pinning a lower corner of the blackout to a staple to keep it tight so that the lights could be turned on. His sisters, who had been covering the upstairs windows, were coming down.

'Like what?' he asked again. 'A girl like what?'

'Kind of la-di-da you mean?' Moana said. 'Stuck up?'

'I didn't mean anything,' Ani Rose said. 'I didn't mean anything about *her*. And you don't have to go trying to put me in the wrong,' she said to Pita, 'the way you always do with your sisters.'

What was it about him?

'But there's some who take their pick. Is that what you mean?' Sophie asked. 'Some who know how to get the job they want, in a bank or something, or driving, or they join the WAACs to get out of the manpower.'

It wasn't the first time Sophie had mentioned the Women's Auxiliary and he thought she could be thinking of joining. Ma would never agree to it.

'Too good, you mean, for our kind of jobs?' he asked, trying not to let it come out rough. He was wild with his sisters and Ani Rose, but at the same time recognised what he was doing to them, attempting to make them say the things he often thought about himself. As Ani Rose said, trying somehow to put them in the wrong.

'Too good for you and me?' he asked.

'We get the jobs they don't want,' Moana said, 'the low-pay jobs. That's what Pauline reckons.'

'And you have to listen to her all the time?'

'All born equal in the sight of God,' Ma said, coming in and switching the light on.

So he let it be. Why all this, when he'd decided long ago to put Jess out of his mind? Jess wasn't for him, so why try and pin blame on his sisters and Ani Rose because of it?

The room was shadowy, the light as dull as candlelight. He liked the shadows, the blackout. He enjoyed Sunday nights and being enclosed in a room with them all at home. He liked the way the ceiling disappeared, liked the thick weight of the mantelpiece – on it the photos, the holy pictures and the pieced-together virgin. He liked the darkness of everything, the undefined furniture that The Uncle had brought in before their arrival, the solid floor, the unlit passage which was indistinct behind whoever came in the opened door.

He took their pack of cards from the drawer and dealt a hand for each of them, took a packet of wax matches from the mantelpiece and shared them out.

'She's mucking out at the hospital,' Ma said, 'washing and scrubbing. You don't get much messier than that. She said hullo to me when I was on my rounds.'

'Scrubbing for victory,' Moana said, sitting down and taking up her hand.

'Canneries for victory.'

'Tin hats for victory.'

'Wool up your nose for victory.'

'Blow yourself up in a bomb factory, for victory.'

They were all having a try at shifting a mood that he had caused. But this was the way they could enjoy each other's company, he thought, at home with the world blacked out. Away from posters and advertisements telling you that you had to be happy to do your duty, that you should be working harder and putting up with adversity so that you could help win the war, that if you didn't keep your mouth shut the ships in your harbour could be blown to kingdom come. It was all adding up to victory.

He thought of chicory, essence of coffee, a question he couldn't answer. He thought of Victory Red, a ruby lamp, the statues and altar candles, the serpent underfoot, the quiet pews.

In his hand were red hearts, a full flush. There were glassy wrists and pale hands that he didn't want to think about. He raised the stakes and spread his cards down.

'Victory,' he said. It gave them all, including Ani Rose who they all thought he should marry, an excuse to laugh as he spread the full hand down and collected his pile of matches. Life was good, even if there was a war. It only needed the conflict to end, the end to bomb-making, their brother at home, to make dreams a reality, to forge their family future. There was no girl prettier than Ani Rose.

But he'd been thinking more and more that it didn't seem right for him to be just waiting for the end of the war, enjoying his comfortable Sundays, without being prepared to go and help finish it. Now Brother Tu was wanting to join up. On a recent weekend visit Tu had said that he wanted to leave school at the end of the year and enlist.

'Others my age have gone,' he said.

'There's others your age in their graves by now,' Ma reminded him.

'You're stopping at school,' Pita told him. 'You don't have an education just so you go and get your brains blown out.'

And Tu had stood up to him, argued with him, angered him.

'There's time,' Tu said, 'when the war's over, when I've done something to help end it. Then I can take up my career.'

'No. That's that. And you don't have an education just so you can make your mouth smart,' Pita said. 'You want a war, I give you one.'

'Listen to your big brother,' Ma said. 'One's enough from a family. In fact one's too many.'

But Tu had already said the thing that had been on Pita's mind for some time now, about needing to do something to help end it.

Pita was sorry he'd reacted the way he had, sending the boy off angry, feeling the boy's eyes on him for the rest of the weekend, as though accusing him. He knew that it was he, not his young brother, who should be the one going to help. Making bombs was something older people could do, something that women could do in order to free men to be soldiers. He'd heard women talking about serving their countries at home to enable men to go to the front.

It was not long afterwards that they heard that Rangi was coming home on furlough because of something to do with his eyes.

Letters from Rangi, by now a veteran of Greece and Crete campaigns, told little of the action of war. They told of being on the move, settling into the routines of camp life in preparation for the next encounter '. . . who knows where . . .' and how they filled in the many days of waiting. '. . . training, arranging a few games, scrounging round the villages for food. A few chooks here and there . . .' Only occasionally were letters interspersed with the sights and encounters of war, but all sensitive information had been blacked out by the censors: '. . . well that was a thing to see, hundreds of gliders over   all these hundreds of parachutes coming down like it was a paddock full of mushrooms, only the mushrooms were coming down out of heaven. All colours. It was down   to earth to take   . None of them dropped near us. We were only watching from our possie, but the ones defending that part, well they really got it in the neck. Anyhow, later we had to clean up a few of these   when they come snooping around, and also had another go round when a pack of Huns made out they wanted to surrender and threw a grenade instead. That got us wild. We went for them. Good job. That's how we got ourselves out . . .' '. . .   and glad of a rest and a few days leave. Went to the hospital to get a few splinters out. Pretty girls around this place but no chance . . .' 'You all had that news long ago about our cousins . . .' '. . . pretty quiet these days. Training, training, training. And the weather   Don't know what's coming up. All this waiting around but hoping to get back into it soon. Anyway, a good game of rugby today, New Zealand against South Africa. We gave them a good hiding . . .'

It would be a good time for him to go now that Rangi was coming home, Pita thought. Once his brother arrived he was going to tell him to stay with Ma, their sisters and Tu, even if his eyesight had fully recovered. One was enough from a family.

28

chiefs

I write my notes in the dark side of our *casa* after completing my watch. There's something on my mind, and though sleep does its best to overtake me, I keep myself upright, push my pencil across the page as I wait.

Men settle themselves after another day or night of fighting that was like the ones before, times in which days themselves have become nights, being ever darkened by the thick, choking grime of smoke and the damp, hanging nets of cloud and mist. Above us all, no matter what attempts have been made by Yank, Indian, Brit or Kiwi soldiers, ol' man still stands, looking down, barring our way to Rome.

But although we are all worn down, flea-ridden and shitting fluids, we've cleared all infiltrators from our triangle of ground and taken hordes of prisoners. And since we've now been able to make a route safe for our carrier platoons, hot food has been delivered to us safely every night.

Something else delivered along with rations and ammunition is the *Cassino Evening Post*. It's handwritten on army paper by some of the reserve boys standing by in the town jail. There are news items from the BBC and a few jokes and anecdotes included. Good on them.

One day two chiefs came out with us to fight. Which day? It doesn't matter. The two chiefs were Hemi and Gary. The scrollwork on their rifle butts has been completed now and they have rubbed into the designs a mixture of gun-oil and ash which has made the patterns stand out in dark, connecting whorls.

I suppose it was because there was nothing more they could do on their rifles that Hemi and Gary looked for other surfaces for their artistry. All they could find were the faces of each other, so they began to draw the olden-day patterns of chiefly moko on each other's skins, beginning in the middle area of their foreheads. They drew wide patterns at the top which came to a point between their eyebrows. In this area – which shows the status and authority a man has – they have made twin scrolls, the ends of which open towards the tops of their heads to allow the inflow of sacred, life-giving waters. The direction of the coils also shows where chiefly authority lies.

On either side of the scrolls are rows of lines over the remainder of their foreheads, beginning in the space between their eyebrows and extending upwards before taking a downward curve at their temples, telling the story of rank. If these 'stripes' were mirror-imaged on to the sleeves of their battle dress, Hemi and Gary would be army sergeants. When I mentioned this to them they shrugged and opened out their hands. They knew nothing of the meanings, they said, only knew these patterns they were drawing were the same as the ones chiselled into the face of their ancestor.

Lines and spirals on nose and cheek tell where the tipuna was from, who his parents were, who his families were and his position in those families.

There are markings to do with birth and lineage, and you can read on a man's face what he is known for. But although I know the areas of the face where this information is etched, I am unable to read what its wearer is expert in – whether he is known as a seer, a man of medicine, a carver, a war leader, a grower of food or a fleet commander. It is Uncle Ju who has explained the old patterns to me, which he did as he carved the wooden faces at the top ends of our taiaha. But there is more for me to learn once all this is over. I look forward to that.

Though they enjoyed the joke of what they had done to each others' faces, and gave no more attention to it once it was finished, I thought what fine artists Hemi and Gary were and how great they looked. They were true in their hearts, I thought, loyal and brave in spirit. They made us all light-hearted.

On that day there were four of us approaching a building that we thought had enemy hidden inside. This was confirmed when a burst of fire sent us down behind a mound of masonry. The ground ahead, though cluttered, had no decent cover and we knew any move from us would draw more fireworks. We tested this, Anzac and I, by taking off our helmets and holding them above our barricade on the tips of our rifles. Sure enough we were in the firing line, and well within range. Anzac's helmet hurtled twenty yards while mine wasn't hit at all. I took this as a good omen.

'It's a sign,' I said, putting my very good tin hat back on my head. I looked about and could see that there was a shadowed way round the thin edge of the firing line that I could take.

'Keep it up,' I called, away and running with my bombs.

There were new bursts of fire as helmets bobbed about, but Jerry wasn't fooled by that for long and soon the firing ceased.

But the sight I saw, as I circled towards the *casa*, was of a great tattooed chief, leaping three feet in the air from one side of our barricade, arms flung wide, tongue dropped two yards out of his head. The chief let out a mighty yell. As this first one dropped down behind the barrier another great chief leapt from the other end, shouting and hanging his tongue.

Between the two of them they kept the Spandau busy until I timed my first grenade, whacking it into the room through the doorway and getting out while it blew. The boys were running to join me as I hurled the second grenade and three men came out of the building amid clouds of dust with their hands in the air. Others remaining inside the house were beyond surrender.

One evening we were sheltering in the end of a long cellar, the other end of which had been blasted away, opening it out towards the shattered slopes of Castle Hill and the hunched ruin of the castle itself. The stuttering light of gunfire, the tracer fire and the flares made it seem like a scene passing and re-passing before our eyes as on a movie screen, or like the way that windows of speeding trains flick by.

We had scrambled into this cellar because a squirt of machine-gun fire had crossed adjacent ground only a short distance ahead of us. Not knowing quite where the fire was coming from, nor whether we had been seen or not, we decided we should stay where we were until after dark. But there were only some of us in the cellar. Two of our men had thrown themselves over a low wall on the other side of the alley and were lying low there. One of them was Gary. His cousin Hemi was with us in the cellar.

Our shelter was a solid one, but it was not a good one as there was only one exit and we were trapped in there. Occasional bursts of fire across that exit, though not quite reaching the gap, soon made us realise that our presence was known. Any approach we made towards the opening brought a burst of fire.

About halfway along one side of our tunnel there was a crack in the wall where I posted myself, but my vision was limited to the broken piece of wall opposite, where our other two boys were crouching. Now and again I would spot the shapes of their helmets rising like round loaves above the wall. Because this movement of theirs drew no reaction I guessed the enemy had not sighted them.

But the two behind the wall could see what none of us in our tunnel could see, which was two Huns sneaking up, each with a fistful of stick bombs, coming to explode us confined in our cellar. Our mates behind the wall knew that every bit of the way forward of these grenadiers would be overlooked and protected by their gunners.

What I saw on looking out from my spy-hole was the figure of a fine chief springing up on to a wall. We heard him shout, telling us to charge – saw the arms splayed, the dropped tongue, the whites of eyes as we burst out from the room at a crouching run, firing our guns and making as much noise as we could. The sticks went in over our heads, exploding behind us. And as they boomed, the man on the wall was leaping. By the fanning light of Spandau fire, we saw pieces of him falling.

Earlier today, just as night came, we brought Bootleg out by stretcher to the field ambulance. He had both feet blown off by a Schu mine and pieces of metal from it embedded in his face. Clever gadgets, these mines which produce no hum, which hide them-selves away from the detectors inside their wooden casements. Boof. A face full of screws, clasps and hinges as the explosion takes your feet away. So as well as having limbs torn off, you can end up blind. At least Bootleg still has his eyesight. That's something.

Out in the field, Medical strapped his legs to stop the flow of blood and prepared him for transport. But there weren't enough stretcher bearers by then, so some of us were brought in to assist out in this battleground which we shared with our enemy, where there was only a red cross for protection.

'Just as well you can stand on your head,' we said to Bootleg on the way out. A laugh gurgled up and came out hee hee hee from between broken teeth, bleeding mouth, sliced lips.

'Good you can walk on your hands.'

'No more toe-jams.'

'Clean sheets, a pretty nurse is what you're after, I bet.'

When we arrived at where the field ambulances were waiting, and as we were transferring him on to one of the gun carriers that had been converted to take stretchers, Bootleg asked us, 'How about the middle leg. He still got his foot on?'

Johnny lifted the blanket, 'Good as gold, ay,' he said.

'Right as rain,' we all assured him.

'Ah, champion,' Bootleg said. 'All ready for action by time I get home.'

Hemi was taken out at the same time as Bootleg. After we dealt with the stick throwers the oncoming gunmen took fright and ran, and we departed too, with the Spandau beginning to swing in our direction.

On the way back we picked up a prisoner, and once out of danger stopped and shared cigarettes and water with him. We realised that Hemi wasn't with us, so we waited and he soon came along, carrying his own and his cousin's rifles.

The next thing that happened was that Hemi charged straight at our prisoner and before we realised what was going on the German was lying dead.

No one spoke. We returned to our shelter and didn't mention the incident to anyone.

Hemi cleaned the markings from his face and from then on wouldn't eat. He hardly slept. He was a ghost. Gone. We did our best to find him but he wasn't there, the great chief inside him gone roaming.

Before he was taken away we dismantled the two rifles and packed the etched butts of them in with his belongings. I don't know if that is what he wanted or not.

The book I write in is creased and stained, having been through many misadventures. Some of the writing is illegible and will have to be rewritten once we get out for a rest. I've left the pen behind having decided that it, and the bottle of ink, are not good things to take into battle. There are only a few inches left of the pencil which I now use and which I've sharpened from time to time on my bayonet as I watch men come and go.

Cigarettes glow in the dark, and tonight, high above, there's a piece of moon shedding light into the roofless end of the building. I wait and watch, uneasy. It's a long time since I've heard anything of my brothers.

29

pennies

Mita and Toby, in town on leave, were in the middle of the floor pumping a ukulele and singing 'Pennies from Heaven' when Jess came in with four others. Pita, out in the supper room with Ma and Fred, was waiting for Mita and Toby to finish their impromptu item so that he could announce the supper waltz. These duties were left mainly to him now that he and Timi, who had been turned down by the army, were the only regulars. Often they were the only two men not in uniform. He didn't see Jess come in.

The band tuned in and played along with 'Pennies' and Fred was complaining, wondering how the two inebriated gentlemen had managed to get in, half-cut and bandy-legged as they were, when he himself had stood guard at the door, nosing out drunks and sending them back the way they came.

'They came in late,' Ma was saying, 'after you left your post.'

'Walked in, or rather, stumbled in and took the floor,' Fred said. 'The sandwiches will have their toes curled up by the time supper is announced and we would've wasted our time saving our butter rations.'

'Don't be a fusspot, Fred, there's no harm, people are enjoying it. And their money is the same colour as anyone else's.'

'Dear lady, how do we know they paid?' Fred asked.

Pita had spent most of the night in the supper room, helping make sandwiches, shifting tables and talking to Ma and Fred. Other helpers – his sisters, Ani Rose and other club girls, came in to assist from time to time, but Ma always sent them back out to dance. There was a shortage of dancing partners for the soldiers on a night like this, with so many of their own boys on leave from camps, or home on furlough. And now there was the ever-increasing number of American servicemen about, changing the look and sound of the city and the dance halls. 'Baby-face boys', Ma called them, and Pita thought it true that most of them looked no older than Brother Tu. 'Lambs to the slaughter,' she'd say, and he thought that was true too. The first lot had already gone off to be mown down on Pacific beaches.

'*She's* here,' Timi came out into the supper room and said, 'and they brung Bing and Fred Astaire along.'

Looking out through the servery he saw Jess wearing a blue skirt and silver shoes, looking thinner and even paler than when he'd last seen her. No Victory Red. She was with a woman and man who he thought could be the sister and brother-in-law that she'd spoken of, and with them were two chewing Americans. Jess was introducing them to Ani Rose and his sisters as he went out and announced the supper waltz. He stepped down from the stage and asked her to dance.

The next week Jess's sister and husband and the two Americans came again, but not Jess. He was disappointed, wanted to ask after her, but he didn't. However, at supper time, her sister spoke to him, telling him that Jess had to work so that she could make up her sixty hours for the week.

'If she gets her hours in she'll be able to come again next time,' her sister said. 'She's keen on you, and I suppose she wants to know if she's wasting her time or not?' She stared at him.

He didn't know how someone he didn't know could talk like that to him and he wanted to walk away, wished one of his sisters would come along, or Ani Rose, or Ma.

'Should she just forget about you? That's what she needs to know,' Jess's sister said.

'Yes. Yes. There's a war on,' he said, a foolish thing to say that didn't explain anything. Not that he wanted to explain. He just wanted to be left alone to get on with filling the teapots, shifting the forms and tables in the supper room.

'Dougie and I won't be back,' Jess's sister said. 'Dougie leaves next week. My sister will want an escort, if she comes.'

He felt trapped. All he knew was that he wanted to see Jess again, but also wanted her out of his mind, out of his present, out of his future, out of his life.

'She said she'd be at Courtenay Place at half-past seven next Saturday if you want to meet her. If you're not there, then at least she'll know. You won't hear from her again.'

Out of his mind, but all week he thought of seeing her again. He thought of not going to meet her but knew he would. When they met he'd have to tell her he was going away.

At Courtenay Place he waited for almost an hour, thinking he could've missed her. The junction was crowded with girls and soldiers. The trams were full. People pushed out on to the road from under the verandahs and from the tram shelters on the other side of the street as the trams clattered in. Others stepped down from the trams on to the roads, hurried to the footpaths and went on to the picture theatres and dance halls. Bells clanged. The trams moved off again and so did the stream of cars delayed behind them.

Courtenay Place, but where in Courtenay Place? Her sister hadn't said. He assumed that he should wait for Jess at the tram stop, but then remembered Jess had told him her sister lived nearby and that she often stayed with her in the weekends. She could be walking rather than coming by tram.

She could've decided not to come.

He left the tram stop and walked down past Aitken's Book Arcade, the post office, Adams Bruce, Castle's the Chemist, the drapers and Victoria Laundry. He turned by the greengrocers with its dark doorway smell of trampled fruit and vegetables. People waited in the alcoves out of the wind that flapped the billboards and rattled the tin verandahs. He returned to the tram stop deciding that he would take the next tram home.

Then he'd be free.

But he let the next tram go by, then the next. Jess stepped off the one after that, wearing a coat over her hospital uniform, a beret with a pin through it and her hair tucked up. She looked brittle without her make-up. Her clothes were crumpled from pushing her way through the overcrowded tram.

'They were short-staffed down at the wharf clearing hospital,' she said. 'Some of us were taken down to do cleaning duty before the hospital ship arrives in the morning. It was very dirty. Dust and soot. We had to scour it all and didn't get back until eight. I didn't know whether you'd come, then didn't know whether you'd wait for me.' He knew that if he was to tell her he was going away he should do it right then.

'I'll have to go up to my sister's place to change,' she said, 'just up there, up Marjoribanks Street if . . .' He turned to walk with her and they hurried across the road among a crowd of people heading for the De Luxe Theatre. She took his arm as they began to walk up the steep street, dark in the blackout.

'My brother's coming home,' he said, 'so I can't, so I have to . . .'

'Get yourself free of the piano girl,' she said.

'You don't know about our family,' he said. 'You don't know anything about me, or what's going on.'

'Mystery man.'

She could be laughing at him. He couldn't look at her, but could feel the light touch of her arm as she led him through a gateway and along a path to the front of a house which was lost in shrubbery and darkness. Taking him in along a hall and through to a sitting-room she checked the blinds before turning on the light.

'Now tell me,' she said pulling out the silver pin, taking off the beret, shaking out her hair.

Then he had his arms round her, his face in her flimsy hair, her breakable body against him, and he ached all down and all through him. All he could do was cling to her. He felt such despair.

'Tell me,' she said. 'Tell me what you want.'

'I'm getting married,' he said, putting her away from him, turning to leave. 'I'm going away to war.'

30

awol

So what of sorrow?

Last night after I put my book away I lit a cigarette and blew out the candle. I hadn't seen my brothers.

When I finished the cigarette I lay down and went into a heavy sleep, and deep in the night I heard a ghost call my name, 'Te Hokowhitu-a-Tu.'

Standing in the moonlight on the broken-down side of the *casa*, his face covered in blood and his clothes stained dark with it, was the ghost of my father who had come to speak to me. 'Te Hokowhitu-a-Tu,' he called. He's come for me, I thought. I wasn't surprised.

But as I became more awake I realised that this was not the ghost of my father. Instead it was one of my brothers, but Pita or Rangi? I wasn't sure. Ghost or not, I wasn't sure. This brother was looking for me, calling for me with the sound of both my brothers' voices rolling into one another, wavering and echoing against one another as they called.

'Te Hokowhitu-a-Tu.'

Big Brother is not a big man. He's of medium height, being half a head shorter than Rangi and me. He is broad-shouldered, big-boned like our mother and has her dark skin and black eyes, her strong black hair. The moonlit figure that I could see was too tall and thin to be Brother Pita, so I understood as I became fully awake that it was Rangi standing there. Though he looked ghostly in moonlight I soon realised he was not a ghost. He was searching for me.

'Te Hokowhitu-a-Tu,' he called. 'Te Hokowhitu-a-Tu, Big Brother is dead.'

Sorrow deeply felt is like an inner deadness that is beyond tears, a deep softening of bones, walls that fall inward, crumbling and becoming rubble and mud. Sorrow is a gap that cannot be breached by regrets and longing.

I stood and took up my greatcoat as though to go somewhere, but after a moment realised there was nowhere to go. Rangi came towards me and we held each other for a while.

'Bits got him in the head, got him in the chest, got him everywhere,' he said. 'I saw it happen, knew it was him and tried carrying him. It was no good. "Put me down," he said.'

There was movement, there were voices as we sat down together. Men were going out to do their watch, talking, boots cracking over the stone floor, footsteps crunching out in the gritty dark.

'He talked about a Hun kid he sent home to his mother earlier in the day,' Rangi told me. '"Just a boy," Brother said, "with fluff on his face. Nothing to shave." He couldn't do it. Pita couldn't end him. Instead of ending him, the Hun kid, Pita fixed him just bad enough to send him home.' As men went out others were returning from patrol, lighting cigarettes and candles.

'And wanted to know if I thought God would be happy with that ... with him, for sending a Hun kid home to his family. I told him yes, yes God would. He talked about Ma and our sisters, Ani Rose and their baby, and I thought why him? Why him, I keep thinking, him with a wife and kid and who never wanted to be here in the first place? Why not a silly devil like me?'

There was shellfire away in the distance and I knew that somewhere out in the ruins, under a sky where all is reversed and the Cross does not exist, where the Pot empties itself into a back-to-front pool and the slice of moon which seems to wax, is waning, lies our brother.

'We talked about you,' Rangi said, 'there's something we said, something we talked about.' That's all he would say. Then before settling down to sleep he said, 'We go out tomorrow night. You, me and the cousins.'

I think of war. I think of Ma, of my sisters and Ani Rose and how they listen every day for a knock on the door that they hope they will never hear, how they wait every day for a telegram that they hope will never come. But now there *will* be a knock on the door and the delivery of a message. They'll take the envelope into their hands, not knowing which of our names they'll read once they have opened it.

It was awful. Big Brother was a mess. We straightened him out as best we could, put his blanket over him and gathered stones and fragments to make a marker – a pyramid of rock and rubble to ensure the redcaps would find him. We stuck his rifle upright in the ground beside him and made sure he was wearing his identity discs.

It was my cousins and I who did all this. Brother Rangi did nothing but cry, tears just pouring out of him as every now and again he repeated, 'Not tonight, not tonight. Yes, but not tonight.' I don't know what he was going on about. He could've been talking about our brother's burial, not wanting to leave him out there under the moon and stars, but I don't really think so. Anyway, besides it being impossible to dig in ground like this, burying isn't allowed.

Eventually we sent Big Brother on his way, 'Hoki atu ra . . .' and as well as that we prayed for him – 'Eternal rest grant unto him O

Lord . . .', which seemed right for someone like him. Five bob both ways, and a good way to keep flanks and rear covered.

And on the way back we talked about the words of both the Catholic prayer and the 'sending forth' of our Maori heritage. We talked about how in the prayer we ask for a place to be found in heaven for the departed. But we reckoned 'eternal rest' and 'perpetual light' could seem like a form of punishment if taken too literally. The former could be a kind of supine isolation, the latter a torture of light where darkness never gives relief. On the other hand we thought it could seem, from the way we are often told it, that perpetual light is a kind of shining love and enlightenment, emanating from most high, bringing with it the greatest happiness that it is possible to experience. It could seem that heaven is a kind of joyful playground, the place of highest reward, despite a rather stern hierarchy of deity and trinity, and the less dour mother, saints and angels. This heaven is attainable according to what you do in life. It's your sainthood if you get there. If you don't reach it, too bad for you. We talked about 'rest in peace' perhaps being too much of a good thing in some ways, but at least preferable to hellfire for all eternity.

'Hoki atu ra' is not a prayer but a permit from the living. Your death is you going AWOL, but to a higher state. That's what we reckon. 'Hoki atu ra' is giving you leave so you can march out and go off to join the ancestors in that other dimension. It's your living friends and relatives allowing you to go, telling you to get yourself off to the homeland. But it's not meant to be your reward. Your rewards and punishments have been dealt out already, in your earthly life. All that belongs here, stays here. That seems like a good thing to me.

So, now in the quiet of the moment, I imagine the homeland reunions, the reuniting, to be rowdy, joyful, unrestful, wicked and full of singing and laughter. These thoughts cheer me, and these thoughts are enough for now. One day, if I live long enough, I might decide that this here on earth is all we get, that there is no afterlife – no God on high with a long grey beard putting ticks and crosses in a book. I may also decide that the ancestors have gone no further than the earth who is called Papatuanuku. Earth is something I believe in (whatever that means).

In the meantime I talk to Pita, 'E te tuakana, hoki atu ra,' and, 'Elder brother, *requiescat in pace.*'

31

manners

When we returned to camp Rangi began to talk to me about something that must have been on his mind, something that happened one day in Wellington when a riot broke out in Manners Street. It was a story of Rangi and Jess, a story of love, a story that could only be told because Big Brother was dead.

But it wasn't right that Rangi should be telling it, not right at all. I didn't want to hear such a story, not with our brother still lying out there under a loopy sky, unattended and not yet in his grave. It was too soon for this story, too soon by years. I couldn't understand Rangi's reasons for telling it.

'I got home on furlough pretty glad of a break,' said Rangi. 'We were buggered, most of us having wounds of some description and some of the boys half off their rockers. As for me, my eyesight was playing up and went quite blind for a while coming out of the desert. But able to see okay by the time I got home.

'Anyhow, home on furlough was when I found out Brother Pita had joined up. Didn't want that. War? It's not him.

'Of course I got letters from him from in camp telling me to stay home. Don't go back when the furlough is finished, he said. Stay home and look after our mother and sisters and our young brother. You already done your bit for God, King and Country and that's your duty now, looking after them. You know how Ma feels, he said, you know what Ma's been through. All that made no difference to me even though I know I could've stayed home because it would've been allowed. There was a big row going on, all the bigwigs having rows, some saying us on furlough should be allowed to stay home now because of all the fighting we done already.

'Well they couldn't make us Maori boys go back because none of us got conscripted in the first place, none of us had to go in the first place. Anyway, in the end, yes, they agreed we got to be let off. The Maori Battalion, and any married Pakeha man with kids didn't have to go back to the front.

'But as for me? I couldn't stop thinking about our poor Battalion, our mates still over there with all of us experienced ones missing from the ranks. There was recruiting going on all over the country trying to fill all those places. New boys still soft from their mothers, homesick, still shitting yellow, all signing up and going off. I couldn't stay behind.

'Anyhow there's Big Brother away in camp, and there's me, home for a while having a great time round the service clubs in Wellington. Plenty of attention in our uniforms. Free drinks and welcome anywhere. And it was like everyone was having a real good time at home: plenty of jobs for everybody now; plenty of money; all the pretty girls all dressed up and going out dancing. All the Yankee boys causing a bit of excitement.

'I like them, the Yankee boys, their jangle and twang all round town. They make the place alive with their money, their stockings and chocolates and flowers for the girls. Honey boys, drunk in Courtenay Place, sucking oranges in the train, handsome like film stars. They know what they want and they want it fast before they all go off and get blasted to bits.

'Wolf whistles too. Wheet whee-ee-oo-oo, Wheet whee-oo-oo,

Hubba hubba ding ding. Hubba hubba what a bubba. And kids all hanging round for chewing gum and badges. Might even get a cigarette or two if they're lucky, or a two-bob bit. White teeth, wide smiles. All of them, the whole lot, got Yankee piano mouths.

'Yes, I like them. It's them looking after our country, saving it from the Japs while we all go off and fight for England. Funny thing that.

'Well one afternoon Timi and me are walking through town with Sophie and Moana, sisters all dressed up looking pretty. Off to the Majestic Cabaret down Manners Street. Timi and me are their escorts, or supposed to be their escorts. Really they are meeting up with a couple of the honey boys that they met at our Club social, but they don't want Ma to know.

'Timi and me took the girls to the milk bar, looked these two Yankees over, then left the girls there ordering ice-cream sodas so we could get off to the nearest club not far down the street. "No running off with Tom Mix," Timi says into the girls' ears as we leave.

'At the club we looked round for who we might know. Pretty crowded with all these Yankees and Kiwis from the services. And going up to the bar, a Yankee boy on a high stool said, drawling away and not too loud, "We don't drink with no darkies here, boy."

'I put a right hook under his baby jaw and he sailed up then went down flat. Lights out. Of course his mates went for us, but a bit late by the time they figured out where the right hook came from. Timi and me already backing and sidestepping our way out. We got to find us some other place for a drink, I thought.

'But while we're doing this, this sidestepping, this getting out, all these Kiwi boys start finding themselves a Yank to bash, as if to serve them right for all their honey talk, all their chocolates and flowers, their stockings, their money, kissing girls in the street, up their skirts in shop doorways. The whole place is busting up.

'Well, I don't reckon it was me, or the slow Yankee boy that started *all* what happened that afternoon. Somehow it was just ready, and it happened. By the time we got out on Manners Street the whole place was a madhouse, Kiwis and Yanks all having a go at each other. Punch-ups all up and down the street, breaking out in side streets, in clubs and bars, civilians jumping off trams to come and join in.

'A proper riot.

'Screaming.

'People up on shop verandahs yelling and throwing things down, shop windows breaking, stuff flying through the air, all the traffic at a standstill, police running round all over the place blowing whistles, and me and Timi standing in the middle of the road laughing. We couldn't move in any direction without bumping into trouble, so we stopped there where we could watch our backs as well as our fronts. What a thing. You, Little Brother, locked away in your boarding school, mightn't have heard a thing about it. Or might-be you did. But all hush-hush you see. Nothing in the newspapers. Anyway, I bet you didn't know it was me and Timi in the middle of it all.

'So it goes on and on for hours. It seems like hours. I start thinking about our sisters, but reckon they'll be okay dancing at the cabaret with their Yankee boys. Hope so.

'Traffic is starting to move, so off we go, making our way along the footpath, through the rubbish and glass. People are still scuffling along, some being helped, some bleeding, some crying. Ha, you go off to the other side of the world to fight for your country and here they are at home trying to kill each other, ha ha. I don't reckon I started it, or that Yankee boy with his mouth, but might-be we did.

'Well we can't get through. Part of the footpath is blocked off because of glass, and the Zambucks are there trying to help. We follow the crowd down a side street to go round the block and back to the Majestic. Side streets are a mess too but we take it slow. And then we turn a corner and come across a girl sitting on a bin, blood on her clothes, shoes in her hand, heels busted off the shoes.

'It's Jess, white as white, glass in her hair and her clothes, rolling her stockings down to get bits out of her legs and feet. We stop and Timi leaves me, saying he'll go and find my sisters.

"'I need to get these splinters out," Jess said, "so I can walk home." I think how calm she is. I think what a corker girl she is. I think our brother is a fool.

'It takes a while getting the glass out so she can walk. Even then I can see walking is sore, and it's a long way home. Legs and arms all cut too.

"'I'll take you down the harbour," I said. I'm thinking of salt water, how good it will be for all those cuts and scratches. It's only a short distance.

'I help her along past the jetties to the beach. The tide is right out and it's flat calm. Jess stands in the water with her skirt tucked up and I roll the bottoms of my trousers up and help her wash her bleeding legs, pick bits from her arms, comb out her thin hair. All this is in the dark of a blackout night, in the dark of shadows that are ships and high hills. Everything is so quiet all around it could be a night in the desert without gunfire.

"'I put my hands over my face when the window came bursting out, luckily," she said. "And I happened to be on the outer edge of the footpath when it all came flying, fortunately." She's strong, I thought. I thought she was lovely.

'Up on the beach I take off my shirt and dry her with it, just careful because there could be more glass. Then I kissed her in the dark, standing on the night sand. It's what I wanted to do.

"'Your brother broke my heart," she said.

'I said, "He's a fool."

"'I don't know why I loved him," she said.

'I said, "He's a fool."

"'He never said one nice thing to me, not once. I was never good enough for him."

'I held her close. She came down on to the sand with me.

'So I just want to tell you, Little Brother, Jess was the loveliest girl. She is the loveliest girl. If anything could've kept me home after furlough it would've been her. I kept with her, stopped with her for the next six weeks until we sailed. Told nobody. Timi might've guessed, but he never let on. Ma only knew I was off round the town, some girl involved, but never guessed who.

'And Pita? No, never. I never would tell him. And the reason I never stayed home from furlough, stayed with Jess, was because of him. How could I? I now realise that our brother wasn't such a fool. I reckon he did right. He chose right, chose the one he could really love, the one who wouldn't let him get away with any of his nonsense.

'Jess's heart? Well, it would've broke sooner or later, that's what I reckon. And his heart too. But I want you to know she's the loveliest girl when you meet her again. When you see her just tell her I said she's the loveliest girl.'

But why tell all this to me? And why now? I'm not his priest, his confessor, his messenger. Why say to me, 'Tell her she's the loveliest girl,' as if I am the only one for whom there will be a tomorrow?

32

bony

The sun has dried the ground, the hills and paddocks are turning green and there are yellow fingertips creeping against the black branches of the grapevines as they come into leaf. In the valley the cherry trees are already covered in blossom and around our rest area are plenty of leafy trees providing good shelter.

It's a beautiful country we find ourselves in, and I try to imagine it unbroken and quiet, with citizens living their ordinary, day-to-day lives. So many of them are homeless now. They come round the camp cook-houses waiting all day for leftovers of food. There are children, some of them no older than five or six, walking about with buckets wanting scraps. These are the refugees who sleep in ditches and dugouts. They have nothing but the threadbare clothes that they wear. We give out food from our parcels. We give them socks and blankets then have to spin a yarn to the requisitions officers who have the headache of keeping us equipped.

Other civilians are on the roads, their carts piled high with furniture, drums, sacks, barrels and utensils. Sometimes they have money but there are no shops and nothing to spend the money on, so when we want extra cash we'll hock off our boots, clothes or other acquisitions, which people are only too pleased to buy. Again we have to account to the officers for these items lost in the course of war. Of course.

To arrive at our present site we had to come out from our zone in the dark under smoke and machine-gun fire, marching what is known as the Mad Mile before we could make it to our transport. The MM is an ugly, stinking stretch of Highway Six, strewn with burnt bodies, rotting dead men, rotting dead mules, and rusting vehicles and equipment. It has to be marched in single file. There's no other route. Enemy guns are fixed on different points along it, and every so often, whether night or day, it's heavily machine gunned. There's no view of what is coming at you from the rear and you have to keep your ears wagging and hope you have time to dive for cover if the gunning starts up. But there's no guarantee that when you make a dive you won't land on a mine anyway. If you happen along there at the wrong time you've had it. Kaput.

Now at least we've had time to get the mud off ourselves, wash our clothes and blankets and clean our boots. It took some doing. Rest is what we need as most of us are suffering from concussion, with headaches and blackouts for which some have had a spell in hospital. Others have developed nervous conditions and have been hospitalised too. Most of us are woken at night by our noisy dreams.

How good it is to have regular hot meals – not to forget the accompaniment of *vino rosso* – as well as uninterrupted, night-time sleep. Night-time sleep in a warm, clean bivvy is the best thing in the world after sleeping wet and filthy in cellars and hideouts, sometimes during the day, sometimes at night, or just whenever you have become too bandy-legged to carry on. Even though you may not have found the safest of hideouts and you think you are likely to wake up dead, you can't help it. You know you just have to go to sleep anyway.

It's a relief to be away from the continual roar of guns, though we can still hear the war going on from here, being about twenty miles inland from Cassino. At least it's far enough away to be able to block the sound out of your consciousness during your waking hours, even if you cannot keep it out of your sleep. There'll be no more war-front for us for a while as we attempt to regain some weight and condition. We looked like a pack of skeletons marching out of Cassino and could hardly recognise each other. We were all a bit mad in the head as well.

YM mobile cinema puts on a new picture every night, my favourite so far being *Ziegfield Girl* starring Hedy Lamarr. We've also seen *Rosy O'Grady* with Betty Grable, and *The Hard Way* with Ida Lupino. I like Hedy Lamarr.

We've been sight-seeing round the local area and take any opportunity to get out to the beach for a swim. I suppose the beaches would be much like home beaches if it were peace time. As it is you can hardly get to the water for wire and debris. The water itself is littered and scummy.

The bombing hasn't been so heavy in this area. Many of the homes are intact or have been repaired, and people are working their land – old people, young people and kids, hacking away at the ground just like backhome people. But at least back home there is a horse and plough. The tools they use here are quite primitive. They grow their crops, hawk their produce. Sometimes in the evenings they attend our picture shows and concerts where we take every opportunity to converse with them, practising speaking Italian. In some ways it's an easy language to pick up as the vowel sounds are close to those of our own language. Once you get used to it there's a kind of familiar flow, and plenty of expression to go with it. We practise on each other round camp. Plenty hands, plenty arms, plenty big-eyes, plenty laugh. And there's this song we've learned and can't stop singing:

Buona notte mio amore,
Buona notte mio cuore,
Sogna tutti i miei baci,
Sogna solo di me.

Buona notte mio amore
Ci vedremo domani
Per tornar più felici di qua
Buona notte mio amore

Tomorrow we go on a day's leave to Pompeii, and though this isn't my first visit, many of the boys haven't been there yet. The Rotorua boys are looking forward to it as they are reminded of their own buried village at home in Whakarewarewa. They'll be amazed at what they see. Once they've made their way through the hundreds of vendors and hawkers and carts and sale-stands they'll find themselves walking city streets on cobbled roads which are over two thousand years old. They'll see the ancient architecture, the carved marble columns, the decorated pillars and archways, and the wall-paintings depicting saints, angels and churchmen done by artists twenty centuries ago. Spooky place. They'll have a look at Cleopatra's bath, visit the arena of the gladiators and come back with their eyes sticking out just as I did.

Though I've read of the eruption of Tarawera I realise I don't know too much about the history of my own country. The history we studied at school was all to do with England and Europe, a history which has only begun to make some sense to me now that I'm here on this back-to-front side of the world. What I learned from Uncle Ju about our own tribal history is not the kind of information you would find in books, and when I get back home I'd like to visit some of the places that boys of other companies come from.

For example, these pals from Rotorua tell us about the weird behaviour of the land in their area. Well, I have heard of geysers that shoot steam into the air in this thermal region. I've seen the spouts on the newsreels at the pictures. And I've heard of the pink and white terraces made from build-ups of silica, that formed over untold time into two sparkling natural staircases which have been described as the eighth wonder of the world. But these terraces were all buried when that mountain of theirs blew its top in 1886. It blew three of its tops, if I remember correctly. Yes, three of its craters exploded and the land all around for miles was covered in mud and rock and ash, and all the villagers were buried alive.

Anyway the Rotorua boys talk of other present-day phenomena – lakes of boiling mud, hot and cold water running in streams side by side, blowholes appearing in their back yards and steam coming up through their roads and tracks and pathways. They don't need inside baths, they tell me, because they can just walk outside and get into a hot pool, choosing whatever temperature suits them by moving round it. They don't need ovens because there is natural steam and natural boiling water where they can put their pots and baskets of food to cook. I think they're pulling my leg. One day I'll see for myself.

But I'm not ready to go home yet. I want to see this war out. We'll soon be fighting fit again and will have another go at Jerry sooner or later.

Rangi hasn't been the same since Pita's death, hasn't left camp and seems to spend an unusual amount of time on his own. He watches me, has now become my father, big brother, watcher – not like himself at all. I never wanted to be a burden to either of them.

Anyway, there's plenty going on to keep us occupied. Besides the nightly picture shows there are organised concerts and sports, and the other day I lost a few lire at the donkey races organised by Twenty-third Battalion. The Kiwi Concert Party has been doing the rounds. What a show. It's the best and funniest I've ever seen. The men taking the women's parts are so good you really can't tell the difference. They have the clothes, the smooth faces, the make-up, the stockings, the high-heels, everything. They even have the voices right, whether they're speaking or singing. The whole place was in an uproar because of the very funny skits that intersperse the programme.

One of the favourite comics of the whole show is our mate Stan Wineera who we've known since he turned up at the Club socials in Wellington while he was in camp. He has large green eyes that stick out like potatoes, and an Adam's apple that moves up and down while the rest of him, including the potato eyes, is perfectly still.

Not that it's a complete comedy show. Far from it. There's beautiful singing, both modern and classical, as well as a variety of instrumental and dance items. It was a rendition of 'Ave Maria' by a female impersonator that had us all on our feet calling and cheering and clapping as if we were Italians.

When we went round to see Stan after the show all the Yankee boys were there trying to get the pants off the Kiwi blokes to make them prove they weren't really women.

Meanwhile the war goes on. There's been a general reorganisation and Eighth Army has taken over from the Kiwis on the Cassino front. The Poles are going to have another go at Monte Cassino. Everyone reckons Jerry hasn't got much fight left and that our Battalion will be back in support pretty soon, once the breakthrough has been made. *Che bella Roma*, here we come.

Since writing my last notes we've moved to a place called Colle Belvedere, taking over from Twenty-fourth Battalion to wait in reserve. From here we overlook Monte Cassino, also the abbey, with great bites taken out of its walls as if walls were biscuits. Much of the masonry has been crumbed and chewed and spat in piles. All down the hillside are the burnt, black remains of trees and vegetation, but in among the ashes are signs of green. Beyond Cassino are the layers of mountains, with Monte Cairo, above them all, still capped with snow.

This is a different view of ol' man from the one which so astounded us on our first sighting. The new perspective is one which shows that what had seemed so impossible to us then, to be possible as we see it now, though it is still a cause for wonder. We're able to see that, rather than the abbey being a building on top of a sheer cliff and covering the whole of the crown of the mountain, there is indeed some space around it – contours and pathways at the top of a winding road. Nevertheless the building of the monastery still seems an amazing feat.

Some nights ago YM set up their cinema out in one of the paddocks and we saw pictures from home of the Victoria Cross investiture at the marae in Ruatoria. The Cross was being awarded posthumously to Moana-nui-a-Kiwa Ngarimu for his outstanding actions in Tunisia. Everyone knew someone in it, the East Coast boys of C Company being the most affected by the viewing. It was their own parents, grandparents, aunties, uncles, cousins and sisters they were seeing, calling out to, waving to, shouting messages to as they saw them flick by on the screen. They had the projectionist show the reel over again in slow motion so they could have a better look at the faces of the people. It's all we talked about for the next few days, and some, especially the C Coy boys, have been pretty homesick since then.

Not long after that we had a visit from General Freyberg who gave out ribbons to those who had been awarded them. He shouted us each a pint of vino as a way of sharing his own award, which he said really belonged to our Battalion. Plenty party. Plenty singsong. Plenty act the goat.

Speaking of vino, Brother Rangi has been really hitting the plonk lately. It flows like water in these parts. *Vino rosso, vino bianco, vino a volantà.* There's Freyberg's seven hundred pints for a start, and there's a party going on somewhere all the time with everyone getting soused and noisy. The Italians are always amazed at the way we drink wine as if it were beer. Down the hatch it goes. It became so rowdy round camp that there's been a new order for lights out and silence by 2300 hours every night.

Rangi's always been a hard drinker but lately seems to have turned from a happy boozer to a sad and more frequent one. I wish he would apply to go home and take himself right away to our backhome mountain for a spell. His heart has gone out of this scrap. He could go and stay with Uncle Ju for a while and camp out in the quiet of the hills. When I think of home I think of that. But I know Rangi won't go. He'd never leave me or our cousins.

One day during my last backhome visit, while I was secretly awaiting call-up, Uncle Ju said, 'One last thing. After that, no more.'

We went out into the yard with our taiaha, practising all the moves I'd learned so far, keeping in mind that for every blow there is a parry, for every action a counteraction and if you're not first you're dead, as Uncle Ju would always remind me.

Of course I'd been 'dead' many times over the years of learning, but had seldom caught Uncle Ju out in any of the moves and actions he'd shown me. As time went by Uncle Ju stepped up the speed so that by the time I was seventeen we were exercising at a fast pace.

On this particular day, after we were well warmed up, Uncle Ju said, 'This time, after we've been through our whole series you bring your stick over and down on my head. Make it fast.'

I had done this action before but never at speed, so I was reluctant. We went through the usual routine and at the end I brought my weapon over and down towards his head, but only half-heartedly. He lifted his staff, two-handed, to counteract, then he said, 'Not like that. Fast,' even though he knew I didn't want to do it. 'Fast and as hard as you can,' he said. 'Look, you got to do it just like you want to split my head with the blade and slice me right down the middle until your taiaha hits the ground.' He could see I still didn't want to do it. 'You got to trust me,' he said.

I sat down and thought about that for a while and knew that I had to do it, had to understand what he could do and had to trust him.

We began again – the stepping, the eyeballing, the expulsion of breath; the stepping in, the blow and parry, the whirl, the thrust. And at the end, with a strong, swift movement I swept back and upward with the shaft and whacked it downwards.

Then I found myself, with the breath shunted out of me, sprawled on the ground behind him. A dead man. Or a man who in other times would be dead with the top of his head sliced off by the sharp edge of a victor's hand-club. (But if the victor thought him worthy, he might honour the man by using the man's own mere pounamu to finish him with.)

Afterwards I wanted Uncle Ju to do the same, come down on me in the same way and I would counteract. We had always changed places, swapped actions, in the past. I needed to practise this last one. But my uncle wouldn't agree to it. He said I was too light and bony to toss him up backwards over my head.

33

buono

We woke one morning and looked out from our perch on Colle Belvedere to see the Polish Sztander flying over Cassino, a proud feather in ol' man's ruined hat. There was a wonderful view of it from our position, and great excitement on seeing the flash of red flapping up against the blue sky, its white eagle flying. There was a big smile on Rangi's face, the first for some time.

'Jerry's had it,' he said. 'Running backwards.'

This seemed to be true.

The irony was that the final battle for ol' man, the mountain himself, didn't happen in the end. The months of endless fighting, the thousands of casualties, all the bleeding traffic passing through, led up to a simple enemy withdrawal to another line. Gone out the back door.

So on coming down from our position a few days later we found no opposition, no mortar raining down. There were no Jerry pockets to contend with, no houses to clear, just a free march to our pick-up place.

From there we made our way, practically unopposed, to a small village where the most difficult task facing us in getting there was finding a way across a river that was too deep to wade. But we came across a man with a boat, persuading him that we needed it for a while. He wasn't happy about loaning it to us as it was a rather fragile flat-bottomed craft, patched and home-made looking. We were not sure of it either. However it did the trick and we were able to come across eight at a time.

On our way round the mountain we came upon clusters of graves, so small that at first we thought they were the graves of children. But there were so many of them. Then we noticed the steel helmets at the head of each grave and the small boots at each end, and realised that they were the graves of the Gurkha soldiers. Many of them died on ol' man's chest after eight days and nights in cruel conditions, and when it came time to withdraw they were so beggared that they had to be pushed and hit and shoved to get them down off the mountain. That's what we heard.

Though it's not unusual to see tin hats placed on the graves of soldiers we hadn't seen boots left in that way before. To us it indicated that these men died bravely – in action, with their boots on. There are none braver than the Gurkha soldiers.

But perhaps the boots had been left there for the living to claim. Those who buried the dead would've seen, as we had, other temporary graves dug away at one end so that the boots could be removed from corpses. People need boots. Refugees are swarming down the roads in their hundreds. Many are without shoes and their feet are bleeding. They're starving and filthy and their clothes are in tatters.

Also on our way over the mountain we saw columns of trucks driven by the women of the Polish Army. They were heaped high with the bodies of the dead.

On our way into the village there were signs of hurried enemy departure. There were ammo dumps, vehicles with flat tyres that had been left behind, and at one stage, closing in on a *casa*, we found an uneaten breakfast all laid out on a table and no one in sight. Beauty. We made short work of it.

Later among the hills we were taking pot-shots at the tail end

221

of Jerry who were scooting off like rabbits. 'Run rabbit, run rabbit, run, run, run,' is the English song that the Germans made fun of our army with, playing it over their radios when New Zealand was forced to evacuate Greece. Well, we have our own version: 'Oma rapiti, oma rapiti, oma, oma, oma,' we sang. It was a dance up there on the hills getting on with the job. Brother Rangi, with a grin going halfway round the mountain, reckoned the worst was over and this was what it would be like from now on. Jerry would throw in the towel any day soon, he said.

Even the next day, with an occasional blast from field guns coming our way, there was little to bother us, and by the day's end we were able to settle into comfortable *case* for the night.

I guess it wasn't only Jerry who had made a quick departure. At some earlier time villagers had left their homes taking whatever they could with them, but were beginning to return by now.

Left behind, and making itself at home in one of the empty houses, we'd seen a large pig. We went back to look for it, bailed it up and clouted it on the head with the back of an axe before making sure of it with a bayonet. Then we took it down through the village on a stretcher covered with a bloody blanket. The villagers, believing we were carrying a dead comrade, came out of their doors crossing themselves – the men removing their caps, the women placing sprigs and flowers round the fallen. Porky tasted good.

It was on 4 June, during our time in that small village, that we heard that the Yanks had occupied Rome and that the British and the Americans had landed on the coast of France. Soon afterwards we were relieved by the cavalry and taken to comfortable quarters where the sun became warmer day by day.

Though we were still training hard we found plenty of time to relax and enjoy the warmth. Rangi was much more like his old self and I felt happy about that. General Freyberg paid us a visit and watched Maori Battalion clean up everyone at the swimming carnival.

We heard that there was still resistance in the north, but as the New Zealand Division wasn't to be involved we liked our chances of finding an easy passage through to Rome. Well, Florence actually. That's where we were all heading.

It was only a week or so before we were on the move again, a journey of fifty dusty miles of winding roads, which brought us to an area of rolling countryside amid creeks and trees. There were villages dotted all along the ridges.

Our instructions were to keep prodding the enemy in the backside as he attempted to withdraw, but though some of the other platoons met with some opposition, we came through with no bother at all. We were impressed to see our tanks working up through the gullies and trees, up and over the hills and tracks, shooting up any place where enemy soldiers could be. But it seemed as though most had vamoosed.

Not all had left however. One day there was Spandau fire coming from in among trees across the gully and we watched one of our platoons go off towards a *casa* to hunt it out. But in the next moment they were caught out as there were snipers in trees close by. There was a call of 'ka mate, ka mate' and in our boys ran with bayonets fixed, 'ka ora, ka ora,' yelling the words of the haka so loud, making such a racket that Jerry took to his scrapers. There we were on the next hillside trying to help them with the haka, but we could hardly do it for laughing.

'Ka mate, ka mate, ka ora, ka ora.' – 'Will it be death, or will it be life?'

Well it could have been either as the crazy devils ran head-on without even considering which of the two alternatives, life or death, it would be for them. But of course there wasn't much else they could do apart from surrender, and they weren't about to do that. Luckily not one of them was hit. Tin bums. They went off and cleaned out the troublesome *casa* after that, and as we came down a little later we could hear one of the boys in the house playing a piano. So we waltzed a little, sang a little on the hillside, and on our way back we discovered a couple of anti-tank guns that had been left behind in the trees.

And now? Now we find ourselves ensconced in a warm, beautiful Tuscan villa among green paddocks, fine gardens and groves of poplar trees. The people of the villages are good to us, giving out wine and flowers and handing us babies to cuddle. *Buono*. At the same time they keep an eye on their daughters. Who can blame them? Every evening at sundown every mother from every doorway, from every second-storey window and from along every narrow street, is heard calling Maria. Every girl is named Maria and every Maria is called in a different way, the tones rising and falling, the syllables lengthened and shortened in all the variable patterns: *Maree-a, Maa-ria, Mari-aa, Maaree-aa, Maa-ri-aa*. Also – *Maria Vitto-o-oria, Maria Tere-e-sa, Maria Elvi-i-ra*. We practise this.

The sun is hot, the grapes are ripe and the wine is flowing. Last night we stayed up all night drinking wine and singing Italian songs: 'Buona Notte Mio Amore', 'Sul Mare Luccica', 'Mamma', 'O Sole Mio'. Beauty. I could lap up plenty of this. This is war? Box of birds all chirping.

Buona notte.

34

tigers

So much for all that. There's more rough stuff going on and more to come. A major bite-back is taking place and we've been called up. There's a rumour the Tigers are waiting for us. So we're ready, waiting, going out to face the dreaded Tigers. Real business. It's not going to be the easy march we first thought.

Rangi has lost his good humour again, looks as though he hasn't had any sleep. Also he's been drinking too much, which is not the thing when waiting to go into battle. I hope there won't be trouble because trouble often surrounds someone like him, making him one of the most promoted and demoted soldiers in the whole army. He's a kind of lone ghost soldier, disappearing into the dark or into gunsmoke, into groves and ground or into any night or day landscape, often defying command by acting alone. But every time dispatches are read out his name is there because of extraordinary soldiering.

About camp or on leave he's not ghost-like at all, nor is he a lone man. He's as solid as mountains, without being either cold or distant. He's a man full of warmth and fun, loved by everyone. And he doesn't care or even think about the acclaims. Dispatches, medals, ribbons, stripes, mean nothing to him. Nor, I think, does his life, though he appears to take it by the scruff and enjoy every moment when not out fighting. Or did once. My cousins and I are the ones who revel in his escapades, his notoriety, his fearlessness and his reputation. I'm proud to be his brother.

But I want him to go home. There's no one in the Twenty-eighth who has served as long as he has, and only two weeks ago there was an opportunity, when the Taupo leave scheme was announced, for him to be one of those marched out. He refused to have his name in the ballot. What's wrong with him? He's taken Brother Pita's death very hard, but there's more to it than that. I don't know what's going on.

I could've told Rangi my own story of love. It is a boy's story. Of the three of us I was the first to be in love with Jess.

It was only a few days after our arrival in Wellington that I found Jess. Right from the start Wellington was a wonderful adventure to me, and no matter how much Ma and Pita tried to prevent me, I galloped about its streets and alleys, played in its jetties, inlets, parks and plantations. I visited its shops and halls and picture theatres. As I grew older I rode the buses and trams and explored the wharves and railway sidings. I went up on to the scrub-covered hills from where I could look over the whole city and the harbour, and I felt like a great adventurer. There was no one in the family who knew the city as well as I did.

In the first week, two blocks away from where we lived, I found the cake shop, being attracted to it first by the smell of baking, then by the fabulous window display. By reading the finely printed cards that were spiked into the baking by long pins, I soon learned the names and prices of the goods in the window. There were madeira cakes, caraway cakes, plain and filled sponges, marble cakes, fruit cakes and ginger cakes. These could be bought whole or by the slab. They were plain, or iced with lemon or chocolate icing, or otherwise just dusted with icing sugar.

Melting moments, louise cake, queen cakes, vanilla slices,

lamingtons, marshmallow squares, meringues, cream puffs and sponge drops were the names of the small cakes which cost a penny each. At varying prices from a ha'penny to fourpence were biscuits, buns, pies, savouries, scones and pastries and fancy loaves of bread.

Inside the shop there was Jess, and one day as I was looking in the window she saw me and smiled as she reached for a portion of caraway. She had a bright face that creased when she smiled. I remember the glint of her eyes and how pale her skin was, framed by short brown hair. Her lips were pink-lipsticked and her cheeks were rouged high up by her eyes.

The next day I stopped again at the cake shop, this time standing inside the doorway as I took in the display of goods on the shelves and cake stands. There was a three-tiered wedding cake – decorated with white lacy icing and trails of roses – on a silver stand in a tall glass-fronted cabinet.

'Hello, Handsome,' Jess said. I felt myself go red at that. It's not the sort of greeting that you can reply to, not even you as a seven-year-old boy. 'I saw you yesterday looking in the window,' she said. 'Do you live round here?'

I told her where I lived and answered all her enquiries about how long we'd been there and where we'd come from. From then on I called in to see Jess whenever I was passing, and if she wasn't too busy she would talk to me. Her Aunty Peggy also always had time for me whenever I went in, and I found that if I called in late in the day Aunty would give me a butterfly cake or a gingerbread man. They always talked to Ma too, when she called in for coffee buns or something special like that.

Of the three of us I was the first to be in love with Jess.

When I went away to boarding school I was homesick for a whole year, missing Ma and the family, friends from the Club, my friend Alec Ching and his little brother who we called Chinee Boy. But I also missed Jess and Aunty Peggy. I missed the streets of Wellington too, and the adventure that I found there among its people, its buildings, its lights and vehicles and its battling trams.

My brothers didn't know about this friendship. They left for work early in the mornings and came home after the shops were shut. They didn't know our neighbours, or the people about town, or the shopkeepers the way Ma, my sisters and I did. We didn't speak of these friendships to Brother Pita. This was years before Pita ever saw Jess.

After Jess and Pita met he was all she would talk about when I called in to the shop. She wanted to know everything about him and I'd tell her what I could. But I guess I had my loyalties. There were some aspects of our lives, and of his life, that I could speak about and some that I could not. Also there were many things about Pita's life that I didn't know, that I have only begun to understand since he and I have been on this other-way-round part of the world together. Jess asked me more than once to take messages to Pita, but I knew better than to do that.

On the night of the Centennial Exhibition, sitting beside her with her arm around me as we came down the Jack and Jill slide, I knew that I was deeply in love with her, no matter that it was my brother she was interested in. And that night as we all made our way up the hill to her house, though she didn't notice me as I walked nearby, I took in the soap and powder smell of her, watched the light on her skin as we passed beneath the street lamps. At the top of the hill, when she looked out over the whole lit-up world in those days before the blackout, I was so sorry to be leaving to go to boarding school. Tingle tingle, thump thump. They say it's fear that makes hair stand on end and hearts beat sixty to the dozen. I'd say it was love.

But never mind all that now.

We'll move at any moment to open up a fight that will shove the enemy back across the Arno River, thus breaking what is proving to be a strong thrust against us. We'll push forward to a road junction where we'll link up with Sixth Brigade, putting us on our road to Florence.

Off we go.

Maori Battalion march to glory
Take the honour of the people with you
We'll march, march, march to the enemy
We'll fight right to the end
For God, for King and for Country
Aue! Ake ake kia kaha e.

Today I'll write . . .

35

bleed

1 November 1944

Today I'll write. I'll write because it'll help me sort out what took place and how it all happened. Now that I've begun to remember, there's nothing I can do to keep half-formed recollections from making their way into my head, and nothing to prevent these scraps from gathering themselves together and becoming whole memories. It's too late to forget.

Writing will help me to sort out what sequence of events has brought me here to the hospital in Senigallia, what it is that I can bring out from the shadow of days that will help me, since there's not enough that can remain forgotten to make forgetting worthwhile.

I have to go back to the last time I was writing in my book, which was when I wrote down the boy's story of love. How long ago? Three months, four months? Too long ago to recall writing it. I see that by the time I finished it was time to leave. 'Off we go,' I wrote. We were starting out for Florence singing the Battalion song.

There are inklings now that I must pull up out of memory which will be formed into words on a page. These words will be grouped together to become sentences. These sentences will then speak to me and tell me my story.

What do I see?

I see tanks moving up. They are our own tanks. I hear the sound of mortar bombs – the grunt, the dull, jarring smash as they break apart and the fragments spray out. There are shatters of rock flying. Big guns are in my head with sounds that enter dreams.

Around me there's a stink of smoke and cordite that channel up my nose and throughout the broken bones of my face as I push these fragments on to paper, piecing the puzzle together. The pen is heavy in my hand as I attempt to keep it moving along the lines. It's too late now to forget.

I know it wasn't mortar fire that put me here, or tanks, or traps or sniper bullets.

We are starting out over a flat area among tree-cover and rows of vines, heading towards a large villa. There's a Tiger up ahead. We're on our way to locate a Tiger. We can hear it. Shells break up the ground. They skin the vines, decapitate the trees. Men fall.

As we move forward I watch my brother disappearing. He's a shadow moving ahead of me, ahead of all us, becoming smoke and trees, just as he has in the past become smoke, trees, vegetation, night, water, rock, sky, rain, rubble, walls, sunlight, snow, horizons, earth. That's him. In a moment he's gone. There's heavy fire, big guns, one of our tanks blown to pieces and blazing.

And there's something in my heart as Rangi goes off on his own but I can't find what it is now as I try to remember. I know there's something in my heart.

In smoke and trees he disappears and there's a feeling I have.

That's all.

That's all I remember, except for my name being called. I think.

Never mind, another day will do. The nurses are here with charts. They talk about me and to me, say I'm doing fine sitting up and writing in my book. I'll be up dancing in no time they say. Some sensation has returned to my damaged arm, which is good progress they tell me. I yelp when they stick me with pins, which is a good sign. These are the good things they want me to know. I can move the arm a little and it will mend in time. The physiotherapist has given me a coloured woollen ball, a large pompom, which I am to keep squeezing in order to get strength back into my hand. I try to remember to do it because she's kind. My jaw is mending and after many weeks of tubes and feeding myself through a straw I am now able to chew a little.

Doing well.

The remembering can wait for another day.

Today I'll write about a bumpy journey by stretcher from battle-ground to field ambulance, from there to the advanced dressing station, and from there to the main station. These emergency posts are no different from battlefields where men are meat. Men bleed coming in on stretchers. They're stuck pigs spilling blood from throat wounds. They're butchered cows, mortared mules, red sluicing against the sick whiteness of fragmented bone. I'm one of them, stitched and bandaged and with someone else's blood pushing through my tubes.

Yet I'm not one of them, because inside a dark place there's a story that takes away my belonging. I know the story, not because I have been able to remember everything that happened, but because of what I have been able to deduce as I lay in my hospital bed. I sit here now, pen in hand, ready and unwilling to bring the story out from there. Sounds rush through my head, my dreams, like trains. Mingled with those sounds I hear their voices.

'Te Hokowhitu-a-Tu,' I hear my brothers call, but that was long ago when I woke to ghosts on a night of blazing stars. That was the first time.

'Not tonight, not tonight,' I hear my brother tell my brother, but that was long ago too. 'We do it but not tonight,' making a promise under a backwards sky.

'Te Hokowhitu-a-Tu,' I hear my brother call again, but that was not so long ago on the day of the Tiger. That was the second time.

These buildings were once a holiday place for kids. That was long ago, once upon a time in normal days. Sometimes I hear the voices of children coming from behind white curtains, hear children stepping with bleeding footsteps along white rows.

Broken angels.

The land is covered in snow.

The hospital is situated on a large expanse of sand with the sea only a hundred yards away. Sometimes I know it is not children but the sea I hear. It's the sea that I hear whispering and stepping in my mind.

It was autumn when I arrived here, after being in the main dressing station for some weeks. The weather was still warm and people were out in the fields gathering grain as though their lives were ordinary. I saw them. They were out there working as though these were normal times. Yet there are mountains which bleed, bleeding rivers, bloody snow like markings on sheep's backs, red flowers that push themselves up out of bloodied fields. There's ruby mud. There are rusting hill-slopes, cities of garnet and ruddy angels, where men are meat that low and bellow and bray. All this I see. Blood inhabits my dreams. There are tourniquets made with gun barrels, olive boughs, arm-bones of the dead.

O what happened, what happened to olive boughs?

I know what happened to me. Once I write it I know it will be true.

The conflict in Europe is coming to a close, everyone says. They tell us that the battles have been hard and long through Florence, Fortunato, Marecchia, Orsoleto, the Uso and Rimini.

Names.

Names and places we hear and read about.

Every few weeks there is a new place, a new name. I would've been there, but who am I now that I cannot be Te Hokowhitu-a-Tu? Jaw and face bones smashed, a bullet wound, a cut from shoulder to ribs, a hole in my side like bleeding Christ.

This is what I must write, blue-black on a white page:

My brother did this to me.

Now it is written.

Rangi disappeared, waited for me, being part of smoke or a rock or tree, from where he called my name, 'Te Hokowhitu-a-Tu.' It's my name that I hear inside that dark place, my name being called. I hear it, Brother Rangi's voice calling my name. I hear my brothers' voices calling my name. Coming through gunfire, explosion, ack-ack, it's the sound of my name that I hear, their voices fluctuating, intertwining, echoing as though in tunnels. I'm wet, sweltering, breathing fast, as though running in hot rain. There's a smell of smoke and burning, of flesh, of ether and antiseptic, of fresh blood.

Here I am, running towards my name, and even though I don't remember it there's a shot that bends me, a glancing pistol shot causing me to stumble, a shot from a Luger. I know that.

'Te Hokowhitu-a-Tu.'

There's a blow to the side of my head which can only be from the butt of a swinging rifle. It lays me out. After that there's a careful removal of clothing and a careful bayonet cutting that is done exactly, sufficiently – an operation which will ensure that for me the war is ended.

Just this one time in my life, a bullet in the side and distracted by the calling of my name, I'm not quick enough to be first.

'Te Hokowhitu-a-Tu.'

This is what they chose for me, my brothers, making sure I had injuries enough to send me home or keep me in hospital until it's all over, making sure I'll never steady a rifle again. This is what they talked about on the night that they were dying and living under the upside-down moon and stars.

But 'Fight right to the end,' what about that?

They might as well have killed me.

I can't forgive them for the shame I feel at being among all these men who have been wounded in battle, who have been smashed by enemy fire while fighting for whatever belief they have, or whatever pride. Men prepared to lay down their lives.

I was one of them once, ready for whatever came to me on the field of battle – all for the honour of the people, the pride of my beloved Battalion, my own pride. I am, was, a man of my Battalion until my brothers decided to take me away from there.

Who am I now that I will never again hold a rifle, and that my brothers, not meant to be my enemies, are the reason for it? How can I ever face the people at home if they come to know these wounds were inflicted, not in battle against an enemy, but by brothers who decided I was not man enough to withstand the consequences of where I had placed myself – brothers who had made themselves my keepers.

After slicing me I know that Rangi would've bandaged me, fetched the stretcher bearers, gone with us to the field ambulance before running off again, into smoke, into trees.

Now I'm an impostor.

Being removed from my job by dishonest wounds bears heavily on me.

I have come across some men with feigned or deliberately prolonged illnesses, and some with what are probably self-inflicted injuries, and now feel I have no right to despise them. I envy the true wounds of the men around me, most of which are much worse than my own.

There are times when I envy them their deaths.

36

skin

It's months since I've written anything. My wounds have healed but I've been transferred to a medical ward because of pneumonia and hepatitis from which I'm slowly recovering. I can't eat meat, can't eat much at all. The skin hangs off me like bandages but what does it matter? What I'm afraid of is being well enough to be sent home. I don't want to go home to be treated like a hero.

It's all right here. People are kind in this place of white walls, white beds, white uniforms, white smiles, on these shores of the Adriatic.

Much of my time is spent reading. There are always plenty of books as the mobile library visits regularly. Reading intrudes on thought and takes a man away from so much self-pity. People leave me alone when I'm reading and it pleases all these nurses that I'm doing something. They're always kind, and having a conversation about a book is not too much trouble as it is a sign to them that I am coming out of myself. They tell me I'm improving and they're right about that, too. I believe reading keeps me out of the funny wards. I don't want anyone to know of the clamour that goes on in my head, the places that thought and remembering take me to, for fear of where I'll end up.

As for writing, I'm done with it. I don't know if I'll ever write here again as it's all much too self-indulgent. There's no comfort in it. Letters have arrived for me but I haven't opened them because I am unable to face their words, and though I occasionally begin a letter home I never get past the first line or two. Now I intend putting this notebook away with all the unread letters, then I'll do better. I have to do better. I have to try and take part in conversations and card pools, watch the entertainment, listen to the news, get myself up off this bed.

37

spirito

At the beginning of April I was brought down to Base Hospital after being taken by ambulance to the port in Ancona where I was loaded aboard a barge by wharf crane, stretcher and all. We were taken out and slung aboard the hospital ship, sailing off down the Adriatic Coast to Bari. Ambulances took us to Bari Base, where I remained for the rest of the month for assessment before being brought to convalesce here in Santo Spirito. I'm doing fine.

A few days after our arrival the war in Europe ended and there were all sorts of celebrations going on. I had to take it quietly because my chest is still playing up and I continue to suffer the effects of jaundice. Jaundice is the main problem. I still get the shakes, with headaches and giddiness from time to time, but mainly it's the jaundice. Every so often I'm shoved back into hospital for a spell. Apart from that nothing has stopped me getting out and about. I've made good friends here.

There were rockets going off, flares lighting the sky, and everyone was talking about boarding the ships for home, hoping they wouldn't be transferred to the war in the Pacific.

No more war for me, though I must say I'm not in a frame of mind to go home either. What I want is to return to my unit, especially now that the fighting is over, but the main problem is weight loss. I'm feeling well, in good spirits and having a pretty good time, but they won't let me go anywhere until I put on a bit of condition.

Santo Spirito is a pretty place. The headquarters, a fine two-storey building which is set among almond and olive plantations, must have been a nice family home once. The beach is just across the road and we're able to go for walks there, swim, or paddle about in little boats. The accommodation is mainly in Nissen huts, which are movable quarters made of corrugated iron, like long, closed-in tunnels with windows and vents in the front and sides. Not very impressive to look at but they make comfortable sleeping quarters at most times of the year. In summer you fry and have to get out and sleep under a tree. There are twenty beds in each. On the other side of the main building are the tents for the Jerry prisoners who do most of the work, including the cooking.

On the whole I enjoy it here. We can take up different interests such as crafts, gardening, building maintenance or motor upkeep. So I've tried my hand at carpentry, and as well as that there are always vehicles in need of repair. I like going and making a nuisance of myself among the mechanics. Apart from that I go for walks, spend time at the club or at one of the cafés, or I go off into the dunes with Lila.

Otherwise I spend many hours reading but I think I'm running out of books. We receive the papers from home – *Weekly News* and the *Freelance* and sometimes a bunch of old dailies and a few magazines. There are light duties in the kitchen from which I am exempt, and also I have not been given guard duty – considered necessary because of the *banditi* operating around these parts.

At the back of the camp is a railway going up a steep hill. The *banditi* jump on the railway trucks as the trains make their way up. They toss goods off and later jump down to collect what they've thrown out. However I haven't seen any of them round camp since I've been here.

I've had a visit from Cousin Anzac who came down with one of the transport officers, following up on a couple of vehicles that had been stolen. For the first day we sat around yarning. It was so good to see him. The next morning we went out in a dinghy. Anzac rowed me round for a while telling me all about life up in Trieste where the New Zealand battalions are encamped now. It was a warm day with just a light breeze blowing.

In the afternoon we went with a bunch of others down to the village to watch a soccer game. It was very funny, more of a fight than a game, and it ended up with the referee being chased down the street by the losing team. You couldn't see the old ref for dust. It reminded me of some of our backhome rugby matches, but backhome it's not so much the team that disputes with the ref. It's usually the onlookers, the aunties giving him hell, running on to the paddock and bashing him with their walking sticks or laying into him with their bags.

There's a good café bar in the village where you can enjoy a drink and that's where we went afterwards. Alcohol is off-limits for me but I still had a few, knowing I would suffer for it later, and we just stayed there talking, singing along with these Italians, until I remembered I was supposed to be meeting Lila. Lila's a driver and chaperone who works mainly between Base Hospital, Santo Spirito and the ports. She's one of those who looks after us when we're taken over to Bari Base to the flicks, or to see one of the shows they put on over there.

There were a few of us who started meeting, having a drink together from time to time, or going swimming. Lila would join us on her days off. She's all right, Lila. She likes fun, likes a good time and she's good-looking. Quite beautiful, really. She's someone you might think would set her sights on an officer instead of a dog-tucker, whiskerless boy like me. I was surprised one night when we all met in the club after one of the shows that she sat down beside me and began talking. I was pretty pleased when she continued to single me out. All my mates think she's a bit of all right and I think they envy me.

We talked a lot about Wellington. Lila's from Kelburn, Wellington, only two tram sections on from where our family lives. The secondary school she attended is in the street next to ours.

'Where we learned to wear hats and gloves and sit with our knees together,' she said. 'And where we walked with books on our heads to teach us deportment. We practised aour, raounded, vaowels and learned to be ladies. You would've seen us.'

Yes, we'd seen the girls every day on the footpaths, going to and from school in pairs and threes. We'd watch them as they stopped now and again to look into each other's faces, stepping into their own conversations, stepping back, baring their teeth, widening their eyes, their laughter exploding four inches behind their gloved hands. None of the girls we saw would have been Lila though, who would have left school at about the time our family arrived in Wellington when I was seven.

'No matter what the weather,' she said, 'no matter what the season, we were decked out year after year in aour heavy serge gym dresses with broad box pleats from the yoke to below the knee. Legs and feet suffered all through hot summers bagged in thick wool stockings and lace-up shoes. Our heavy, braided blazers, our gloves and big felt hats had to be worn at all times in public places, no matter how we sweltered. And we were pinned at our throats from daylight to dark in enormous, floppy, stripy bow-ties. No wonder we had scaly legs, pimples and dandruff. Tits like boxes.'

Well I was unable to imagine Lila with any of those ailments. She has beer-coloured hair with the same shine as beer but with a good soap smell. She has a clear, fair skin with quite a few freckles below her eyes, which thin out lower down on her face and can just be seen faintly beneath her make-up. Her eyes are beer-coloured too, lighter than her hair. There was nothing flaky or scaly at all that I could see. Tits, big and lifted, shaped by whatever garment it was that saddled them.

'And I'm still no lady,' she said leaning towards me, tilting her head, sparking her eyes – which all had my heart thumping round in its skinny case of ribs like a tolling clock.

My own school uniform with its wool trousers, thick socks, blazer, cap and tie was probably just as hot and uncomfortable I suppose, especially on summer days. But if I'd thought about this discomfort at all I would never have dreamt of saying so. My school uniform was more than just a uniform. It was part of a pathway, part of my mother's dream, part of The Uncle's wish, part of my brothers' and sisters' work and money, part of our family's hopes. It was the pride of everyone including the backhome grand-mothers, grandfathers, uncles and aunts and cousins.

'When we arrived in Wellington,' I said, 'I thought the railway station was our house, having the idea that when we stepped off the train we'd walk straight inside it.'

Lila laughed, throwing her head back, leaning back and swinging her chair up off its front feet until I thought she might fall backwards. I held her chair, leaned into her ear.

'We should go for a moonlight swim,' I said.

'So we should,' she said, and stood up straight away.

We peeled away from the others and Lila went out to the transport and picked up a blanket and a bottle of wine on our way down to the beach. Well, I'm prepared too, I thought, remem-bering the packet of rubbers that had been sitting hopefully in my top pocket for some time.

Taking off our shoes we walked along the shore past the pier, with the water easing round our feet until we came to the far end of the beach among the dunes. The hard, knotted roots of the dune plants protruded from slips in the sand, and the dune grass lay flat and sleek over the mounds and contours of the hillocks.

The far end of the shore is a favourite place for couples, especially on summer evenings. We put the shoes and the wine down on the sand and spread the blanket, then Lila stripped off all her clothes and walked down to the water, followed – after a slow-fingered fumbling with belt and buttons – by this naked, running-to-catch-up skeleton. We swam and splashed and laughed. Her breasts, free from garments, swooped. They scooped like big ladles. I dived, came up behind her, hands under the ladles and spronged against her backside. She took me by the hand and we went up on the beach and down on the blanket.

'You don't muck around do you?' she said when we were lying back on the blanket smoking. 'You go for the direct hit.' She laughed. But it made me think there should've been more – for example, kissing standing up like film stars, more talk, more time, more feeling.

'Aim, set, fire,' she said.

'At least I got the gumboot on,' I said.

'So you did.'

She laughed again, tossed the end of the cigarette away and rolled on to her stomach. 'Pass me another one,' she said.

I thought she meant a cigarette at first. She reached her hand into my groin, working away there and as soon as I sprouted, dressed me up, propped herself and started swinging. It was a bit of all right. Then she began laughing, spreading her arms out at her sides calling out, 'Yippee. Yippee-ay-o,' like a cowboy.

I did my utmost.

She's all right Lila, full of fun, nothing too serious in it, which is how she wants it to be. It suits me too. Nothing's permanent, even though I love her in a way. I know that it's because of Lila that I've mostly been able to leave the shaking miseries behind, even if lack of weight is still a problem.

Now here I was standing her up just because my cousin had arrived. I went off to our meeting place over an hour late with Anzac in tow, both of us drunk and singing. She wasn't there. So I knew I had probably had it with Lila.

Anzac says they were treated like kings when they entered Florence, though they had a tough job getting there. It was forty miles on foot in lousy weather and fight, fight, fight for every inch. Our cousin Manahi was shot down at the top of the hill over-looking the city, Anzac said. He was stretchered off but was dead by the time they arrived at the field dressing station.

The civilians of Florence shook their hands as they entered the city, showered them with flowers and gave gifts of fruit and wine. Tanks and vehicles were decked out with roses and people scrambled up on them to ride through the streets. For the whole of their stay they were shown great generosity, and many of the Battalion boys were billeted with families they came to love. Anzac had photographs of his 'family' which showed their house 'stuck up on the ribs of a mountain,' Anzac said. I know what he means. Villages here are often set in against the hilltops, and the narrow roads ascend in looping zigzags which have less and less width nearer the top. Seen from afar they appear, I'd agree, like a set of ribs on these ol' fella hills. There are pretty girls in this family and I think my cousin is in love. He told me that the boys are speaking Italian all the time now.

The Allied army, including the Maori Battalion, left Florence, fighting their way north, liberating the cities. It was tough every bit of the way. Real war, but they made it through and were welcomed everywhere with banners and flags and singing.

Now they're all having a great time up in Trieste, according to Anzac, with parties and dances going on all over town every night. Wine gardens are the thing, and open-air dancing. The Maori Jazz Band is very popular up there. They have piano, sax, trumpet, drums and any number of singers. Anyway, Anzac said he was pleased to leave there for a few days to have a rest from it all. Even when they're broke they manage to get themselves tanked up every night, and he said there's hardly a night without trouble in some part of town – black eyes all over the place. He also said the beaches there are covered in rubbish, including two-man Jerry submarines which were scuttled on shore by the departing enemy. There are the remains of U-boats and other vessels that have been blown up and are sticking out of the sea. You can't get into the water, he reckons, without bumping into an arm or a leg.

I really miss him now he's gone and intend asking, at my next doctor interview, if I can rejoin my Battalion. They won't send me home yet as they say I'm still not fit enough for a long sea journey. I have to build up. That's all right as far as I'm concerned, about not going home, though I have to face up to it sooner or later. For now I'd be happy to get back to my unit.

Before Anzac left he asked me, 'You still write in your book?' I remembered the book and thought it was time to get it out again as writing in it has helped me in the past.

Rangi is dead and so is Johnny. They were found together on the road to Rimini.

38

over

I've been away from my unit a year. But now that the Maori Battalion has been brought down from Trieste to Lake Trasimeno the doctor doesn't see any reason why I can't join them as long as I remain under medical supervision. Here's hoping he'll recommend it.

Anyway there's plenty to do and much to see, so I've been making the most of it. Last week we were taken on an outing to see the Grottos. They are large caves of stalactites and stalagmites which make a kind of eerie pink light in the dark caverns. I was amazed by them. I believe there are caves like these at home but I've never seen them.

From there we went round the coast for a swim in a deep river pool of beautiful clear water, which made me think of summer days in some of our backhome swimming holes. All these reminders. Am I more homesick than I want to admit? But I'm still not ready to face the home people, can't think of returning home, etc . . .

Enough of that.

There've been other enjoyable times too. The Andrews Sisters came to Bari to put on a show. We were taken over by truck to see it. The Sisters were much better in real life than on film. They played up to the Yanks who nearly went crazy every time the girls hitched their skirts above their knees. They had the Yankee boys hooting and howling and trying to scramble up on stage.

Afterwards we all went over to the Services Club for a few drinks where I had more than was good for me. Lila was there. We had a reunion.

The best night of all was when we went to see the Bari Opera Company performance of *Tosca*. The Bari Company is said to be the best in Italy, having many of Italy's finest singers. I believe it. We were escorted to our boxes – each holding ten people – where we were seated in large, comfortable chairs with a good view of the stage and audience. We were given programmes with the opera written in English for our benefit, but I found that once the performance began I didn't want to look at the programme, being just completely absorbed by what was going on.

There was a forty-piece orchestra, and the singing, the voices, somehow just get right into your insides – into your mind and into your heart. The local people love it, love their singers and their music. They stand and call and applaud and really know how to show their appreciation of their performers. I won't forget it. Came out of there floating. This is such a spooky country.

On this day, 15 August 1945, the war has come to an end. The Japs gave up much sooner than expected. Apparently it was these new bombs that did it. We had a special thanksgiving service this morning and later a special victory dinner with all the trimmings, including two bottles of beer each. Now there are preparations underway for a big celebration. We've decorated the mess with victory signs and streamers, also with bunches of condoms blown up with cigarette smoke inside so that they look like white balloons. Everyone's talking about boarding the ships for home.

There were mess parties going on all over the place and we ended up going from one to another. I ended up crook from too much celebrating so I've been in hospital for the last few days but should be out later this morning.

What happens now?

39

mosaic

Everyone's hopping mad about the decision to send all of the Maori Battalion home as one unit, especially those who were due to go home on furlough just as the war ended. No other battalion has had to do this. We've been waiting for two and a half months for a ship that has enough space to take us all. Everyone's given up dreams of having Christmas in Aotearoa, though still hoping to be away from here before winter truly sets in. Nobody knows what's happening and they're fed up. As for me I'm just happy to be home with my Battalion which I rejoined in Florence not long after it was transferred from the lake camp in Trasimeno to winter quarters here.

So we've been out and around this lovely city of Florence, taking in its architecture, its fountains, its marble and paintings and statues – and to hear its music and its singing. I've attended Mass in the Duomo.

That was with Maria Maddalena.

It's true what Anzac told me, the boys are speaking Italian much of the time now. I'm racing to keep up with them. If not speaking

Maori we speak Italian, even to each other, as though English has become a forgotten language. But as far as writing is concerned, well English is the only language I've been schooled in.

Though the weather is becoming colder, we have warm, comfortable quarters, and the New Zealand Forces Club, which has taken over the Hotel Baglioni in the city, is really top-notch. It's a beauty, helluva posh. There are bars all over the place. It has several dining rooms, each with its own crystal chandeliers, gilded mirrors, marble pillars and intricately carved furniture. The easy chairs are all upholstered in brocade and velvet.

All the walls and ceilings are carved and patterned, and in the halls are alcoves where there are marble statues done by famous sculptors of the past. You can walk out on to the roof of the Club and look down on to the large square where the main feature is a memorial of our fathers' war. Their fathers, our fathers. And seated out there you can look over the whole of Florence. How would this grand hotel look back there under our backhome mountain, I wonder. Still no match for our ol' fella mountain I guess, when you come to think of it. Am I thinking of home?

Bells ring in Florence.

People sing, and sometimes Italian musicians take the stage in the Club's music room. Otherwise there are plenty of shows on round the city, including the Kiwi Concert Party which is really popular here. There are queues a mile long every night and some of the locals have been to see it several times.

Much of what we do here centres round the Club, where we prop ourselves up on its bars, have a feed or attend the social evenings. Also the Club will arrange trips to Rome or other places as we are all rostered for four-day leaves, going off in trucks in groups of six. The Club sells tickets for concerts and shows, and there are boards advertising the dances on round town.

It was at one of the dances that I met Maddalena.

I've been once to Rome and intend going again, but it would take weeks to see Rome and the Vatican properly. What I can't get over is the wealth of the church, St Peter's being so heavy with gold and jewels and mosaics that I doubt you could pray there. This is not to mention great marble statues, some twelve feet high depicting the saints through the ages. There are statues in every piazza, every nook, every hallway. As well, there are hundreds of painted renditions of the teachings and stories of the testaments, as well as the religious tapestries. It's overwhelming really. And tiring. I went to sleep on the broken terraces of the Colosseum even though it's a place full of ghosts, and afterwards went off with the boys to find a drink as we'd all had enough of sight-seeing. In spite of the fame of all the great halls and plazas and the marvel that is the Sistine Chapel, I think I prefer strolling round the streets of Florence.

It was on the second to last day of leave in Rome that we decided to have a look through the catacombs where the early Christians used to meet secretly and hold their underground masses. We were led through the passages by an old monk carrying a candle on a pole. Our own candles, which we'd bought at the entrance, made their ten lire worth of shadow and light on all the bones, domes, jaws and teeth, ribs and toes and fingers and things that were stacked all along the way. And we found it so horrible and so extremely dreadful down there, where even a whisper echoed and vibrated, that we all felt like laughing. Couldn't help it. You'd been out on all those battlefields. You'd seen what it was like. Now you'd chosen a place like this to visit – all the more skeletons to gather into your dreams. What fools.

Anyway we were nearly through when one of the boys stuck a cigarette in a gap between the teeth of one of the poor old martyrs. A little curl of smoke went up and we couldn't hold on to laughter any longer. It was pretty noisy after that.

I bought rosaries in mosaic boxes, and statues and holy pictures blessed by the Pope, for my mother, my sisters and Ani Rose. One of our Battalion mates has a job at the Rome Club taking sight-seeing tours. He knows his way around so he took all of our little parcels of rosaries etc, put our names on sticking plaster which he stuck on to the packages, and took them round to a Swiss guard at the Vatican who would see to the blessings. I imagined His Holiness lifting a hand at a certain time each day to give a mass benediction to all these items. Some of the boys put their greenstone tiki in with the rosaries for a good old papal blessing too. Our mate went back for them the next day, then delivered them to us.

I bought garnet rings and collected holy water from a special fountain to take home and on my way out of the Vatican purchased a copy of *Il Vaticano*, a book depicting the Sistine Chapel and all the beautiful arts and constructions of Vatican City.

After two and a half days we'd had enough of walking the city and went off into the side streets looking for wine bars and girls, and hoping to find cheap restaurants. Everything's pricey in Rome.

It was at my first dance in Florence that I met Maddalena who was there with her family. There's always a surplus of men at these dances and my mates and I usually head for the bar and spend most of the night there. Anyway we'll always have a few drinks aboard before taking to the floor. I liked the look of Maddalena and the boys were egging me on. She's slightly built with muscly calves and small ankles. On that night she wore a pale green dress made of some soft stuff, and pointed shoes. When she walks or dances her back is straight and her feet point outwards. She has a light, smooth skin and black hair pulled back neat and shiny, and dark brown sleepy kind of sticking-out eyes – meaning that her eyelids come partly down over her large eyes and give them a half-shut look. She has a slow, angling neck, and long, straight, dark lashes. Her eyebrows are black and bushy, high and evenly curved. She's light and easy on the dance floor.

It was supper time by the time I asked her to dance. We didn't talk much, but during the last dance I asked about seeing her again. She said she would be at Mass on Sunday at the Duomo. I didn't think I would go there but I did, taking Anzac with me. After Mass, Maddalena's family invited us home.

I think I've fallen in love with a family. They're kind, and the food they cook suits me. It's because of Maddalena's family that I feel myself becoming stronger, because of them that I'm able to eat and add a bit of stuff to my bones. There are times when I think of remaining in Italy, in the music of Florence with my new language and new family and Maddalena. I love it here.

But I know I can't stay. I know I won't. I'm of no use to them. Once everything is over there'll be nothing to offer, not even army pay, or rations or food parcels. I'm of no good to Maddalena or her family, and of course I wouldn't be allowed to stay here anyway.

And I'm no good at love, except with someone like Lila when I know it can only be for a while. There's this feeling which inhabits me, telling me that I belong nowhere except with my Battalion. It tells me that after a time, no matter where I am, these scraggy thighs will move me on.

There are men away in the mountains, soldiers, some of them New Zealanders, who live there now. They have wives and children and work in the fields with new families. These men have been there for over two years – ex-prisoners-of-war, who escaped to the hills in the confusion that occurred at the time of the armistice. Some walked out of the gates after Italian guards left the camps and went home. Others climbed the prison fences, or cut holes in the wire, not sure whether it was true or not that Allied troops were coming to escort them out, or whether they were going to be evacuated to other prisons in Germany. There were men who jumped from trucks, or who rolled into ditches while being marched or transported to railway stations. Some threw themselves from cattle trucks and moving trains while en route.

Not all escaped to the mountains. Some found a way back to their regiments or to the coast, from where they were shipped to other countries. It was September then, still warm enough to sleep under hedges or in the fields, but many of the escapees were cared for by civilians.

Once in a while these stories come down to us, and sometimes I think of going off to live in the mountains too, but I know I can't go there. It's not a serious thought. I have nothing to offer to anyone.

Anyway I can't leave Anzac to return home without me, taking so many backhome deaths with him. He and I are the only ones left of our backhome brothers and cousins. There are all those who died in Greece and Crete and Africa before I'd even left home. Since then there have been Tama, Matey, Tipu, Choc, my brothers and Manahi. Also there's Johnny. To top it all off there would be my absence. Cousin Anzac couldn't be made responsible for taking my absence home. Besides, we are not permitted to stay here. To remain I would have to be a fugitive.

Also I would not be allowed to take the beautiful Maria Maddalena home with me – that is, if I could love her enough for that – as we have been told by our command that no permissions will be given to apply for marriage licences. Our officers have made it clear that they will not allow us to add insult to injury to the women at home – so many now without husbands or prospective husbands – by permitting us to return with Italian wives. They mean it. They say they'll lock us up before they allow that to happen. They'll throw us on board ship unconscious if they have to. Well, they're the ones who'll have to answer to the people at home, so who can blame them.

I do love Maddalena but not enough. She's beautiful and gentle. I've held her close to me, taken in her scents and her softness. We've kissed.

And that's as far as it's gone with Maddalena, which I suppose is right. She's the good kind, the serious and everlasting kind, the family kind who deserves a promise from me – a promise that I will send for her, return to her, at least write to her – but I can't give a promise. And I don't treat her well, sitting at a bar punishing my insides when I should be dancing; or arranging to meet her, but instead, making up a six to go to Rome. The worst of it is that I am not true to her, finding easy company in the streets of Rome or round the edges of camp from time to time. If only I could love her enough to make a break, jump ship and stay, or even make a promise. Or at least I could be true to her. I know I'll leave her, not only because it'll soon be time to go, but because I cannot think of a life beyond life with my Battalion, a life with men who know what it's been like.

A feeling of impermanence inhabits me.

40

artery

23 January 1946

Once the rough weather and high seas have abated we'll enter the Heads, leading us through to our final harbour. Who will I be then? And what will I write about as the *Dominion Monarch* plies back and forth waiting for the winds to die down and the seas to lighten? There's no sun. The clouds climb down. What can I write that will lighten me?

The boys are out on the decks where they've been since early morning. I was with them earlier, but the sea journey hasn't been good for me because of bouts of my stomach complaint and a return of anxiety. The rocking of the boat has churned my insides, causing me to throw up white froth. I've taken to my bunk.

Never mind. I'll write.

I'll write to occupy time. I'll write to keep fear and madness out of my heart. Writing will settle me, then I'll rejoin my friends. Maybe there are words that I can find that will help me untangle the jumble of questions and contradictions to do with my experiences of the past two and a half years.

Am I sorry that I went?

What I know for certain about the days leading up to my enlistment is that I could not have not enlisted, could not have not gone to war. There was no other choice for me, no other choice in the heart of me, in my Tuboy heart.

I understood when the war began that the Battalion was where I belonged, when, as a fourteen-year-old at the Centennial Exhibition, I watched the soldiers march in, this pride of the people with their buttons, bayonets, boots and faces shining. They were lauded and applauded by hundreds as they formed their guard of honour and I knew that was where I belonged from that moment.

It's where I belong now.

They are me. I am them.

For a boy living away from his mountain, they were his new mountain, and just as my mountain was part of me and I part of my mountain, this gleaming Battalion was part of me, I part of it. On the day the Exhibition opened the Battalion became another home-place and I waited for the time when schooling would be done, the boy's things over with, and I would become a man of the Battalion. It's what I prayed for. I promised God that when the soldiering was over I'd do whatever my family expected of me, take up any role in life that was laid out for me. I meant it at the time.

On the day that Rangi left on the *Aquitania* when I was fourteen, and I looked across the water and heard men singing, I felt myself there with them, aware that some on board were not much older than me. In my dreams was a silver ship, sailing away to adventure somewhere in the world. There was a Battalion of men and I was among them. They were our pride and I belonged there with these kin, these comrades, some of them men from our Club who had always looked upon me as a favoured young brother.

After the departure of the Battalion we held our breaths, waited for news.

Some must have waited in dread, for announcements of loss

and death. In my eagerness I waited for word of triumph and glory.

It came.

From the time of the first reports coming from Mt Olympus where the Battalion forced an enemy withdrawal, how tall we stood in our race, how proud we were. This Battalion was us. We were it. Soon we were to hear of actions against paratroopers around the Platanias River, the attack against the enemy-held aerodrome in Maleme, the routing of enemy at bayonet point in Suda Bay. We learned of the taking of Schollum Barracks, the siege of Halfaya Pass, bravery at Fort Musaid, the ambush at Menastir, action at Tobruk, the rout at Gazala, the breakout at Minqar Qaim. It stirred us. It stirred me.

Then there was Alamein, El Mrier, Munassib, Miteiriya Ridge. Above all were the stories of hand-to-hand fighting in the struggle for Point 209, the attacks and counter-attacks for the rocky hilltops at Tebaga Gap, and the skill and daring at Takrouna.

Olympus, Platanias, Maleme, Halfaya, Musaid, Tobruk, Menastir, Gazala, El Alamein, Tebaga, Takrouna. These names were on our lips, in our hearts, as we listened to news reports, or heard the stories told by friends who had been invalided home. So in my mind there was never a question of not going to war, even though I knew so little of its causes, so little of what it was really about, so little of what men are capable of doing to one another.

While the reason I joined my Battalion was because I saw it as a home-place, I know that others joined for different reasons. Some joined for a coat and a pair of boots, for food, army pay, and so as not to be another mouth to feed at a time when there was no work, no money for them. There were some who had been ordered by elders to go, some giving up their schooling to be part of this 'pride', this new Battalion off to show itself to the world. There were those who were running away from monotony, who were off to see the world, off on the biggest adventure of their lives. Others had absconded from marriages or difficult family situations, or from trouble with the law.

But for all of us there was a desire to belong to something, be part of what was going on, perhaps be important and smart in a uniform, or to have excitement and to test ourselves. It was for comradeship too, very much for that, but also I came to know it truly was for 'the honour of the people'. I understand that now.

The sea is still cranking though the wind has died down. The mist is low as our ship staggers into the last artery. This artery will spill us into the grey harbour under the ash skies of home. On the wharf, a short time from now, there'll be ceremonies that bring us home and release us from war, ritual incantations that take us out from under the mantle of Tumatauenga, god of war.

Who will I be then?

There will be weeping and farewell and prayer for the spirits of the dead who we carry home with us, and further ceremonies, in the days to come, on our own backhome marae after our Battalion has been disbanded.

In half an hour we berth. My Battalion is my home, but soon it will no longer officially exist.

Who will I be then?

I'm not ready to arrive, or to be any place in particular. I have no wish to be welcomed as a hero.

Footsteps pound the decks and stairways. The voices are loud and the laughter is joyful. I look for joy as my heart rocks, my hand trembles, my insides lurch.

I have not enlightened myself very much about recent experience. War is not for untangling, not by this little soldier anyway. All I know is that it would be too easy now to say I shouldn't have gone, that we shouldn't have gone, that it wasn't our war, that there should never have been a Maori Battalion.

The ship thrusts, the tourniquet is loosed and we spill through this artery into the turning harbour. Anzac has come for me. The boys are up on the high decks, he says. Some have climbed the stacks and funnels, and as the boat shuttles towards the docks they are singing our Battalion song. Traffic lines the hills and shores of Wellington as people converge to welcome us. I have to put this away, have to leave it now. I come out from behind white paper, remembering that in Santo Spirito and Florence I was well enough. I'll be well again. I'm going to join my friends, climb to a high place and sing:

Maori Battalion march to victory
Maori Battalion staunch and true
Maori Battalion march to glory
Take the honour of the people with you
We'll march, march, march to the enemy
We'll fight right to the end
For God, for King and for Country
Aue! Ake, ake, kia kaha e.

There was a war. I had to go. It's over. I'm glad I went.

41

remnants

We were the eight hundred, the remainder, as we marched the short distance from our place of disembarkation to Aotea Quay where the crowd waited. I was one in our midst. But what I remember experiencing on that day is a floating sensation, a distinct feeling of being above as well as outside of myself, a watcher, looking down on everything that was taking place. I had emptied my gut into the ocean and hadn't eaten since then, so maybe it was the emptiness in my stomach that was making me so light. The seagulls swirled about in the wind, rising to sit on the ledges of the waterside buildings before reeling out again. Perhaps my bones had hollowed and lightened like the bones of birds. This crossed my mind.

As we neared the gates the crowd stood silent and I could hear the pipping and piping, the raucous breath expulsions, the huffs and coughs and exertions of the challenger coming to meet us across the wharf yard with his taiaha. I could hear the rattle of the piupiu that he wore as he danced forward, hear the slapping of a hand against flesh.

The taiaha that he held switched from end to end, swept from one side to the other. He extended it forward, drew it back. It leapt and spun. I could see the man's facial expressions, the wide-open eyes which rolled, stared, glared, switched from side to side. His tongue flicked like the tongue of a lizard with spittle flying – but sometimes his tongue elongated, dropping from the back of his throat, down and over his chin. The extent of these facial exertions showed in the corded sinews of his neck.

He was an old man, a big man, a master of the art of taiaha, who reminded me of my Uncle Ju as he came forward on the balls of his bare feet in prancing steps – long steps, short steps, steps that sometimes did not bring him forward at all but were quick patterings, hammerings on the ground. His calf muscles bulged and the sinews from his ankles elongated, tensing the rounded muscles of his big frame.

The taiaha itself was an impressive piece. Unlike the scraped sticks that I learned these martial arts with on the backhome hillsides with my uncle, this was an old, carved piece similar to the one on Uncle Ju's wall, being extra long in the shaft and darkened by time and polishing. Though I couldn't make out the details of carving on it, I could see the inlays of paua shell glimmering in the dull light, the white flashing of feathers as the challenger twirled it or swept it in large semi-circles before him. Or as he clutched it, two-handed and upright against this or that shoulder, thrusting and threatening before finally and slowly, with grimace and expulsion of breath, and while not moving his eyes from the face of our leader, he took the dart from his waistband and placed it on the ground as we halted at the gateway.

The calls that brought us forward were coming from the crowd from all directions – from the old women of all the tribes as we made our way in. They were calling the ancestors to accompany the spirits of the dead, as we, the men of Tumatauenga, bore these deaths home to them. On and on, on and on went the karanga, coming from every corner as we made our way to the seating that had been prepared for us. All around was the calling and crying, the keening and wailing, and the pouring forth of sorrow for the faces not among us. I felt the weight of it, somehow the guilt, and as the grieving continued I thought I would have preferred to be in the place of my brothers rather than to be the one returning without them.

Following this time of lamentation were the ceremonies, prayer and incantation that freed us from the tapu of war and brought us out from under the mantle of Tumatauenga, handing the men of the Maori Battalion back to the people. There were speeches and songs. There were action songs and haka by costumed groups that had come from all over the country, foremost being performances by our own Ngati Poneke Club, their voices as fine as ever.

Of course the ceremonies had to be completed before we were free to go to our families, but from where I sat I could see Ma and my sisters, uncles, aunts and relatives, there with the Club members. Sitting barefoot on the ground in front of the concert group with their taiaha, wearing dark clothes and bands of green leaves on their heads, their faces painted with the marks of mourning, were the old women. Among them, sometimes in the arms of my sisters, sometimes playing, sitting, toddling about among relatives and friends, or scrambling in and out of a pushchair, were two little children. I didn't know who they were.

Even as I write I realise there is something I don't yet understand about the two children.

When it was time Anzac urged me to my feet and we went together, the remnants, to greet the family, and during all of this I had the feeling, not only of being somehow above the ground, but also that I walked forward in someone else's shoes.

My sisters came hurrying out of the concert lines, putting jackets on over their Club costumes and picking up one each of the children as they came to wait with Ma and the others. The children were presented to me as Pita's children, Benedict and Rimini, but I had known only of Benedict. I looked about for Ani Rose.

Sorrow had entered my sisters. Sadness was what emanated from their laughter and their eyes, but what I can say about seeing Ma that day, walking towards her as the returning runaway, was that I was struck by her beauty – her brown glowing skin, her eyes of dark sharp light, her full figure, hair folding back from her face like layered black leaves.

There was a feast set out for us in one of the wharf sheds. Here were all the foods we'd dreamed of while sitting in rain-filled hideouts and snowed-in bivvies. Now, though I was unable to find real appetite, I was able to eat enough to ground me, stick me to the seat and keep my bones together. I could laugh, join in the singing that went on as we feasted, and I began to think that it was good to be home after all.

Later that day we had to say goodbye to our Battalion mates as they boarded the trains and boats for different destinations. Those from our region stayed and boarded a bus the next morning. We were returning to all our different home marae to repeat the mourning and welcome ceremonies with those who were waiting for us in our backhome places.

Though I had no desire to go backhome to be treated like a hero, I understood what a breach it would be not to go. I had no desire to stay in Wellington either, or to be in any place in particular.

It was on the bus journey that I received a hint of the reason there were two children of similar age, supposedly belonging to Pita, but I asked no questions knowing that some of the answers would be in the letters I had never read while I was away.

If I'd read the letters on receiving them I would've known in advance that one day Jess had come knocking on Ma's door bringing a nine-month-old granddaughter who Ma knew nothing of until that day. She was Pita's daughter, according to the letter from Ma. There was no mention of Brother Rangi. I don't understand Ma's reason for allowing everyone to believe Pita is father to both children, unless it is because she wants the children to think of themselves as true brother and sister. I don't think so. Ma is only ever interested in the truth. So there's no good reason that I can think of, but if that's the way she wants it then my own lips must stay sealed. Perhaps one day there'll be an explanation.

If I'd read the letters at the time of receiving them I would've known, prior to arriving home, that Ani Rose had been taken into a tuberculosis ward in Wellington Hospital, leaving her baby to be cared for by Ma and my sisters. Having read I would have guessed that like many others who died in the tuberculosis ward Ani Rose would never come home from there.

There were four buses and several cars in our convoy of people who had come down from our region to take part in the wharf ceremonies. There were also relatives now living in Wellington wanting to accompany us. It was a hard time bearing all that death homeward, and the days, though so recent, distort in memory, congealing into sounds of wailing and weeping, a line of smiling photographs of the dead, mortar fire and bomb blast, ground exploding, dreams of white ships. But never mind.

Of the men of my generation there were none there to greet us at our home-place. That's all I have to say about that.

After all the formalities and the greeting and feasting there were enough kegs of beer rolled in to keep a party going for three days. I was glad of this, even though drinking made me ill and laid me low for a long time afterwards.

Anzac and I stayed on for two months under our everlasting mountain, but there was no work and we didn't want to be a burden on the home people. They were so few by then, many having died or moved away in search of work. We returned to Wellington.

My cousin has gone to live with an aunt in Kilbirnie while I remain here at Ma's, hiding behind my book and pen.

I know I can't stay here.

Since this finds me on the last page of my last notebook, this will be all. I'll shove the books away somewhere with the stack of letters. As yet I am unable to burn them but one day I will. In the meantime they can be the private mementoes of this twenty-year-old soldier of the Maori Battalion, home from war. His other inheritances are: a hotch-potch of memories, a few scars, some reconstituted teeth and a mended jaw, a gammy arm that is good enough to get by with, a troublesome stomach, exploding dreams, sometime tremors, and a kind of madness in his heart and legs that won't allow him to be still.

That's all.

Te Hokowhitu-a-Tu
13 March 1946

Dear Benedict and Rimini,

Dear Benedict and Rimini,

I know how useless I've been, but never mind all that now. I hope the diaries have helped you find the information and understanding you were seeking. I write this letter in addition, as there are thoughts that I've had since rereading the notebooks that I need to add. Maybe it will further illustrate my brothers' lives and answer some unanswered questions. Also there's a plea that I must make.

From believing that your relationship to each other is half-brother and half-sister, you've now discovered that you are cousins. Since rereading I've puzzled again over Ma's reasons for keeping this knowledge to herself, but have now come to the conclusion that Ma doesn't know, never did know, that Pita is not father to both of you. I believe that the information will be as much a revelation to her as it must be to you. The reason she doesn't know can only be because Jess didn't tell her.

I don't know Jess's reasons for secrecy. All I can do is think about how unhappy and desperate she must have been at the time, having been turned away by her family, with nowhere to live and no way of supporting herself and her child.

It could simply be that Jess came, bringing Ma's grandchild, that there were no questions asked and that she allowed assumptions to remain. It's possible there wasn't a word spoken, Jess simply handing over her baby and hurrying away. Ma would have taken her grandchild unconditionally anyway. The more I think about it, the more it becomes obvious to me that Ma didn't know about Rangi and Jess. If she had known she would never have kept the information from Ani Rose. I can't think what it was like for Ani Rose when Jess came with 'Pita's baby', this baby being just three weeks older than her own. What was it like for Ani Rose?

In one of the letters I read after I came home I learned that Jess married an American and went to the States to live. Maybe you hear from her, or perhaps she has disappeared from your lives completely. Try not to blame her as there are always reasons for what people do. The message that I was once given to pass on to her, I now pass on to you, Rimini, and to both of you. Just think of her, Jess, as the loveliest girl. It's true. She was beautiful, bright, warm and generous. But what can we know about the state of mind that led to her decisions?

The facts are that Pita was in camp during the time Rangi was home, but as far as Ma, or anyone else knew, Pita could still have been seeing Jess when home on leave. Maybe I'm the only one who came to know this wasn't so.

It wasn't until a few weeks before Pita went off overseas that he wrote to Ani Rose and asked her to wait for him and marry him on his return. Ani Rose, who felt she'd waited long enough already, wrote back and said she wanted the wedding to take place before he left, and with one week to go before departure they were married.

It's probably neither useful nor enlightening to go into any of the details of what went on for the next few years of my life after we came home, but I do feel a need to attempt to explain my disappearance from your lives, despite Ma's strong desire that I should be part of it.

Right from the beginning I realised I couldn't stay with Ma and all of you in the house of heroes, with its photographs, its medals, its shrines and, most of all, its expectations. Though not wanting to make you my confessors it's enough to say I found myself in pubs and clubs most of the time, drunk or recovering. I knew I was no good to anyone and didn't want to upset a peaceful household with my drunkenness, or to allow others to suffer the consequences of a choice I had made. I'd rather be dead than do that. I moved on.

Moving on was what I did for the next couple of years, staying in one place for a while before going off again. These places that I moved to were small towns, sometimes cities, where I caught up with Battalion pals. These were men whose eyes I could look into and find understanding, where I could detect a kind of knowing reflected back to me. We could laugh and sing and yarn without too much picking over the bones of war, yet war was something that stood among us, recognisable. Also, these were the men who understood how misshapen we had become, and how unable most of us were to manoeuvre back into places where we had once belonged. This had become our belonging now, with each other.

Wherever I went I found work – on wharves, in factories, in forests, on farms, but always temporary. Also from time to time I had spells in hospital because of recurrences of my interior condition, these flare-ups being self inflicted of course, always a result of hard living. Never mind. Apart from having itchy feet and jittery legs, moving on was often precipitated by love, or fear of love, or a fear of not being able to offer enough to love.

Perhaps you remember Doreen who I brought with me when I came home to Uncle Ju's funeral? I remember you well, beautiful ten year olds, fussed over by everyone, though rather shy of this uncle who had refused to be part of your lives.

Doreen certainly met with family approval. I watched Ma, my sisters, my aunts and cousins pin their hopes on her over those days of the tangihanga – that is, their hopes that I would find happiness, settle down, take my place in family life.

Before Doreen there were others. I walked out on everyone of them, no good to anybody. There was just no place for me, or I couldn't find it except in Returned Services clubrooms.

I treated Doreen badly, being unable to suffer four walls, or walls of any kind. And just by way of explanation as to where you found me when we next met four years on from there, I'll tell you this. One morning I woke up, sick and stinking, on the kitchen floor with blood up my arm, broken glass scattered and a hole in the wall.

I wanted to be dead.

I went out on to the footpaths where I walked for the rest of the morning. In the afternoon I caught a train and took myself off to the lunatic asylum not knowing what else to do.

They wouldn't take me in at first, until I began ranting. Then they took me in a headlock and dumped me in the lockup. It was a relief. That got rid of me for a while.

Since I'd been living away from Wellington for some years by then, and had only rare contact with the family, it was some months before Ma and my sisters knew where I had put myself. I wrote to Doreen and left it at that. From Doreen my mates found out where I was and it was through them that Ma came to know.

You were fourteen when you came with your grandmother and aunts to visit me.

Seeing you startled me.

I don't remember Pita and Rangi as fourteen year olds because I was only three or four when they were that age. I remember them only as men. But you, Benedict, at fourteen, were already holding on your shoulders Pita's man's head, having the same wide forehead and cheekbones, the same thick, black hair that needed no oiling to keep it sculpted back. There was a dark clarity to Pita, a lustre. His face, his black eyes and dark skin drew light towards them in a way that stopped you. From love? From fear? I don't know which. A glow, or a glower? But perhaps I'm inventing feelings now that he's gone. Perhaps I've become closer to him since his death. Perhaps writing down his stories and rereading them has made it easier to know or invent him.

And Rimini, you are so like Rangi in looks and build, having a similar long-legged, rangy stature, the same brown skin, crinkly black hair and changeable eyes. They are eyes that can be brown, amber, yellow, khaki, green or any mixture of any of those. These are looks that he (and I) inherited from our father, so we're told. That inheritance includes our father's laugh, his smile, his mannerisms. So we're told. But our father, as I remember him, was a fat, pale, clammy man with broken and discoloured teeth who we did not see laugh or smile, even though the soldier photo shows him differently. I do remember occasions when he spoke to me gently and touched my head.

I wasn't greatly insane compared to those I observed in this place where I'd put myself, but knew I was better off there. Those who loved me were better off with me out of the way. If I wanted to beat on walls there were walls there that I could beat on. Any shouting that I did was easily drowned out by the noise of others. My shakes, my blues, my raving dreams were mine and mine alone.

Anyway once I stopped boozing the ranting simmered down, though the dark places remained. Every so often I fell into them. But too bad about that. Too bad. I had put myself in a war, in a place, in a time. There had to be a legacy.

What I liked about my new place of residence was that no one took much notice of me at all. I was just someone in a corner reading a book, someone at a table eating, or someone making himself useful from time to time, in corridors and gardens. There were times when I made a mild nuisance of myself, but not enough to be questioned, examined or treated in any way. Thank God for that, that I had no treatment. The so-called cures that I observed were many times worse than being struck down by madness.

On the day you came Ma intended signing me out, but I was unwilling to leave there at the time.

Afraid?

Yes.

I laugh now, having read through the notebooks, regarding my boy's impressions of what it would be like to be scared, and of the ideas that I had of fear being simply a physical thing. What interested me then was knowing, I suppose *wanting* to experience this thing called fear. Even terror. However I've discovered terror to be a lonely and awful state, little to do with the day-to-day business of war as far as I'm concerned.

At the time of your visit I'd already been thinking about getting out of the looney bin and living alone somewhere, perhaps working a piece of land. Having you come that day encouraged those thoughts. You'll remember that Moana brought Kapa to meet me. Their wedding was planned for January, three months away. Great excitement, since there hadn't been a wedding in the family since Pita and Ani Rose were married. Though I was not ready to come with you at the time, I promised I'd be at the wedding to present the bride, in the absence of The Uncle who had recently died.

I kept my promise and made it to the wedding, even managed to make it through that short time, in sobriety. Afterwards I came here to our backhome place under our mountain, where no one lived any more.

Uncle Ju's and Aunty Janey's place was the strongest and least dilapidated of the houses, so I found boards and sheets of iron from our other broken down homes and made the old place watertight and comfortable. Under our mountain is where I like to be, far enough back under his folding and unfolding brow to make me feel at home. Being here has enabled my wobbly legs to settle down.

So I'm all right here with my few sheep, old Ju's dry stock and this year's weaner brought down from the hills to feed up on scraps and garden leftovers. I'm okay here, out of everyone's way, growing my spuds and puha.

It's not that I want to give the idea that I'm a complete isolate. I have the reputation of being somewhat of a hermit, because of living off the beaten track and mostly alone, though once or twice a year Bootleg comes to stay. His wife Chrissy brings him here and leaves him for a couple of weeks at a time. Glad of a break from him I'd say, though she's a good sort, reckons she always wanted a man who couldn't run away.

If this all sounds like an old man's existence, then I suppose it is, but it's all right.

Saturdays find me seeking out mates at the clubs and snooker parlours, downing a few whiskies and jawing the night away. Can't take too many whiskies without ending up a cot-case, so these days I'm just killing myself slowly instead of all in one hit, ha ha.

I have an old truck that I won in a snooker game from an old fellow called Brimstone, who was the local champ but short of a stake. Yes, my lame arm has become strong enough to be able to steady a billiard cue. My hands have lost their shakes, enabling me to line up a few good shots. Old Brimmy put up his truck and I beat him for it. We had to go and drag it out of his paddock where it was up to its middle in grass and thistles, a broken-down wreck.

But I patched it up, tinkered with it and got it breathing.

So this is where you found me, along with my coal range and lamps and stack of firewood; my animals, my garden, my houseful of books and my views on life.

Here I am, living the life of an old man whose wife may have died, whose children could have left home and whose family could have cut him off, refusing to visit him any more; the life of an old man who lives on boiled sheep guts, fish heads, puha and cabbage – which is food for an old toothless one with a dicey stomach.

The difference between me and the old man I describe is that I have never had a wife, have never wanted children, and it has been my own choice to keep distant from my family.

The difference is that I have a full set of teeth, some natural, some made for me by a careful dentist in Santo Spirito.

The difference is that I am thirty-eight – not seventy-eight, or sixty-eight or even fifty-eight.

The stomach? It's still dicey.

You and Bootleg are not the only ones who have visited me. This is where *they* find me, the nosy parkers with their notepads and pencils. They come in search of war stories, or material for their Anzac Day rags. Gory detail is what they're after. They get sooled on to me by mates who credit me with having the gift of the gab and a tendency to analyse.

These busybodies have heard from somewhere that during my time away I wrote in books. It's been said that I wrote while in dugouts and trenches with bullets flying overhead, in sewers and drains, hidden in vineyards while the vegetation was being strafed six inches above our heads, guts-up in mud, in night trenches in the snow. It's all a load of rubbish.

I wrote mainly during rest times, during waiting times, or in guarded *case*. I wrote in hospitals and on board ships. I wrote when I felt like being alone.

The stickybeaks ask me for the notebooks. I send them packing, tell them I threw the books overboard in the Tory Channel on the way home – an old man's grumpiness.

Benedict and Rimini, how abandoned you have been so far, in your young lives. We think that when we see children looking well and cared for, that they are protected from all the raw deals.

And speaking of abandonment, I know now that in Southern Italy, in and around Orsogna and Cassino, the New Zealand Army, and all our battalions, took part in the most stupid and meaningless sector of the whole business. That's my opinion. We were left in mid-winter with not enough of anything to do the jobs we were sent to do, abandoned on roads and snowbound ridges, on railways, in mud and on mountainsides and in the mess of a town. It wasn't until our whole force was fought to a standstill, after all this experimenting was over, that the real plan was formulated, which would take the Allied Army beyond Cassino to final victory.

This *real* plan, which was carried out two months after New Zealand Corps had been withdrawn, was the one which would have a chance of success, being the one with enough of everything, the one that would take place at a favourable time of the year in suitable dry weather. It was the plan where help from the air was forthcoming and the one that was able to make a way through for tanks. It was the one with enough armour and enough surprise factor to set the enemy back. It was the one that was able to put enough soldiers on the ground in order to sustain a three to one loss of life, as this had to be a war of attrition.

Okay. This is my soapbox rant. This is the box that I get up on when I have more than a few whiskies aboard. It's the rant my mates are sick of hearing and when I start on it they try to shut me down by pouring enough booze in me to put me out and under the table. They usually succeed.

I think too much, read too much, don't drink enough or sing enough is what my pals reckon. But the more I read and discuss, and the more I now discover, the more I understand how ad hoc our battles round Cassino were, how ill-conceived, and how much to do with the whim and fancy and desiderata of politicians – as well as the blundering, indecision, failure and ego of high command. I want you to know how futile I think it was. There they all were, playing marbles. We were their little glassies, stinkies, steelies, bottlies and bully-taw.

I want you to know because I have a plea to make.

Weather, moonlight, lattices of mines were readily accepted as reasons for defeat at the time. We, the little popgun soldiers out on our arses, were reconciled to blaming fates and misfortune on so much death and destruction, but the laugh was on us, truly.

I remember the uncle-from-parliament saying at the time the Battalion was formed that once the brown man had fought in the white man's war, maybe then he'd be deemed equal. All up and down the country similar views and sentiments were being expressed among those who thought about such matters, and I know the different tribes were offering their sons, encouraging them to enlist, even demanding that their youth be part of this new Battalion which would show the world who we were and what we could do, what heights we could reach.

That was what was in the air at the time, and in the hearts, though I heard all of this with only half an ear because these were not the young man's reasons, not the Tuboy reasons for soldiering.

It was being said too that war was part of our inheritance, part of our history, and that because of this we must have some kind of inborn aptitude. Here was an opportunity to show this special ability to the world.

It was being said that this was the opportunity to demonstrate pride of race. The pride, the hopes of the people, were pinned on this Battalion of volunteers. The spirits of the people, the whole of Maoridom would be uplifted, or not, according to the performance of this new force. It was not to do with Hitler, though Hitara features in songs composed at the time, 'Hitara sugar mouth, obstinate man' or 'Purari Hitara e tangata hao' and others. You probably know them.

These matters were not only being talked about but were the subject of articles, letters and reports which I've only read recently. They're all about being true citizens, being equal, proving worth, having a prideful place. It was nothing to do with God and King, and we were too far away for it to really be about our country.

Freedom was what was being talked about, loud, loud, with a sound like banging on mess tins. But if reasons were to do with freedom, the freedom we meant was our own freedom, the freedom and status of the people.

Our citizenship.

It was our citizenship that was discussed by our elders, by Maori politicians, by Maori in authority in the cities or back in our home-places, round the gatherings of the time. There was a sense that if the Battalion didn't do well our people would die, would be shamed to death and not be worthy of a good life. That's how it was. We would be doomed, scrapwood, unable to be citizens in our own land.

But now the question being asked is, was the price too high, this price of citizenship of which our elders spoke? It's the price that has left our small nation beheaded, disabled, debilitated. That's what they're saying now. I want you to know this.

Well, Niece and Nephew, a charge without delivery of goods? A price without gain, or with minus return? Of course it was too high. It was too high. We took full part in a war but haven't yet been able to take full part in peace.

On the way down the gangway after the berthing of the *Dominion Monarch*, just as the last of our Battalion disembarked, a voice drifted down to us from up on deck, 'Back to the pa now boys?' it called – which I think about sums it up: Now that you're home, know your place Maori boy. Yet during our time away the other Kiwi battalions had been more than pleased to have us at their side. These things were quickly forgotten.

And now that's enough.

The trouble with being alone so much and doing so much reading and thinking, is that there's a great mountain of stuff being absorbed that eventually bogs up the head. There it remains, this build-up of sludge, until your brain begins to sicken from a chronic type of constipation. The moment you get hold of someone's ear the muck begins to loosen and splash out all over the place in skittery diarrhoea.

That'll do. But I want you to know.

I want you to know also that I forgave my brothers years ago. They had no choice but to do what they did. The moment that Big Brother shifted his eyes upwards from the spot that makes a man not a man, the moment Pita raised his eyes beyond the Hun kid's furry chin and looked into blue eyes, was the moment the thought came into his heart. And that was the moment the war ended for me. There wasn't a choice. Pita and Rangi could not do for an enemy soldier what they would not do for their brother. They could not do for a German mother what they would not do for Ma.

There's a letter, handed to me by Ma on my return. It was found among Rangi's belongings and addressed to me. I put it away at the time, being unable to face my brother's apologies or his reasons for what he'd done. I'd forgotten about the letter until I dug it out along with the notebooks.

Apologies and reasons? Why, knowing Rangi, would I believe he would offer them?

Dearest Brother,
If this is found with my things it means I'm a goner, pushing up weeds in someone else's country. Anyhow, all I want to say is we think you are a number one soldier. This is one of the things Pita and I talked about when he was dying in Cassino, so I tell you from our hearts we are proud that you are our brother.

Give our love to Ma and our sisters and everyone.

Rangi

Now, Benedict and Rimini, this is what I want to say to you: Please know how precious you are. Sister Sophie has never married or had children. Moana and Kapa are childless. I've had no wish to have children for fear I'll desert them.

You are the only ones.

Benedict and Rimini you are the only ones. We're lucky to have you. We went to war for boys' or men's reasons, Pita, Rangi and I. It would've been the end of all of us if it weren't for the existence of the two of you. It would have been the end of all of us if it hadn't been for speaking – if a Yankee boy on a bar stool had kept his slow mouth shut and if Ani Rose hadn't said she would wait no longer. Spoken for. People spoke for you. There's more than just coincidence.

So I ask one thing because there'll be other wars. It's my plea. I ask you not to follow in our footsteps, your fathers' and mine. That's all I'll ever ask.

If you agree I'll know there's a reason why I am alive, and even if it did not need words from me to persuade you, just knowing that I have lived to speak becomes worthwhile. Having kept the stories, which tell of your fathers, and having lived long enough to hand them over to you, I am now able to feel that I may not be an entirely useless piece of rubbish taking up space on the planet.

If you agree there are things to do.

And I believe you will agree because of what I saw in you when you came. I saw Ma in you. Also you made it clear it was not soldiering that interested you. In having this belief I can't tell you how happy I am to be alive now that I can see reasons for it.

I want to take you to Italy. Part of you lies there. If you accept, we'll make a journey – the two of you, Ma, your aunts, Anzac and me. There'll be others who will want to come. There are your fathers' graves to visit. There are graves of uncles and cousins. There are places to go to, people to meet, music to listen to. It's a beautiful country, old and eerie. You'll find we haven't been forgotten there in Cassino, Santo Spirito, Tuscany, Florence, Trasimeno, Rimini, all of those places – and not just because we stole the villagers' pigs and chickens.

There is a way for it to happen too. All I have to do is sell the herd. They're Uncle Ju's dry stock, which were poor and lean and few in the days when they kept our whole village from starvation. But they're fine animals now. They've multiplied ten times over, doing well on the hill-slopes with no help from anyone. I'll bring them down, select a few to keep, take the bulk of them to the sales and they'll pay our fares for us. Uncle Ju and Aunty Janey would have been more than happy with that.

It's good to be alive as I end this letter with a warmed-up pen, which I now mean to keep on using. I had forgotten my pen. In between planning and making a journey, and no matter what else happens, writing is what I'll do from now on. There are more stories to tell, more to pass on. When we return I'll rebuild the herd. I'll renovate the house and keep it warm for family. There's much to do as I end this letter with a warmed-up heart – and a new dream.

I hope I have honoured my brothers.

Your loving uncle,
Te Hokowhitu-a-Tu

Author's notes

Early in 1944 my father left for war to join Maori Battalion reinforcements in Italy and, while away, kept a notebook for a brief time. It was after reading the diary, almost twenty years after his death in 1983, that I became curious about what it had been like for this band of volunteers. Why did they go to war, I wondered. Why did they commit themselves to a war so totally? What was their cause?

The ability and bravery of the Maori Battalion in the field of war is legendary. In battle they were known for their truculence, especially in close quarter combat, and sometimes for their unsparing vengeance. They had a reputation also for good humour, high spirits, unorthodoxy and acquisitiveness. Dan Davin, Official Historian for the Battle for Crete, has said that neither witnesses nor future historians 'would hesitate to award to the Maoris of 28 Battalion the credit for the most conspicuous élan and valour'.

To us as children these fathers and uncles didn't look or seem particularly valiant, but brave or not these men were our heroes all the same. They were funny. They laughed and sang. They teased. They played and joked with children. They had new languages that they liked to show their knowledge of, and had German, Greek and Italian songs which were passed on to families, some of the songs still being remembered today. It was obvious that while away they had formed special bonds with each other.

But these men, I guess along with thousands of others returning from war, came home with a silence also. They had their ghosts.

Though my father sometimes spoke of Italy and the Italian people, and had some amusing anecdotes regarding mischief and escapades during their time away, he never spoke of the action of war itself. His notes begin with the words 'Left Papakura by train', and cover only the journey by sea and train until reaching camp in El Maadi where preparations began for the campaigns in Italy. He took up his pen again on 13 December 1945, after the war had ended and when he was about to leave a rest camp in Florence: 'So after many months of varied experiences I take off again . . .' His diary is just twenty-five pages in all.

I can say now, that at the completion of research and writing, I have been on a journey too, especially as far as understanding more about the overseas war experience of the soldiers is concerned. It was an engrossing and illuminating journey on the one hand, on the other, one that was both sad and horrifying.

On this journey I have had generous support from many people. At the beginning, on mentioning to him what I hoped to do, Wira Gardiner, author of *Te Mura o Te Ahi, The Story of the Maori Battalion*, offered me his complete file. The letters and personal accounts by soldiers were invaluable. Friend Putiputi Mahuika Snowden when she found out what I was engaged in, sent me her father's memoirs, *Aku Korero*. I am indebted to Wira Gardiner for his generosity, and to Manawanui Mahuika, wife of Captain Nepia Mahuika, for the privilege of reading what was recorded mainly for their family.

I have talked to many people and have been assisted in many ways – via conversation, sharing of memories, advice, direction and insights. Foremost among those people has been my mother, Joyce Gunson, whose enthusiasm for what I was doing was equal to my own. We have spent very special time together going through boxes of mementos – my father's diary, photographs, letters (which I had written to my father, though not my mother's and father's letters to each other), newspapers and clippings, magazines and memorial programmes, and a book of personal data belonging to a Maori Battalion Signal Platoon.

The cover photograph, from a family album, is of one of my father's battalion friends.

I am indebted to Monty Soutar for valuable contacts, and to his brother Barry with whom I have had several long-distance and enlightening phone conversations. I enjoyed time in fruitful discussion with Taina Tangaere McGregor, researcher and Oral Historian Maori for the Alexander Turnbull Library; also with Ola Hiroti, Riria Utiku, Val Head, Margaret Smiler and Mihipeka Edwards, early members of the Ngati Poneke Club which has been in existence since the mid-1930s and which still holds its practices on Monday nights. I have spent time at the Museum of Wellington City and Sea with Loreen Sadlier, Karen Wheeler and Wendy Adlam, looking at pictures and models of ships which had been re-dressed for war then re-dressed again later. Two of my sons, Wiremu Grace and Himiona Grace, in the course of work and research of their own, came up with material that proved to be important. Mike Peehi, through his database of information and contacts for 28th Battalion and their families, has given valuable assistance.

When I spoke to Paul Diamond of Radio New Zealand about a reference that I'd seen to an outdoor concert in Italy, he knew what I was talking about and was able to provide a tape of Christmas messages and songs by the Maori Battalion, recorded in Taranto in November 1943. I listened to the messages of leaders and to the mass singing of the Battalion, knowing that some of my uncles would have been there gathered around the large campfire on a 'beautiful clear night in Southern Italy . . . on a hillside looking down on the moonlit valley below' – none of them with any knowledge of what was to come. This was a battalion of young men, referred to by their leaders in their messages to the home people as 'ou koutou tamariki', your children. 'Here are your children, singing, celebrating and thinking of you.' 'Your children send you greetings.'

Antonella Sarti of Florence in Italy, who is the translator of a collection of my stories, helped me with Italian vocabulary. I am grateful to Antonella for this assistance and also to her husband Chris for the trouble he took in relaying messages to me via last-century technology, i.e. fax machine.

My husband, Kerehi Waiariki Grace, has always given moral as well as practical support to me in my occupation. There are some people in the world, perhaps many, who understand maps. Waiariki is one of those. He has been able to explain the many maps, charts and diagrams which I needed to have demystified for me. It required fortitude. I'm really grateful.

It is my good fortune to be not too far away from several of our excellent libraries and museums. Of utmost importance to me in my research were The National Library of New Zealand: Te Puna Matauranga o Aotearoa (General Reference Service and Music Room) and The Alexander Turnbull Library (Research Centre and Newspaper Room, the Oral History Centre, Manuscripts and Archive Section, the Pictorial Collection and Photographic Archives). I received assistance also from The Settler Museum in Petone, The Museum of Wellington City and Sea, The National Film Archive, The Defence Archive, Porirua Library, Radio New Zealand Replay Radio and Sound Archives, and the Carter Observatory.

The books which formed the basis of my research were: *The 28 (Maori) Battalion* by J. F. Cody; *Te Mura o Te Ahi The Story of the Maori Battalion* by Wira Gardiner; *Cassino, Portrait of a Battle* by Fred Majdalany; *Italy Volume 1, The Sangro to Cassino* by N. C. Phillips; *Cassino, New Zealand Soldiers in The Battle for Italy* by Tony Williams; *The Silent Migration*, eds. Patricia Grace, Irihapeti Ramsden and Jonathan Dennis.

Other texts were: *Aku Korero* by Nepia Mahuika; *Angel in God's Office* by Neva Clarke McKenna; *Up the Blue* by Roger Smith; *The Women's War: NZ Women 1939–45* by Deborah Montgomerie; *Women in Wartime: NZ Women Tell their Story*, ed. Lauris Edmond; *Ma te Reinga* by H. G. Dyer; *The Price of Citizenship* by A. T. Ngata; *New Zealanders at War* by Michael King; *War Stories Our Mothers Never Told Us*, ed. Judith Fyfe; *The Monastery* by Fred Magdalany; *Official History of New Zealand in the Second World War: Prisoners of War* by W. Wynne Mason; *Men Against Fire* by S. L. A. Marshall; *New Zealand at War WW2: The New Zealand Perspective* by Paul Smith; *Kiwis in Khaki* and *Home and Away: Images of New Zealanders in WW2* by David Filer; *Te Iwi Maori me te Inu Waipiro* by Marten Hutt; *Nga Toka Tu Moana Pohatu Whakaea: 50th Anniversary of Ngarimu VC and Reunion of C Company* published by Ngarimu VC Anniversary and Organising Committee in Association with Te Puni

Kokiri; *Ta Moko* by D. R. Simmons; *Mana* magazine, 'Anzac Issue No 27' published by Mana Productions Ltd.; *The Maori Battalion Remembers*, Vols 1–5, ed. Harry Lambert; *Golden Jubilee 1940–1990 The Maori Battalion Remembered*, ed. Harry Lambert; *Wartime Memories*, ed. Peter McQuaid; *Official History of the New Zealand Exhibition, Wellington, 1939–1940* by N.B Palenthorpe; *Official Guide to the New Zealand Centennial Exhibition 1939*; *NZ Centennial Exhibition: Newspaper Cuttings Vols 1–3 1938-1939*; *NZ Centennial Exhibition 1939-40: Dominion Court Guide, 1939*.

Although all main characters and most minor characters are fictional, there are some who make a brief entrance into the story, who did in fact walk the earth. Te Puea Herangi was an outstanding figure in the history of our country and needs to be granted the honour which her own name gives. Kingi Ihaka and Fred Katene of the Ngati Poneke Club were such distinctive men to all who knew them that it didn't seem worthwhile reinventing or renaming them. Stan Wineera was one of the 'uncles'– my father's relative – and a stand-up comedian of the Kiwi Concert Party which, as a child, I had the privilege of seeing when their show was brought to Wellington after the war. Ruru Karaitiana (Danny) wrote the song 'Blue Smoke' on his way to war and first performed it at a shipboard concert. It was sung by Maori Battalion soldiers throughout the war. Later, in 1949, with singer Pixie Williams, it became the first all-New Zealand hit record ever, topping the radio hit parade for six weeks. It was recorded overseas by Anne Zeigler and Webster Booth, Dean Martin, Al Morgan, Teddy Phillips and Leslie Howard. I remember one day when I was about ten years of age that on going into Begg's Music Store in Wellington with my mother and brother, we were excited to see Ruru in his soldier uniform, sitting at the piano playing and singing 'Blue Smoke'. I guess he was there promoting the new record.

Patricia